A Pride & Prejudice Reimagining

Faith & Family

Pride, Prejudice, & New Adventures
Volume VII

NEY MITCH

FAITH & FAMILY
Copyright © 2025 by Ney Mitch

ISBN: 979-8-88653-381-1

Published by Satin Romance
An Imprint of Melange Books, LLC
White Bear Lake, MN 55110
www.satinromance.com

Published in the United States of America.

Cover Design by Caroline Andrus

Good day, Reader!

Thank you so much for pursuing this adventure to the finale of the series.

You all are amazing, and I appreciate the fact that you are here, at the conclusion of this series of mine.

I also wish to give a thank you to Jane Austen, for as you can see, she has inspired many of us, and due to individuals such as yourself, she will always prove to do so.

A special thanks to my family, friends, publisher, and everyone else who helped make this series possible.

But, at the end of the day, the reader is the one who deserves the most love, because without you lot, we writers are just a voice howling to the wall.

Therefore, this is for you.

To the end, my friends...to the end!

PROLOGUE

Standing in the dining hall of the inn, Charlotte and Captain Wentworth looked at each other, perturbed. All around them was much conversation about the much anticipated but equally dreaded call for war, and it was apparently sweeping over Lyme, as it must have done so all over England.

"Upon my honor," Charlotte whispered, "I had hoped that it would not come to this, but it has."

Captain Wentworth began to speak when they were suddenly interrupted.

"Frederick! And Mrs. Collins!"

They both turned and Captain Harvill had entered the inn, seeking them out.

"Captain Harvill," Charlotte said suddenly.

"I was told you were both here and I was called to summon you," Harvill continued.

"Were we sent for?" Charlotte asked.

"Yes, your sister Maria has requested your presence with her at Cumberland, and Admiral Croft and your sister seek you out, Frederick. They are starting a search party to retrieve Benwick and Miss

Crawford, and given our history with him, I volunteered us both for the assistance."

"Oh, of course I shall help," Captain Wentworth replied with haste, "Let us go then."

Charlotte retrieved her bonnet from her room and joined both men in the barouche box that Lady Russell had loaned Harvill. They left immediately.

As the box rolled along the streets of Lyme toward Cumberland, Charlotte groaned inwardly, bitter at Harvill's sudden appearance at the inn. Captain Wentworth and she were finally going to arrive at an understanding—and he was on the road to confessing something. Very much did Charlotte wish to know what it was, and now there was a possibility that she would never find out, for the situations in the world had intervened.

Harvill looked between them and sensed that there was a tension, a feeling of words not being uttered, yet appeared as if they should have been between them.

"I hope that I had not intruded upon you both with my arrival," he said by way of excuse.

"Oh, not at all," Charlotte lied. "If my sister needed me, then I am happy you were willing to do the service of retrieving me."

"Do Mr. and Mrs. Crawford have any idea of what route they had taken?" Captain Wentworth asked. "Surely this was not a sudden scheme, but one that Benwick and Miss Crawford had thought out, which means that they had to have places of refuge along the way to their destination."

"You are right, Frederick, for Benwick is a man who never does something on a whim. Yet he is a clever and sharp man and looks on life as he looks on commanding a navy vessel."

"Oh, blast it!" Captain Wentworth groaned.

"What do you mean?" Charlotte asked. "What is more amiss?"

"That Benwick is not just a lovesick puppy. He is methodical and being a sea captain makes us men of strategy."

"Precisely," Harvill added. "He knows that we are coming after him, therefore his mission will be to do the unpredictable."

"He will not stay at locations that he knows we shall search, and he also knows that they have to travel swiftly, because they can be tracked and traced if they are slow. He will change horses."

"And not just horses," Harvill said, "but maybe even clothing. Think on it. A wealthy and fashionable woman such as Miss Crawford traveling with a naval Captain who is in uniform will most certainly be noticeable and memorable to people they come in contact with. They will have changed their clothes, to make themselves appear as everyone else."

"Oh," Charlotte sighed, "then if that be so... they will be nearly impossible to find. Unless of course, her parents have some form of art, some likeness of their daughter with them, a small pocket portrait. For when you trace them, you shall at least have a picture of her to show to innkeepers and stable boys along the way."

"That is a marvelous idea!" Captain Harvill said. "Thank you and I shall bring that observation up when we return to Cumberland."

They rode on and as they did so, Frederick and Charlotte eyed each other with curiosity and also confusion.

Both remained indecisive on how to approach one another, as well as being impotent for they could not do so when in the presence of Harvill. Being left at an impasse, Captain Wentworth turned to the window and gave voice to his frustration.

"Foolish... damned foolish!"

Little did Harvill know that Wentworth was not only speaking of Benwick's actions, but also at his inner annoyance at not having spoken faster when he was within Charlotte's room and had his only opportunity of having her alone rather than in company.

As for Charlotte, her mind was very much in turmoil. She was a little angry with Maria for summoning her, for what could her presence at Cumberland achieve? Nothing. Every action that had now occurred would be so without her presence there amongst it. Her coming to Cumberland would not bring Miss Crawford back to Lyme, nor would her venturing out from her room have kept the war from occurring.

No indeed!

Charlotte Collins was a small piece of a large world, as insignificant to its ways and workings as a leaf was in the wind. Therefore, she regretted the words not spoken between her and the Captain and would continue to do so for the rest of the day.

Eventually, they arrived at Cumberland, entered and when coming into the sitting room, they were bombarded by many approaching them. All were repeating the same sentiments and sentences from 'Isn't it all most shocking' to 'War is upon us', for the interruptions of the outside world had burst in upon them.

Then through the crowd, Charlotte saw Mr. Darcy and Elizabeth.

I

IT IS A TRUTH, GENERALLY UNRECOGNIZED

When Charlotte entered with Captain Wentworth and Harvill, I felt a slight pity for her—and relief. For in the midst of being at Cumberland did I notice that Captain Wentworth had quit the house to seek her out, and it would be either for her benefit or for her misfortune.

Yet upon them entering, and seeing their comfort with each other, I could see that the interaction had not been a tumultuous one in her case. Upon seeing Mr. Darcy and me in the crowd, Charlotte immediately began to make her way toward us. Before reaching us, she was intercepted by Maria, who took her hand and spoke some very desperate words. I saw Charlotte pat her shoulder and then they both made their way toward us.

"Distressing business this all is," she said when she had approached.

"To which are you referring to?" I asked. "The elopement or the news of war?"

"Both," Charlotte said.

"Yes, it is very hard."

"And harder for them," Mr. Darcy said, eyeing Lady Russell, Mr. Russell and Miss Elton.

"Yes," Jane said. "For this was meant to be their time of happiness, and now it shall forever be etched in their memory as the engagement party where two of their guests eloped and war was announced."

"They have been overshadowed by tragedy then," Jane Austen acknowledged. "But only if they let it."

"What do you mean?" Jason asked her.

"I mean that, at first, they must be frustrated today. Then tomorrow it shall be a bitter wound, the next day it shall feel as if it is an annoying cut, then the day after that, it shall be an interesting memory. And then the day after..."

"It shall be a good story," Colonel Fitzwilliam finished.

"Precisely."

"However," Georgiana said, "I do not think they will view it as so."

"No, they shall not," I replied. "And therefore, we had best to find a way to show it to them in that manner."

"Oh," Maria said, "it could be regarded as such. But I am still thinking of our mother, Charlotte. She must be so frightened."

"Our mother?" Charlotte asked, startled. "What does she have to do with any of this?"

"Oh, you did not make the connection?"

"No."

"It's Samuel. War has finally started right when Samuel has gone to America!"

Charlotte's face became immediately flushed as she realized that her brother was then traveling to the very country that ours was now declaring war upon. Feeling suddenly guilty for not having thought of him sooner, she blushed.

"Oh, poor Samuel!"

"Do not worry," I replied, doing my best to offer solace, "I promise that he shall be fine."

"But we do not know that," Maria cried. "He could be attacked or arrested when he arrives there."

"He shall not be. Samuel is smart and he has known how to conduct himself. Also, Philadelphia has too many ships traveling from England to arrest any of their passengers upon arrival."

"Yes," Jason replied. "Having lived there I can tell you that it will not be so terrible for him. Look at it any way that you like. If he is wary and says nothing that could be regarded as controversial, he shall be well."

"What is the matter?"

We all turned, and Captain Wentworth had approached us and overheard the last of our conversation.

"Forgive me, but I could not help but see that there is a different sort of alarm with your lot," he began.

"No apologies are needed," Charlotte said. "It is only that another shocking revelation has reached us."

"Of course, for we did not have enough of those," he replied, trying to make light of it all, "for it never rains, but it pours. What has occurred?"

"It is our brother, Samuel. Weeks earlier, he traveled to America."

"Is he there now?" Captain Wentworth asked, his brow furrowed.

"If he has not arrived already, he will soon be."

"Oh... I am sorry, Mrs. Collins and Miss Maria. That is indeed distressing, yet there is hope. He will be fine, I can assure you."

"Are you certain?" Maria asked. "There is no guarantee sir."

"You are right, there is none. But Miss Maria, never lose hope." He then turned to the rest of us. "I have just come to tell you that our search party shall begin, and we are about to take our leave in search of the runaways."

"Do you not need our assistance?" Colonel Fitzwilliam asked.

"Many of us men in the company shall depart for them, therefore you must remain, to look after our gentlewomen and keep everything calm."

"How long do you plan for your search to last?" Jane Austen asked.

"Whether we find them or not, we do not plan to be gone for more than four days. Worry not, we shall hopefully find them."

"Good luck then," Mr. Darcy said.

Captain Wentworth bowed to us slightly, gave Charlotte one last look and then he left with the search party.

Charlotte watched him as he left and all the other guests wished them well, with much anticipation. As they were all distracted with the heroes' departure, I approached Charlotte and whispered in her ear.

"Come this way and walk with me. For there is obviously something you are withholding."

Charlotte nodded, compliant and she moved away from the throng and followed me as we took a turn about the room.

"You came here with Captain Harvill and Wentworth," I began, "but I am quite certain that Wentworth had left earlier. Do you know of this?"

"Yes, he came to the inn to see me."

"Did he see you in private?"

"It may have been improper for him to see me alone and in my room, but Elizabeth, believe me, it was quite necessary."

"I am not judgmental; I am simply wishing to make certain that the interview went well."

"It went...it was unfulfilled."

"How so?"

"We did not get the chance to say all that we wished to before Harvill came in upon us."

"What did you speak of?"

"Of my own folly."

"And what folly is that? Given the circumstances, I daresay that your jumping into the ocean is now regarded as miniscule."

"Not only that, but my actions with Benwick. Lizzy, even Wentworth believed that Benwick and I had formed an attachment. He had come to *The Queen's Right Hand* to offer me his condolences, which means I allowed myself to appear as if I was...a flirt."

"You were not being a flirt, but only social."

"And now I am not so sure. Perhaps I was being overtly kind for I was happy to have had an ally at Cumberland, and now I fear censure."

She placed her hand on my arm. "Lizzy, if Wentworth and the rest of our company thought so, then that means all the other guests thought so as well. Now I shall look as if I am the one who was either used for the ruse, and was a dupe, to which Benwick made a fool of me. Or I would be viewed as their accomplice. It is more likely that it shall be the first as opposed to the second, but now they shall ridicule me when my back is turned. They shall look on me with pity and will not believe that I have not been injured by this all."

"Oh, Charlotte, you need not fear their thoughts. And surely they will not think so, but hopefully will only be preoccupied with the news of war and the search party."

Yet it was not to be so.

For after the search party left and the subject of the war had been quite exhausted, Charlotte would prove to be correct. Many in our company began to speak of the eloping couple and there were many subtle looks at Charlotte.

"Indeed," Lady Russell had said, most guardedly, "this is all so much of a shock. For in regards to them both, I would have thought Miss Crawford's attentions were elsewhere... as were Captain Benwick's."

"Indeed," Mrs. Applegate said. "It does go to show you just how we often never know people. No matter how we think we do. And of the inconstancy of affections as well."

"Yes, but it is all so vexing!" Miss Elton exclaimed "For this to happen under our very roof here, it makes one feel so forlorn and almost to blame."

"You are not to blame," Mr. Russell said.

"Very true," I said. "Miss Elton, you have been a delightful hostess as well as offering us many diversions. You cannot control the actions of others, nor shall you ever be responsible for them."

"No indeed," Mr. Bingley said, "And this is your engagement party. Pray, Mr. Russell and Miss Elton, do not let the rash actions of a couple deter you from enjoying this most special time of your lives."

"Indeed," Mrs. Applegate said. "That is what makes their elopement all the more scandalous. They chose to do it in the wake of your blissful moment. Utter selfishness."

"I do not think any time would have been a good time for it," Mr. Darcy said. "Mrs. Applegate, and it will never be so simple to tie them down to wishing to ruin Mr. Russell and Miss Elton's happiness. All that we can tie them down to is being rash and selfish. Yet malicious intent is not something that should be laid at their feet."

"Either way, this is a most alarming affair," Lady Russell said. "And will be much talked of."

"Oh, pray," Miriam said. "For the sake of Mr. and Mrs. Crawford, who are devastated and have taken refuge in their room, let us speak no more off it. As well as not spread the news ourselves, for this is already hard for them, and would be even harder if we spoke in a way that the rumor shall spread and followed them even when they leave this place."

"Oh," Miss Elton replied, "of course. That is very wise."

The subject of the conversation then shifted to the newly declared war that was up ahead, and we all pondered how long it would last, how much of Parliament's money would go into financing it, and would it be as much a war fought with our navy as with our armies. This would call both kinds of men in our military to the fronts.

What was more devastating, men such as the Admiral and the Captains were acquaintances who we all had a mutual affection for, might be swept up in it once more. Indeed, it was most distressing, therefore I very soon decided to not think of the Captains and the Admiral being taken away from us as soon as they had come.

While the conversation continued on the subject of war however, I knew that the people, when they left Cumberland, would spread this news to everyone in their social sphere. For it is a truth, generally unrecognized, that humans have a tendency to not be able to tell when they are being inwardly hypocritical. We often speak of the decorum of not spreading rumor and scandalous news. Yet when it does occur, we are the first to cling to it, dwell on it, and wishing to spread it and not care for the harm we do.

This is the even-handed dealing of the world. We speak well...but we spread harm. And if there is one thing that is almost as frightening as war, it is the high circles of the ton, and the fright of being amongst the vicious elite.

❧ 2 ❧

MEANWHILE

Yes, Caroline Bingley thought to herself, *This is the even-handed dealing of the world—and it makes me sick!*

For while the occupants of Cumberland were lost deep in the news that was the arrival of war being waged and the flights of the two lovers, on another side of England, in London to be exact, Caroline Bingley sat in the sitting room of her sister's townhouse. Louisa and Mr. Hurst were absent for the moment, for they were overseeing the plans they had for a re-design of their music room.

Caroline knew very well that she was not invited to the meeting. Mr. Hurst had a very short temper with her often in the manner that he was curt and implied with his actions that he would not have wished for her to be present.

Her omission from the meeting did not vex her at all, for more and more, she had spent much of her days in reflection that she usually did not undergo.

Ever since Elizabeth and she had the confrontation at Canterbury in America, she had been secretly disturbed. For so long she had determined that Mr. Darcy's choosing Elizabeth over her was a fluke of nature, utterly nonsensical, and that Mr. Darcy, a man whom she had revered, had lost his senses. Yet too often the mistake of her not being chosen as a suitable wife had been occurring. And others being chosen over her, while at first it was a simple annoyance, now it was a pattern.

"Everyone seems to love any woman but me," she said aloud. "And I do not understand it."

Caroline groaned inwardly, trying to see the reasons for her not securing a husband while what she regarded as many lesser individuals had. She had beauty, a sizeable dowry when the Bennet women had none, and also had refined manners. She was the product of good breeding and all the benefits that could come along with the life that she possessed were at her disposal.

It was Charles, she told herself. Charles still had an interest in trade, making many connections and still owning factories, attaching himself to the very trade their father worked hard to separate them from. What were all their father's labors for if not to elevate them, which it did, until Charles decided to revert back to the very life that they should have rose over.

And he also married to clearly disoblige her and his family. Along with the wealth that their father had found for his children, he believed, as did she and Louisa, that one's trajectory was to always strive to go upward. In marrying Miriam, Charles gained no connections, no prestige in the eyes of the ton, and made their family less, as opposed to more.

Caroline also had felt thwarted by the match because it was against her choice for him. Believing her plan to be perfect, she had always desired him to court and wed Georgiana. And thus, her master plan would have been complete, for one set of matrimony in one quarter always could possibly lead to another match within the families. If Charles had wed Georgiana, then she would have been thrown even more in the path of Mr. Darcy. And his sister's fondness for Charles would have led to Darcy's eventual desire to attach him to herself. If Charles and Georgiana had become a couple, then so would she and Darcy, making it a double wedding of pleasing proportions. And she, Caroline Bingley, would make the ultimate triumph—marrying not only a man of great wealth and title, but to attach herself to the most illustrious person in the lands... it was a dream. But for one moment, the dream had been attainable.

Yet now, all had come to naught.

Mr. Darcy married Elizabeth Bennet.

Colonel Fitzwilliam married Kitty Bennet.

Mr. Henry Darcy married Lydia Bennet.

And none of them married her.

And it even made the question rise up within her... did they feel disgust with her?

No, it could not be so. She was the mark of an accomplished woman, for she excelled in music, playing, singing and dancing—and something in the air and manner of her walking must have been pleasing to the eye. And her address, tone of her voice and expressions were all perfect, well-calculated and always thought out. Never did she speak without care and precision.

And yet... Mr. Darcy looked on her with disgust once, and did not respond to her in the way he responded to Elizabeth. Colonel Fitzwilliam never cared one way or the other about her person, and Mr. Henry Darcy, well—when Caroline did her best to rectify his error, and tried to most kindly do her duty by informing him of the impropriety of allying himself with such a frivolous woman with a repulsive past, she was the one who was rebuked by him.

Therefore, could the very problem be within her?

No, it was not to be endured! She, Caroline Bingley, was simply ill-used and was not seen for the wonder that she was.

ॐ

CAROLINE'S THOUGHTS were interrupted when Louisa entered, holding a piece of upholstery fabric in her hands.

"Caroline," Louisa said, "what think you of this fabric for the curtains in the music room?"

"My opinion is not really needed, is it?"

"Oh, Caroline don't be cross."

"Why should I be anything else? If Mr. Hurst had wanted my opinion, I would have received an invitation to your meeting."

"Oh, pardon a man who thinks that he and his wife ought to have the only say in their home decorations. Honestly Caroline, sometimes I believe that you look to be offended."

"That is nonsense."

"It would be nonsense if it were not true sometimes," Louisa said, sitting down on the other sofa. "Caroline, please dear, do not be sullen, for there is no reason to be."

"How am I being disobliging?"

"By being forlorn for things that you could not control."

Caroline turned to Louisa warningly, but Louisa, who had grown up with Caroline, was so used to her moods to know that she was harmless and only looked intimidating.

"And what can I not control?"

"That you are heart-wounded."

"Heart-wounded? That is not a proper phrase, Louisa. And you are not Shakespeare, giving you no right to create your own words."

"I do not see why he was able to, and I am not given that right, yet that is neither here nor there. Caroline, I mean this in all delicacy and remember that I wish to help you."

"Help me?"

"You are wounded because you are dwelling on things that you cannot control. On disappointments."

"And what disappointments are those?"

"You know very well what they are without me giving voice to them."

"Louisa, sister, I am sure you have me wrong."

"And when have I ever? I am on your side, as always, but this time I cannot deny seeing where your shortcomings lie."

"My shortcomings?" Caroline gasped, leaning forward. "And what would those be?"

"Caroline..."

"Tell me!"

"You dwell on men who never loved you, and then you do not understand why they did not—even when you gave them no reason to find you worthy."

Caroline flinched, alarmed that her sister, Louisa, who had often been her main ally, would say such a thing to her—especially when they saw eye to eye on so many things.

"Louisa, how dare you?"

"You pushed me to my conclusion."

"You are saying that I am not lovable?"

"You are lovable, Caroline. However, you make yourself not likeable."

"And how so?"

"You try too hard."

"Is trying too hard a sin? For I find the error of humanity to be not trying hard enough," she said, jumping up and beginning to pace. "No, I will not suffer under so misguided a notion."

"It is not misguided in your situation. However, you must see how in many cases, you overwhelmed the men you were pursuing with your overbearing manner—and your paltry tricks to bate them."

"What?"

"Tell me Caroline, how did you try to woo Mr. Darcy?"

"I... I complimented him at every turn and showed my admiration for him always, as we were trained to do in finishing school."

"And what did that ultimately lead to? It led to everything you did coming across as false perhaps, or as if you were trying to force your good opinion upon him. Do you not see? You were trying too hard, and it made Darcy feel cornered and suffocated. And from all that I observed of you with Mr. Henry Darcy, you did the same thing with him. Also, you performed the sly act of trying to gain their affection by slighting the women that they admired. On men of weak inclinations or weak character, that works often, but on men of stronger resolution, that only makes you look like the villain, because you are offending the woman he adores."

"That...that is how it made me look?"

"Yes. When a man loves something, and you mock it, you become grotesque to him because you place yourself on the opposite of where his affections choose to lie. One catches more bees with honey as opposed to vinegar."

"Well, that, I admit is logical, but the rest I cannot agree with you. We were trained to compliment men and allow them to feel as if we agree with them in every turn, to show our suitability."

"That works for some men, yet for others, they prefer tenacity. And you never saw that Mr. Darcy was that sort of man. And also...you need to forgive Elizabeth for being the one he did choose."

"I could never learn to like her, or the Bennets!"

"Perhaps you do not like them because you wish that you were them."

"Pardon?"

"I have been speaking with them more of late, when we were all in Philadelphia, and I must say that I see the charm that they possess, especially to a man like Mr. Darcy, and Mr. Henry Darcy's position. You actually owe them a great deal."

"I owe them?" She felt mortified.

"Yes, for they saved you."

"How have they saved me?"

"Because I am now quite certain that you would have been miserable if you had wed Mr. Darcy."

"That is preposterous."

"No, I do not believe so. Your natures are too much not in unity with each other. Or they do not complement each other in the slight-est. He is too sardonic for you and needs someone who brings him out of his shell. Elizabeth Bennet does that for him, while you need something else. You are a spirited speaker, and you need someone who will argue with you."

"What?"

"Yes, you need someone with spirit as well, who is willing to accept a challenge and enjoys a good row."

"You are saying that I inspire verbal altercation?"

"I am saying you need someone who will stand up to you."

At her wit's end, Caroline turned away from Louisa and paced most frantically. Louisa and she were usually of one mind on most things, therefore, to be so at odds with each other was overwhelming to say the least. Feeling greatly offended by her sister's words, her first impulse was also to not listen to Louisa's advice, for they appeared to be nonsensical. Yet to add more injury to her insult, Caroline now felt alone. For even if a situation had not ended to her liking, Louisa had always been there to agree with her on all matters.

Yet now Louisa was objecting to her, and it made her feel quite solitary in her heart. Whatever the case however, when one's emotions are hurt by someone that they are not accustomed to it being so, logic and consideration of the truth are never what follow, but only rage, quick reactions and decisions based on pride. A person is left to reacting in a terrible light; and they shout. And thus, when she had calmed her nerves, she turned back and began her counterattack.

"And what of you, Louisa? You married a man who not only you did not love, but who also did not love you. Therefore, who are you to lecture me?"

"Sister do not speak so."

"It is very well for you to speak ill of me, but you do not wish to know the truth of yourself? And the truth is that you are a woman who has suffered disappointment as well."

"Yes..." Louisa said, resigned. "Yes, I do know it."

"What—what?"

"Caroline," Louisa began, her voice growing heavy and weary. "You do not think I know that I live in a loveless marriage? Well, I do know it."

"And..."

"And I am now resigned to my fate, yet that does not mean that I have to sit here and do nothing. That does not mean that I will not try to save you from making the same mistake that I had. I married for position, and Mr. Hurst practically sleeps through our marriage. You wanted to marry Mr. Darcy for his position, and he would have slept through your marriage as well. You are lucky for Elizabeth, believe me, for she protected you from your own nature, and you hate her for it."

"I..."

"Please believe me; you do not wish to suffer the same fate that I have. The image of the perfect married couple is worthless if there is nothing real behind it."

"I do not wish to talk of this anymore," Caroline said sternly. "Please..."

Louisa beheld her sister's resigned expression and thought it wise to desist.

"Very well," she said, standing up. Yet before she left, Louisa showed her the curtain she had picked out.

"You still have not given me your opinion on them."

"They could be fancier," Caroline said.

"Oh."

Louisa smiled at her and then left the room.

Now being left alone, Caroline sat back down and wondered if she would be right to let herself cry.

After a moment's deliberation, she realized that it would not be worth it to do so, and therefore, she grew still, as a statue for a moment, wondering how it all had come to this.

Louisa had forsaken her and claimed that she had not wanted Caroline to make the same mistake. Yet Caroline did not see that she had made a mistake.

No, she would not allow that!

Her plans and schemes had not worked in the past because she simply did not try hard enough. Therefore, if the opportunity ever presented itself more, she would do all in her power to show more affection for the gentleman than she was feeling, and not less if she was to secure him.

Indeed, she would prove she was right in the end. And that was a comforting thought in that troubled moment.

Also, she was certain that she would not spend the course of her life married unhappily, but with the perfect image of a man. Surely, he must be out there, waiting for her.

Thus, meanwhile, as the rest of the outside world in Britain was speaking of war in the streets, Caroline Bingley sat in her sister and brother-in-law's townhouse, believing herself ill-used and the most unfortunate of souls.

3

THE DEPENDENCE OF
FRIENDSHIP

Four days had past until the occupants of Cumberland and *The Queen's Right Hand Inn* witnessed the arrival of the search party—and still missing the two people whose appearance meant the most.

"We have not been able to trace them," Captain Harvill announced when all waited upon them at the Plateau. "Unfortunately, they have covered their tracks all too well. Therefore, Mrs. Crawford, our apologies, but they were swift in their journey and will have already booked passage to Gretna Green."

Mrs. Crawford sat down, looking pale with alarm, and Mr. Crawford looked barely any better. Mr. Nelson, on the other hand, looked put out, for he must have felt himself greatly abused on the matter. For there he was, thinking himself to be on equal footing with the woman he was trying to woo, and all the while she had been concealing an engagement she had with a sailor. Yet what was worse, in his eyes, was the rank difference. He, Mr. Nelson, was a gentleman, and Captain Benwick was merely a man who was rendered distinguished due to his profession. Feeling passed over for one who he regarded as lesser than himself, Mr. Nelson had much weighing upon his mind that was enhanced by the grief of abused pride.

When Captain Wentworth arrived with the rest of the search party, Charlotte met his gaze, and they looked on each other with wonder. Both greatly wished to know what the other had been thinking, yet being in a public place had offered them no choice but to linger in ignorance of each other's thoughts and intentions.

An hour into their arrival, suppertime had come, and they all went in to eat. At first no one knew what to say, for the discussion of their search party had been exhausted while they all congregated in the sitting room. However, they were two less in party, for Mr. and Mrs. Crawford immediately quit the house, leaving under the excuse of hiring a professional group of investigators in London.

Charlotte was not omniscient, yet she knew Captain Benwick to be smart. He would not have gone to London, for he would have known that would be the first place her parents would look. And a man of such connections would easily have booked passage on a ship that would travel to the coast of Scotland rather than ride to it. There was no way of being certain, but she would not have been surprised if they had actually traveled to Portsmouth, purposefully out of their way, to thwart people, and then took a ship to Scotland, where then they would travel to Gretna Green. Benwick was a clever man, and as fate had proven, Miss Crawford was also a shrewd woman. Thus, they would not be found, for they did not want to be.

As she sat there amongst the group, Jane Austen moved from her previous spot across the table and sat beside her.

"One thing that I never understood," Jane Austen said, "is not the elopement, for I can always understand the impulse to elope— but the morning after."

"What do you mean?"

"Well, one elopes because one is very much in love. However, the morning after the wedding, what do you do? You have to go back and face your families, therefore how does one act afterwards?

What if the family forsakes you both? With elopement, there are so many repercussions, for the better and for the worse. Even at the best of loves, would all the possible censure be worth the sacrifice? If a family is forgiving, then yes, it is all for the best in the end. But if the family is severe and unyielding, then what is to be done?"

"Yes, it is difficult indeed to think on so. However, when you were in love with Tom Lefroy would you have eloped with him if the chance would have presented itself?"

Jane Austen looked ahead, her eyes growing wistful.

"Charlotte, while I wished to say that I would have had the self-control and presence of mind to have withstood resorting to such an extreme action, I cannot tell you. Honestly, I do not know if I would have been able to have denied him or not."

"Yes, I can see how there is no answer to that question."

THE NEXT DAY was the last that the Cumberland party would remain in Lyme. As Charlotte and the rest in her company returned to the Plateau to offer their last bit of congratulations to Miss Elton and Mr. Russell, for which they promised to attend the wedding which would take place in London in a few weeks' time, everyone did their best to be merry.

However, as they all remained in the sitting room, waiting for the mid-day meal hour, Captain Wentworth had to confess that he wished to borrow some papers to write a letter to the family of Captain Benwick, informing them of their brother's situation. He could not write in his room, for he had been negligent to have forgotten paper back in London. Lady Russell most readily attended to him and Wentworth sat at the writing desk and began to compose his letter.

Charlotte, not wishing to appear idle and run the risk of casting her eyes upon his studious frame, stood up and walked to the window to look out at it. However, the post had already been taken by Mr. Nelson, who was staring out of it as well. At first Charlotte decided to move past him, yet his eyes fell upon her, and he nodded.

"Mrs. Collins," he began, "you find me enjoying the pleasant view of Cumberland."

"Yes, I do," she said, finding no choice but to approach him and stand at his side. However, the distance she had between herself and the desk which Wentworth remained writing did not go unnoticed. They were close to one another, but hopefully not so close that he could overhear she and Mr. Nelson.

"And you have anticipated me," Charlotte said, standing at the window. "Excellent prospect, is it not?"

"Yes, the view is quite lovely."

"I shall miss this place actually, for I have grown to love Lyme."

"I confess it to be of little beauty in my eyes, and I never wish to return to it."

"You are letting your pain and disappointment cloud your judgment, Mr. Nelson."

"Oh, am I?"

Charlotte knew she ought not to have said such a thing, but Mr. Nelson's feelings were not primary in her eyes, therefore she did not fear veracity at the present time.

"Yes, you are. You have felt a great loss and so you associate Lyme with it. That is not an uncommon tendency of human nature to allow one's opinion of something to be affected by the incidents that happened within it. Yet I tell you now, not to fear it. Do not dread the sight of something that has once caused you pain if it can offer you pleasure another time. Life changes so utterly and completely, Mr. Nelson. Yet I am sorry for your disappointment."

"Thank you for your kind words."

"Yet, if it is any conciliation, I do not believe Miss Crawford meant to hurt you."

"And that makes her crime any less?"

"No, it does not. It only means that the infliction was not only not intentional but also forced upon her. If her parents had allowed her to wed Captain Benwick freely, then she would never have had to resort to such a base plan to follow her heart. I am certain that she meant no harm, and perhaps even did not think that you would be in any way affected by her actions in the end."

"How could I not be?"

"Sir, it is a theory, universally acknowledged, that sometimes a person may appear as if they are serious in their attentions to another and ultimately was just doing so with no real intent upon them."

"I can guarantee you that I am not such a kind."

"Indeed, perhaps you are not, and most likely are not. Yet Miss Crawford perhaps told herself so as to relieve her of her guilt in leading you on. On your part, it is a cold business, and a careless one, I will never deny."

"It makes me dubious of all women now, to know that they can be capable of such willful deceit."

"And how is this act of deceit more treacherous than the acts of deceit committed by man?" Charlotte asked, her eyebrow raised.

He flushed. "Forgive me."

"You are forgiven, but you must not make that sort of generalization, even though generalizations are an easy thing to make—but never do so in this circumstance."

"And why ever not?"

"Because you do not take into account what occurs to a woman's heart when she falls in love. When we do so, a desire to be with the man always becomes our priority. Miss Crawford was in love with Benwick, and though this may be hard to hear, I had seen hints of it with my own eyes in subtle glances. Her devotion to him was not disloyalty to you, for loyalty could only be given to the one who had her heart, which was Benwick. If she had loved you in his place, she would have held the same amount of devotion. When you find that lady, whose heart is filled with love for you, then trust is something you need never worry over. For if her love is true, then she will always wish to be bound to you. And she would not forget you easily."

"Will she not?" Mr. Nelson said, hanging on Charlotte's every word.

"No, she would not. It would not be in the nature of any woman who truly loved."

"Do you claim that for your whole sex?" Mr. Nelson smiled.

"Yes," Charlotte smiled also, "we certainly do not forget you as soon as you forget us. That is why Miss Crawford eloped with Benwick, because she could not forget him so soon as to turn toward you in his stead. Even though you be very worthy, I am sure. It is, perhaps, our fate rather than our merit. We cannot help ourselves. We live at home, quiet, confined, and our feelings prey upon us. You are forced on exertion. You have always a profession, pursuits, business of some sort or other, to take you back into the world immediately, and continual occupation and change soon weaken impression. Your freedom and allowance for activity give you leave to gain and lose new experiences as well as gain and lose memories."

He nodded. "Granting your assertion that the world does all this so soon for me—which, however, I do not think I shall grant—it does not apply to all of us surely, for there must be some who when busy can still have their perpetual flames of passion burn inside their breasts."

"True, it can be so, yet at the end of it all, it must all result from what is within; it must be nature, man's nature, that chooses if it wishes to remain constant to the same woman or turn away to different prospects and forget her when entering the world."

"No, no it is not man's nature, I will not allow it to be more man's nature than woman's nature to be inconstant and forget those they do love, or have loved," Mr. Nelson countered strongly. "I believe the reverse. I believe in a true analogy between our bodily frames and our mental. And that as our bodies are the strongest, so are our feelings, capable of bearing most rough usage, and riding out the heaviest weather."

"Your feelings may be strongest," Charlotte retorted, "but the same spirit of analogy will authorize me to assert that ours are the tenderest. Man is more robust than woman, but he is not longer-lived, which exactly explains my view of the nature of their attachments. Nay, it would be too hard upon you, if it were otherwise."

"We shall never agree upon this question, Mrs. Collins. "No man and woman would probably. But let me observe that all histories are against you, all stories, prose and verse. If I had such a memory as my father's, I could bring up fifty quotations in a moment on my side of the argument, and I do not think I ever opened a book in my life which had not something to say upon woman's inconstancy. Songs and proverbs, all talk of woman's fickleness. But perhaps you shall retaliate and say that these were all written by men?"

"I very well can, for it would be a very politic point, and if you please, it would do best not to use the examples of books. Men have had every advantage of us in telling their own story, for when are we women allowed to be given the right to publish our own works?"

"Miss Austen over there writes and is published."

"Miss Austen, over there, has risked much for her passion to do so, and know she will always do so. The times are changing, but they are changing a great deal too slowly for my liking, but for men? The pen has always been in your hands, and because the written word has for so long been in your domain, and yours alone, I will not allow books to prove anything."

"But how shall we prove anything?"

"We cannot, for there is no full proof to be had," she replied gently, "and I am content with there being no answer to our dilemma."

"I prefer to always have an answer."

"Of course you do, for an answer makes everything clear, simple, and with no answer, everything seems chaotic. Yet sometimes chaos is the truth, in its many tedious but erratic ways, it is so. We each begin probably with a little bias towards our own sex."

He glanced away to the window. "And upon that bias builds every circumstance in favor of it which has occurred within our own circle," Mr. Nelson concluded, "many of which circumstance, circumstances such as my present one which strikes me the most, many be precisely such as cannot be brought without exposing us to the world in immense ridicule, for it is a private matter that has been made public. It is a great shame."

"Whatever shame the world looks upon you with for this, do not take heed to it. The world is cold, judgmental, and sometimes makes the victim of a circumstance the villain, because the victim was the one who suffered the humiliation. And Mr. Nelson?"

"Yes?"

"I do not undervalue the feelings of man, and your capability to feel strong emotions deeply. I should deserve utter contempt if I dared to suppose that true attachment and constancy were known only by women."

She thought a moment. "No, I believe you capable of everything great and good in your married lives. So long as you have an object. I mean, while the woman you love lives, and lives for you. All the privilege I claim for my own sex, and it is not a very enviable one therefore you need not covet it, is that of loving the longest, when existence or when hope is gone. Put simply, Mr. Nelson, we women, even if we are the ones who rejected the man that we loved or were the ones rejected, we still love him and wished that our fortunes had turned out for the different."

Charlotte and Mr. Nelson were interrupted, for Captain Wentworth had dropped his writing pen and accidentally made a commotion in picking it up. Yet she had quite forgotten that he was so near in proximity! Surely, he could not have overheard her, or could he have?

"Is everything all right, Wentworth?" Mr. Nelson asked.

"Yes, quite all right, I merely was being clumsy at the moment," he replied hurriedly, and then he continued working away at his letter.

Mr. Nelson turned back to Charlotte and smiled down at her gently.

"You are a good soul, Mrs. Collins."

"Thank you Mr. Nelson and you deserve your happiness."

"May I find it."

"I am certain that you shall."

Mr. Nelson then moved away from Charlotte to go and speak with Mr. Russell while Charlotte looked out of the window, staring at the view of Lyme.

Indeed, it had followed that her time along the sea was most pleasant in the end, for it had brought her to face what she had been running from for too long. Should it then have followed that only by running away from something, will you inevitably run back to it? Or that the past, as much as we wish for it to remain so, will sometimes rise up and become the present.

It frightened her to know that it could not always be escaped, even if a person had the right to let their past remain where it should have been: behind them. However, some things should not be allowed to rest, it could be assumed. Charlotte needed Captain Wentworth to find her, to confront her for what she had done to him, and only then could she confront the worse parts of herself and eradicate it. Charlotte Lucas was Charlotte Lucas before she became Mrs. Collins, but even Charlotte Lucas had not been correct in the end and had dug a larger hole for herself when she took on Mr. Collins's name. Only at present did she feel that she had done something that Charlotte Lucas should have done long ago.

"Captain Wentworth!" Lady Russell called, "how goes your letter sir? Do you need another pen?"

"Oh, thank you Lady Russell, but you need not do so," he replied, with slight agitation in his voice. "I am now just finished."

"Oh, very good sir."

Despite herself, Charlotte turned to him as he folded and sealed his letter, then he stood up and turned to her most directly. He placed his hands down on the desk and Charlotte saw underneath his fingers a paper that was folded up carefully.

Within his eyes the message was most clear: it was something else he had written, and he meant for her to read it.

After he nodded to her with understanding, he turned, excused himself from the company and quitted the room.

※

AT FIRST CHARLOTTE did not move toward the desk, for fear of bringing attention to herself. Waiting patiently for a couple minutes, her curiosity burned most acutely, until she noticed slyly that no one was paying attention to her and therefore very slowly, she moved toward the writing desk, sat down and took the letter under her palm.

Once more she looked around and beheld all in their own conversation or wrapped up in the intimate space of daydreams.

Therefore, seeing that her actions went unnoticed and unheeded to, she raised up the letter, opened it and began to read most voraciously.

> *I can listen no longer in silence. I must speak to you by such means as are within my reach. Very often I have tried to appeal to you in the proper way, yet each time we have been thwarted, whether it be the actions of others or the threat of war, we never seem to be offered the chance to speak, to restore our confidence within one another. Therefore, this mode of writing you this letter breaches the rules set down by society, yet I care not.*
>
> *You pierce my soul. I am half agony, half hope. Tell me not that I am too late, that such precious feelings are gone forever. I offer myself to you again with a heart even more your own, than*

when you almost broke it all those years ago. Dare not say that man forgets sooner than woman, that his love has an earlier death. I have loved none but you. Bitter toward you I have been, enraged at your refusal of me, I have been as well, yet never inconstant. I know you are wise, Charlotte, you are prudent— but you have passion! You simply forgot it for a moment of time when you should have remembered it. You were once romantic in nature, and you believed in that moment of romance with me. Remember it again, Charlotte. Remember that you once were brave enough for love.

I must go to assist Harvill now at present, but I shall return to Queen's Hand to see you. Though I know that we shall not be alone, it will not deter me. All I require from you is a word, a look will be enough, either a smile or a shake of your head, to indicate your sentiments, and to decide whether I enter Hampshire to ask for your hand or never.

F.W.

When Charlotte closed the letter, her heart was filled with much amazement, for such a message was not to be soon recovered from. At first, she could only sit there, fixed and motionless as a statue, except for her face, which must have held a constant state of surprise. Every moment rather brought fresh agitation; it was an overpowering happiness.

How could it be? That he still loved her despite her mistakes in the past?

As well as being filled with such wonder, she regretted her present state of being within company, for it posed all the problems of being a woman in need of solitude to quiet her thoughts and being forced in a public situation.

She needed to be alone!

For every moment in company would expose her to even more

remarks than was her wish. She knew that she looked agitated, and perhaps ill from hearing such news would naturally make her appear as either very flushed or red in the face. Either look would not bode well, for already most of the guests thought her the injured woman from Captain Benwick. Seeing her looking ill at ease would only confirm it and lead to her being subject to even more looks of pity or ridicule.

No, she must not remain at Cumberland. Therefore, acting up on the dependence of friendship and the cushion that it offered her, Charlotte crossed the room and approached Jane Austen and Elizabeth, who remained separated from the rest while they spoke on some matters or another.

"Charlotte," Elizabeth began, but taking one look at Charlotte's face, she halted.

❧ 4 ❧

FORMIDABLE ALLY

"Charlotte?" I asked, eyeing her with suspicion, for it was not sickness that ailed her, but rather she was disturbed by something, "What is it?"

"It is... Jane and Elizabeth," she whispered, out of breath, "I need to return to the inn."

"What has occurred?" Jane Austen asked, defensively.

"Has someone said something that was offensive?"

"Oh no, quite the opposite." She stealthily took out a letter and handed it to us, "Elizabeth and Jane, if you have any bonds of friendship to me, please I call upon them now."

I was the first to take the letter and Jane Austen read it over my shoulder. As we did so, I felt Jane's breathing on my neck, and it grew hoarser over the course of our reading. When we both reached the end of it, Jane looked at Charlotte.

"F.W.? Then this was from—"

"Captain Wentworth?" I finished.

"Yes," Charlotte said, "he still loves me. He still loves me!"

"That is most wonderful," I said with a happy smile.

"Yet Lizzy and Jane, I fear that I cannot remain here, for my emotions will quite betray me. Please, let us go back to the inn."

"Right," I said, moving to Mr. Darcy with all speed. "My love, if you will forgive me, but I need to return to the inn."

"What is it, Elizabeth?"

"It is only, Fitzwilliam, I feel that I am not well."

My husband, who naturally preferred solitude over massive parties, was all too compliant to the scheme of us leaving. I told him as well that Charlotte and Jane Austen would join us. He was confused by this, but he did not question it. He approached Lady Russell and said that a part of our company had to depart, due to my health, however my sisters Jane, Kitty and Georgiana would remain along with Miriam, Maria, Mr. Bingley, Jason and Colonel Fitzwilliam. Therefore, our absence would go practically unnoticed.

This was all readily complied to, our carriage was drawn, and we were off to *The Queen's Hand*. As we did so, Mr. Darcy turned to me.

"What ails you, dearest?" Fitzwilliam began as we rode along. "And Miss Austen and Mrs. Collins, why did you wish to join us?"

"Because I am not really sick," I said, being honest.

"Then why did you wish to leave?"

"Because Charlotte has received some news that has affected her greatly."

"Elizabeth!" Charlotte gasped.

"Charlotte, you are my friend, and I love you, but I love him more, and never will I conceal anything from Mr. Darcy. I was going to tell him what had truly happened eventually; therefore, it is best we speak of it now."

Charlotte opened and closed her mouth, unable to argue with my inclination toward honesty and Fitzwilliam looked on me with utter confidence and pride.

Within that moment, I then had to accept that no matter what my thoughts were, no matter how much they would make me look emotional or foolish, I had to always share them with him. Honesty did feed love once the love was obtained—only if the person you loved was strong enough. And Mr. Darcy would always be strong enough for it.

NODDING HIS HEAD TOWARD CHARLOTTE, he smiled at her.

"You need have no fear of me," he said. "What is the truth that you are so afraid of revealing?"

"Give him the letter so he may read and understand," I said firmly.

"What?" Charlotte exclaimed.

"Charlotte, Fitzwilliam is the most clandestine and sturdy man ever, he will not break your confidence. Therefore, give him the letter so that he may read it."

Mr. Darcy, even more filled with pride at my wishing him to now always know what was occurring, leaned forward and reached out his hand.

"Do as my wife tells you," he said with such finality that Charlotte gave it to him without hesitation. Fitzwilliam raised the letter to his eyes and began to read. When done, he lowered it.

"This is from Captain Wentworth?"

"Yes."

"To you?"

"Yes."

"Very well, explain why he is sending a love letter to you."

Charlotte began to reveal Wentworth's visit and while she worried that my husband would censure her, he remained silent. When she continued, he breathed out evenly and put her narration into summation.

"I know a little something about refusing the wrong person for flimsy reasons, therefore I always understood your mistake," he said, looking toward me, and then he turned back to Charlotte and continued on. "And do you still love him?" he asked gently.

Charlotte turned to me in surprise, for she had not expected the strong and staunch-looking Mr. Darcy to ask such a delicate question.

"Yes, I do. In truth, I have never stopped."

"Then when he comes to see you, you had best make sure to give him a favorable reply."

"Yes, I shall."

"Very well," he said, handing her the letter. "Then when the moment arrives, go to it, and show more affection than you feel, and not less, if you are to secure him."

"Sir, I cannot show more than what I feel because I feel much."

He smiled at her. "Good answer." Charlotte looked at me in wonder, and I felt all the triumph of seeing my actions lead to good fruition.

"And Mr. Darcy," she continued.

"Yes?"

"Thank you for not being upset with him for sending me the letter or judging me for reading it."

"He communicated in the only way he could, and you needed the communication, or all would come to naught. You may have erred against the rules, but that does not mean that you were in error to have done so. Nothing can be worse than for two people to suffer under the weight of not being allowed to communicate. It is the root of all evil, I have learned."

"Well spoken," I remarked. With no inhibitions, he took my hand on the cushion and squeezed it fondly.

As we neared the inn, Fitzwilliam looked down at the letter one last time.

"I actually must offer him my congratulations," he said suddenly.

"Why so?" Charlotte asked.

"At his incredible prose. It is a well written love letter."

"That is precisely what I thought!" Jane Austen exclaimed. "Oh, forgive me, now is not the time for me to be thinking of words."

Mr. Darcy and Jane chuckled at her outburst and then we had arrived at *The Queen's Right Hand*.

We descended from the carriages and entered the inn.

As we did so, Charlotte walked near me and whispered in my ear.

"Why did you have Mr. Darcy read my letter?"

"I should have thought one of my reasons would have been clear to you."

"No, none of them are."

"Well Charlotte," I began listing, "for one, you are dear to me, but he will always be dearest in my eyes, and therefore I wish for Darcy to always know everything. Second, I knew that he would not be upset with you for your actions. For he is a man who has labored for so long under the weight of propriety while also ironically being one who is unafraid to breach propriety when need be. For him, the sanctity of following rules and the willfulness to break them are circumstantial. And thirdly, now he is your friend."

"Is he?"

"Yes, for he now knows a hidden truth about you. Knowing a hidden truth determines intimacy. And now he will feel camaraderie with you, and wait and see, you shall feel amicability toward him as well."

"Really? Those were all your intentions?"

"I am a complicated woman."

"I underestimated you."

"Many people do," I said, smiling as we walked forward.

As we walked through the inn, whether time would prove to be the culprit behind Charlotte's good fortune, or whether love truly did have a plan afoot, I know not. However, it was a most wonderful sight, for we were not soon into the parlor of the inn when we were greeted by Captain Wentworth.

He faltered when seeing us, for he was sitting in a corner, and we must have come upon him sooner than he had anticipated.

"Mr. Darcy," he said, standing up, "Mrs. Darcy, Miss Austen... and Charlotte," he began, standing up.

"Captain Wentworth," Mr. Darcy said, coming forward, "A pleasant surprise this is."

"Yes, it is. I had simply finished some business I had earlier than expected and felt that the inn would be best for a quick swig of ale."

"Oh, that is very well sir. Inn ale is the best."

"Yes, yes, it is."

At first there was the threat that we would sink into silence, but Jane Austen came forward.

"Well, we had only returned early so to see to William and Caiden, and this is where our company separates. For Mr. Darcy and Mrs. Darcy was planning to see to the boys while Charlotte and I had been desirous of a walk. Yet now that I am back in the comforts of the inn, I think I might be a little tired for the outing."

"Oh!" Captain Wentworth said. "Well, I have finished my drink and if Mrs. Collins would not mind, I should be happy to join her on her walk."

"That... that would be delightful," Charlotte said, her voice hoarse with emotion.

"Very well then," Mr. Darcy said with finality, "it is decided. Enjoy your walk, and Captain?"

"Yes sir."

"Be sure to keep to the public streets on this walk and also be certain that nothing happens to Charlotte along the way that would lead to any form of censure. I have had enough of men not considering a woman's reputation for one engagement party."

"Yes sir, I can assure you I shall do the service with much diligence."

"Very well then."

I looked between Mr. Darcy and Captain Wentworth, and seeing them both looking upon one another, it was amazing how they were both such strong and determined men. Indeed, I felt them to be the stuff of legend.

Captain Wentworth offered Charlotte his arm, she took it, and they left the inn together.

The three of us looked at one another and Mr. Darcy smiled at Jane Austen.

"Miss Austen, when the time calls for it, you make a formidable ally."

She gave him a sly smile. "Yes,it is one of my hidden talents."

We all walked up the steps, we parted ways with Jane and went to Lucy's room where she was seeing to Caiden and William.

While we sat down and played with our children, I often looked up at Mr. Darcy, who eyed me with reverence.

"What is that look for?" I asked.

"Nothing of great importance," he teased. "I simply love you terribly is all."

"You would be wrong to do otherwise."

"And may I never be wrong."

"You are Mr. Darcy...being wrong does not become you."

5

THE GOOD THAT SPRINGS FROM THE BAD

A rm and arm, Charlotte and Captain Wentworth walked out of the inn, and down the street. At first there was nothing but silence between them, for their emotions would not allow them to speak. At last, Charlotte, not wishing to appear meek, thought it wise to speak.

"Your letter...even Jane Austen said that it was well written."

"Oh, did she?" He laughed.

"Yes, she did."

"Then that is a great compliment."

"Yes, it is. And I congratulate you."

"Thank you."

"And I adore you as well."

Captain Wentworth's voice was caught in his throat, for he was not prepared for her to say it at last.

"I am..." Charlotte began, "Frederick... I—forgive me, it is hard to speak just now."

He sighed greatly. "I comprehend your feelings, for my voice is not behaving as well."

"And yet...there is so much I wish to say to you, to speak of, for you deserve to hear so much."

"Why did you never tell me that your mother was the one who separated us? Charlotte..."

"It did not matter. I had rejected you and it was ultimately my actions, my fault and my weakness. My mother would not have been successful, and I would not have fallen victim to over-persuasion if I had only held my argument and committed to what was in my heart."

"Your love for her and sense of duty naturally would have over-whelmed you in such a moment," he said, "and I can comprehend that."

"Yes, and I am happy that you ought to. However, it does not excuse that we could have been married all these years, we could have been happy, and we both could have known love if I had only made the right decision."

"Well, I forgive you."

"And I am happy to be forgiven."

"If you can forgive me."

"What do you have to apologize for?"

"For how I acted when I saw you once again here at Cumberland. I was resentful, and my good opinion of you was most dissolved."

"You were heartbroken, Frederick, and the woman who broke your heart was once again before you. I never blamed you for your actions or words. They hurt me, yes, but they were from the lips of a man who I had once hurt more. Frederick?"

"Yes?"

"You pierce my soul as well—and I love you."

"Do you?"

"Yes, and in truth, I never stopped. Indeed, I never could have stopped. When we first met, I was already in the middle of liking you that I did not even know when I had begun."

Captain Wentworth laughed at her statement, and she laughed as well.

"And yet I do not understand now, as I did not then," she said, "how you could ever have fallen in love with me? Never have I been deserving of you."

"You are a beautiful woman, Charlotte. Just in a very different sort of way."

"I will fight for you," she said. "My whole family can reject me and leave me forsaken for my entire life. Frederick, now I shall do what I should have done. I shall fight to always keep you."

"You would?"

"Yes."

"Now there she is," he smiled gently. "There is the Charlotte Lucas I once fell in love with."

They walked on a little further and Captain Wentworth led her down a side street that held no one in sight. Further down they walked, their bodies close together, and Charlotte allowed her head to rest on his shoulder as they traveled aimlessly.

"Charlotte?"

"Yes."

"I am going to kiss you now."

"Truly?"

"Yes."

Slowing down, Captain Wentworth took one of Charlotte's hands in his own, and pressed the other one on her waist, pulling her close to him. Looking deep into her eyes, he lowered his head, and they kissed.

Deeply and passionately, their embrace was the likes of which Charlotte had never known but had always desired.

As they stood there, locked into a kiss that she would remember all her days, Charlotte wondered at her good fortune. For when she had been invited to Cumberland, the arrival of this man from her past threatened to disrupt the little bit of peace that she once had. But it all had turned around and become for the better! How exhilarating it all was in the end, she felt, as she was locked in this moment of pure bliss, enjoying all the good that springs from the bad.

6

WISHFUL THINKING

Having arrived in Philadelphia the day before, Samuel Lucas woke up in his room in the Society Hill Inn, stood up and walked to the window. It could not have been more than eight in the morning and the street was already filled with people.

Being a stranger in a strange land, Samuel Lucas looked down on the street with trepidation. When he had gotten on the ship from England, he knew there was a national crisis on the rise, but nothing had been made official. Then he had gotten off the boat on the river front of the city and he had discovered that England and America were now at war.

To be in a new country was already daunting, but to be in the country where yours was at war with was the most dangerous. Still keeping his wits about him, when he landed, he immediately asked for the closest inn so that he could get inside and away from the populous as soon as possible and form a plan. It would be best to speak as little as possible, this he knew. Therefore, when a house-keeping woman came to the door to ask if he wanted her to make his bed, he opened it and figured that she of all people would not care about his nationality, for all that she wanted was to keep her employment. Whatever he was would mean little to nothing to her. He inquired about the location of Canterbury estate and upon learning of its whereabouts, he also asked how he could easily receive transport around the city. She informed him of the inn's carriage rentals, which if he paid, he would be driven to any destination in the city's downtown area. When he asked her if it would take him as far as Canterbury, she answered in the affirmative and then he ordered her to arrange a carriage for him, giving her a dime for her services.

When she went away, he went inside, dressed himself in the best attire he had brought, went downstairs to the dining hall, had some breakfast, was informed that the carriage was ready, and he soon was being transported through the streets of Philadelphia toward Canterbury estate.

As he rode along, his nerves were most extreme, for he did not know what to say or how to approach the situation. He was breaking every rule that there could ever be. Also, his efforts could all be for naught. Deborah Darcy would have detested the idea of his coming to see her, as well as her parents of course not wishing to take him to her as well, finding him to be an impertinent snip. All of his time, effort and money wasted all because he decided to act on a whim.

And yet, what if he was fortunate, and everything that he hoped would come true? What if he went to Canterbury and her parents were kind and not apprehensive about this Englishman who came in the midst of war declarations to see their daughter who was a nun? And Deborah had always been a spirited and very outspoken woman —but being a nun now surely would have altered her a great deal. A nunnery was such a strict environment, and it led to even the most kind of creatures eventually turning rigid and stiffly pious. No, he was not candid in his thoughts. Sometimes, as religion was meant to be something that brought liberty of soul to morals of virtue, people used it to the extreme, abusing the very thing they claimed to hold dear and oppressing others with it. What if that life had affected Deborah in any way?

Then he remembered her letter to him, and his heart swelled with hope. She had been the one to contact him first, and how could it be forgotten? No, it must not be. For she clearly was of the same passionate and headstrong character that he had remembered her for. Headstrong in nature was usually a flaw in a person, yet with Deborah, he had seen quickly into their relationship that it was her main virtue. From what he recalled, she had courage, and she fought for the right sort of things that one ought to fight for—and she never had a fear in facing the world and telling it that it was in error.

She had always been better than him.

And he had let her go once.

Oh, to see her again!

However, Samuel Lucas wrung his hands in frustration with his own nature. He worried that he was making a dream of her, and dreamers always have a way of killing the dream they have by puffing it up into something that was never there. His memories of her were fond ones, yet he could have developed such a nostalgia, that she could never live up to the pedestal that he placed her on.

"She is human," he said to himself as the coach rode on, "just as am I. She is bound to disappoint, but only a person of weak character can hold it against her for not being the ideal that no woman can reach."

Thereby, in sheer force of will, Samuel Lucas schooled himself and would not allow his fancies to overwhelm his reason.

Eventually the carriage rolled down the lane and at the end of it was Canterbury House.

Samuel Lucas looked out of the window to behold it, and he immediately felt even more self-conscious. The estate was vast, and he was so small and insignificant that there could be no place for him there. He was not worthy of it.

How had he avoided not ever seeing her house before? Oh, he

recalled how when they met. She was staying at a friend's house in the country, and he wooed her while she was there. Thinking on that memory, he preferred it much more to the reality before him, for meeting a woman he once loved was hard—yet meeting her parents must have been the worst of feelings.

The carriage stopped in front of the house and the coachman dismounted from his seat and opened the door.

"Canterbury Park sir."

"Thank you," Samuel Lucas said, stepping down before the front porch. His legs felt like they were about to give way beneath him, but he gathered his courage, walked up the steps and swung the door knocker a few times. After a couple of minutes, a butler opened the door, and he took off his hat.

"Good day," Samuel Lucas began, "My name is Mr. Samuel Lucas, of Lucas Lodge in Hampshire, and I humbly request an audience with Mr. and Mrs. Thomas Darcy."

❦

SAMUEL LUCAS WAS SHOWN into the sitting room, where he only had the chance to sit down and become comfortable when a large elderly woman entered.

"Good day," she began. "My name is Mrs. Emilia Darcy. Forgive my husband for not coming immediately, but he is held up by business in his study and shall join you."

"Pleased to meet you, Mrs. Darcy," Samuel said, bowing. "I am Mr. Samuel Lucas, from Hampshire, England."

"From England?" she said, her face growing serious, "Good gracious, what would bring you from there? Oh, but wait! You said you were from Hampshire?"

"Yes."

"There are a family of Bennets from there that are—"

"Yes! I grew up with them. The Bennet sisters, Miss Jane, Elizabeth, Mary, Kitty and Lydia."

"Oh, then did you come to see Lydia!"

"Oh, that is right! She must live here because she is married to your son."

"Oh, then you did not come for her?"

"No, though I would be happy to see her."

"Very well," Emilia said, ringing the bell that was on her desk, and shortly afterwards, a maid entered. "Sofie, please bring Henry and Lydia to meet our guest."

"Yes, ma'am," the servant named Sofie said, and then left.

"So, what brings you to Philadelphia, sir?" Emilia continued. "For you do come at a most interesting time."

"Oh, I came to visit a past acquaintance of mine who belongs to this family."

"Oh, you did? Well then, who would—"

"Mr. Lucas!" Lydia's voice came from down the hall. Samuel Lucas breathed out evenly, smiling. While Lydia's nature had always been described as exuberant, he always took joy in seeing her, for he believed her high spirits were the product of her simply being a young woman.

Her footsteps grew closer, accompanied by another and Samuel Lucas stood up just in time to see Lydia enter the room. Her beauty seemed to be at its most prominent, for she seemed to glow in his eyes. That could very well be defined by the man to her left, who clearly was her husband, Mr. Henry Darcy.

"Samuel!" Lydia cried, "I cannot believe it is you."

"Miss Bennet," Samuel said.

"Oh, Samuel, you are not used to my new name," Lydia said, looking up at Henry Darcy to her left. "It is Mrs. Darcy now, and I hope I carry the name well."

"You do Mrs. Darcy, and it looks well on you."

"Thank you, but I cannot take all the credit." She smiled gently.

"As a matter of fact, I can take none, for all accolades must be given to my husband here."

"And he deserves none either," Emilia cried, "for he was born from me."

Samuel Lucas laughed comfortably at their jokes, and he was never happier to see Lydia in the whole of his life.

"And now, if I may," Lydia said, "Mr. Darcy, this is Mr. Samuel Lucas, who is a friend to my family in Hampshire, as well as a neighbor. And Mr. Lucas, this is my husband, Mr. Henry Darcy."

Both men bowed to each other politely, and Samuel Lucas was left in awe, amazed at how Henry Darcy reminded him of Mr. Fitzwilliam Darcy of Pemberley.

"Mr. Darcy," Samuel said, "I must congratulate you on your splendid conquest with Mrs. Darcy here, for she was one of the jewels of Hampshire."

"Oh, Jane was the beauty of the county," Lydia corrected him, "Everyone knew that. But thank you for the good compliment, Mr. Lucas."

"It is nice to meet you as well," Mr. Darcy said, nodding his head curtly. "I very rarely meet Lydia's friends from England that this is an unexpected pleasure. Yet I am curious, what would bring you to America at this time of year, when our countries have now declared war."

"I know it seems foolish."

"And suspicious."

"Oh, Henry please," Lydia said. "I can assure you that Samuel here is not a spy in any way at all."

"Oh, was that the thought!" Samuel exclaimed. "I am mortified if I gave that impression. No, when I left England, war still had not been declared in full, so I thought that I had time."

"You came here on holiday?"

"In a way. I actually came here to once more see an old friend."

"And who is this friend that you say is connected to—wait, you said your name was Lucas?" Emilia realized.

"Yes."

"Then that means...are you the Mr. Lucas that my daughter, Deborah, knew?"

"Yes, indeed! And I was hoping that—"

"You and she courted for a while."

"Oh," Samuel Lucas said, taken aback by the bold declaration."

"What?" Lydia said. "Is that true?"

"Oh well," Samuel muttered, "one could call it a courtship, but we did not ever come to a full understanding."

"And I however," Henry Darcy said, "am left in ignorance on all that you are speaking of. What is this all about?"

Samuel Lucas felt himself very much put on the spot and he did not foresee this quick confrontation.

"Samuel," Lydia began, softly, "you need not fear. We are all very forward in this house because there is no reason to be afraid of one's words, we have learned. Therefore, cast away your apprehensions, your need to conceal, and tell us all the truth."

Samuel looked between them all and realized that he should not have been surprised, for after all, where would Deborah have gotten her frank and outspoken gumption from?

"I...in truth, I did know Deborah Darcy, we had a brief courtship where I did not pursue a more serious attachment, and I wished to see her again."

"To offer her another brief attachment?" Mr. Darcy asked.

"Henry," Emilia said, "you know I always love your need to be overprotective of your sisters but now is not the time. Do not be intimidated, Mr. Lucas. Henry just naturally has a very loyal and protective nature when it comes to family."

"Yes," Samuel said, "I do understand your apprehensions, Mr. Darcy. But she has no need to fear me, for she has already taken her vows, and is beyond my influence. It is.... it is simply I who am not beyond hers, it seems."

"Then," Lydia said, "you really did come all this way to see her again?"

"Yes," Samuel said, gathering his courage and disposing of the last remnants of the timid man he was when he entered the house. "Yes, I found that I could not rest until I had done so."

Lydia, Henry and Emilia all looked at Samuel with wonder, before Emilia blinked and remembered herself.

"Henry?"

"Yes, Mother."

"Get your father. For this one he has to hear himself."

⚜

UPON HIS ENTRANCE, Thomas Darcy was a very large presence, not due to his size, but his energy.

"What is it, Emilia?" he asked when he entered to see Samuel Lucas with Lydia and Henry. "Ah, a new acquaintance!"

"New to us, Thomas," Emilia said, "but old to our daughter, Deborah. This is Mr. Samuel Lucas, from England and he has come to see Deborah, for he has a previous acquaintance with her."

"Ah, you do, do you?" Thomas said, approaching Samuel. "How do you know my daughter, sir?"

"I... I once courted her."

"You what?"

The question was a deafening one, for everyone started, including Samuel.

"Yes, sir, I once courted Miss Deborah Darcy."

Samuel Lucas then proceeded to tell them all of when he had come to Philadelphia and met Deborah, and how they quickly became attached. When they did not offer one another a permanent bond of mutual desires, they separated, but there was always much affection in that case. Over the years, Samuel had never forgotten her. Then one day, she had sent him a letter through Jane Bennet, telling her of how she wished just simply to write to him one last time. The letter had caused him to have hope, fleeting hope that she would like to see him again.

When he concluded his narration, Mr. Thomas Darcy looked on him with a sober expression.

"And that is it?" he said, a little pained. "You came here, from all the way around the world, just to see her again, and therefore confuse her, and wonder why you had never done anything sooner."

"Mr. Darcy," Emilia warned.

"Sir," Samuel Lucas said, "I know this all sounds preposterous, and also that I must be weak. Yet all I can say is that I simply wish to see her again, and maybe she and I can both find peace."

"It might affect her."

"She is a nun, Mr. Darcy. She will never even care that I came perhaps and never wish me to see her. Please, all that I ask is to have this moment. I can assure you that I am harmless."

Thomas leaned back and looked long and hard at Samuel Lucas.

"You should have proposed to her when you first met," he said.

"Perhaps I should have, sir."

"Oh well, I suppose... it is better you try now than never again," Emilia said.

"Now, I did not come to America to take her from her convent life."

"So, you just came here to say hello to her?" Thomas said bluntly. "Mr. Lucas, forgive my pertness, but I was not born yesterday."

❦

As soon as Emilia had accepted his plan, she thought it would be best to not withhold the meeting till the next day. She had the carriage pulled along and she, Lydia, Henry, and Mr. Lucas were riding along, making their way to the convent.

All the way there, Samuel could not help but find himself amazed at how blunt the whole afternoon was. In the presence of the Darcy family, he felt quite naked, for he was never used to people making jokes at his expense or being so intensely honest about everything. However, he got used to the family dynamic of the American Darcys.

Upon arrival, they were granted entry, and they spoke with the Mother Superior of the convent, who sent another nun to fetch Sister Ignatius. While they waited, Mother Superior looked Mr. Lucas over.

"And you, sir, you are from England?"

"Yes," Samuel Lucas said, "I am indeed."

"And how do you know Sister Ignatius?"

"He is family," Emilia said for him. "He is a cousin on my husband's side."

Samuel Lucas flinched at the lie and wondered why it was necessary. But as the Mother Superior looked him over with suspicion, he acquiesced to the deceit because he could tell that she did not trust his reason for coming.

She soon left him alone with Emilia, Lydia and Henry Darcy. Samuel felt that even that was too many eyes on him. Yet he decided it would be best to adjust to the open manner this branch of the Darcys offered him, and so he smiled at them.

"I must confess... I am a little nervous."

"Do not be," Lydia encouraged.

"Yes," Emilia said eagerly. "She will be happy to see you."

"Really? Then she is not fully upset with me at all? I was worried that my hope in her joy at seeing me once more was wishful thinking."

"No, she is not and—"

"Mother!" Came the voice of Sister Ignatius—Deborah Darcy. "And Henry! Lydia, you have all come to see me!"

Samuel Lucas turned to her. At first, Deborah did not see him for she only beheld her family.

⌘

SHE WAS as he remembered her, except in different attire. Yet the strict uniform of a nun did not confine her. She was smiling, full of energy and vigor. And seeing her excitement at seeing her family was all the proof that he needed.

"You three can't live without me, can you?" She laughed as she approached. "And who is with—"

Her eyes fell on him, and she halted immediately.

As she was as he remembered her, he was also as she remembered him.

Both remained looking upon each other, not knowing what to say. Although the amazement was mostly on her side, for Samuel Lucas knew very well that he was pursuing her, and she had remained ignorant of his coming. Therefore, nothing could prepare her for the element of surprise that overwhelmed her sensibilities now.

Yet for Samuel Lucas, he did his best not to cling to the dream, but live in the reality, for wishful thinking really was overcoming him at the moment. She might truly mind his coming or may only tolerate it—but no matter the outcome he could not regret his coming, for seeing her now satisfied his curiosity in full.

Deborah Darcy, he thought, *Once more, we see one another.*

7

REMEMBERING ROSINGS

When the news spread amidst our company that Captain Wentworth and Charlotte were now engaged—so long as Captain Wentworth received permission from Sir William Lucas, then the engagement would be secure—there was great joy all around.

At first there was the impulse to only keep the news within our own company, yet Colonel Fitzwilliam had a different view on the matter.

"If we announce this news to the Cumberland Company," he said, "then this will solve many problems."

"How so?" Captain Wentworth asked, dubious.

"Forgive me if you see my view as me using your news of joy for the benefit of all, but I believe it shall help you as well."

"And how?"

"Charlotte," Kitty began, "as you are aware, there was talk that you and Captain Benwick were beginning to feel a bond with each other."

I saw Charlotte and Captain Wentworth give each other an apprehensive glance, and they could not deny Kitty's words.

"Well," Kitty continued, "if you announce with each other that you are engaged to the group, then it will end all rumors of you being ill-used, Charlotte, and you would no longer be a subject of pity."

"Precisely," Colonel Fitzwilliam continued. "And to add to all this, the scandal that Benwick's elopement has created will make the Russells feel as if their engagement party ended in tragedy. They will never live it down. Yet if you make the announcement and thank Lady Russell for the invitation to their son's engagement party, really acknowledging the fact that only through the invitation could you both have re-met and fell in love, then the Russells will not only see their party as the best of events to occur, but Lady Russell will also look kindly on us all. For we brought Charlotte."

"You both will become heroic in her eyes," Kitty added, "and we will look good-natured for being the means that brought you here. And I am sure that the Russells are looking for a savior just now."

"And there is another addition to this plan," I said. "Wentworth, Lady Lucas once had Charlotte refuse you due to lack of wealth, connections and consequence in the world, yes?"

"Yes," he said, his pride stirred.

"She will not deny you now that you have wealth. But to add to your good qualities, if you announce the engagement here. Then Lady Russell will naturally wish to send a letter to congratulate Lady Lucas on receiving you as a son-in-law. Well then, it will not only enhance your suitability, but it shall also make her fully regret ever telling Charlotte to deny you in the first place."

Captain Wentworth looked at Charlotte, then turned back to Colonel Fitzwilliam, Kitty and me.

"Well," he said, "I daresay that is brilliant."

"How quickly do you wish to tell them?" Charlotte asked him eagerly.

"How quickly can we have our carriages brought round?"

THE ANNOUNCEMENT of Captain Wentworth and Charlotte's engagement could not have gone any better! Upon informing all the company at Cumberland of their union, everyone was overjoyed at the news, but none more than Lady Russell, Mr. Russell and Miss Elton.

When Charlotte thanked Lady Russell for her invitations to our company and to Jane Austen, because only by her coming could she have re-met the man who she was now engaged to, Lady Russell and her son felt a great elation for knowing that they had been the means through which two people could have found such joy. Miss Elton felt quite distinguished as well and openly declared that this would be a story she would tell her children, for it was not every day that an engagement party led to another engagement.

"This day," Miss Elton had said, "joy has truly sprung from joy-initiate."

Lady Russell wished to prolong the party so that this new couple could celebrate alongside her son and his fiancée. But we respectfully declined her offer, stating that we had to return to share the news with Charlotte's family.

Charlotte took that opportunity to ask Lady Russell to send a letter to her family at Lucas Lodge to congratulate her parents on their daughter's good fortune.

"My mother would be exhilarated to know that such a distinguished woman such as yourself has written to her," Charlotte asked. "If I may be so bold to ask you for such an honor."

"Mrs. Collins," Lady Russell said, "I would be delighted, and nothing could give me greater pleasure."

It could therefore be nothing short of correct that Colonel Fitzwilliam and Kitty had joined their minds together and proved to be as great a couple strategically as domestically. I never understood how their souls were so united that they thought of such intricate plans, to the point where they anticipated anything. In that way I was jealous of them very much.

Darcy and I were exemplary in that our hearts were inextricably linked. We weaved a web of comfort and security around us where we fought to catch anyone around us who seemed to be falling, but Kitty and the Colonel were unique in their own manner. It was as if they were two souls who, no matter how far they had moved from one another, the bond did not break, and they would travel any distance to unite. As the same was said for their instincts physically, now the same could be said for their minds. They did not even have long to see the success of announcing Charlotte's engagement and therefore must have arrived at the notion swiftly and organically.

Therefore, it was left for me to arrive at two conclusions:

With Darcy and me, our hearts were linked.

With Kitty and the Colonel, their souls were interwoven.

With Jane always with us, there would always be serene individuality.

With Georgiana and Jason, there would always be daring.

With Mr. Bingley and Miriam, there would always be laughter and tolerance.

With Lydia and Henry Darcy far in the distance, there would always be knowledge that our family stretched far and wide.

With Mary at Rosings, there was knowledge that there would always be another to help build another connection.

And with Jane Austen somewhere in the world, there would be someone to write it all down.

I did not know what Charlotte and Captain Wentworth would bring. However, what was also certain was that all our hidden qualities forged together and created an unbreakable link.

That was why our personalities always seemed desirous of returning to each other, and we could not stay long away. For we all seemed to fit in a strange way.

We were a family—even if all of us were not related, for family does not always need to be.

⁂

Lady Russell promised to write the letter. Everyone's last day at Cumberland passed in happy well-wishes, it eased the sting of the elopement, and that was where the many partings began.

Our company then would separate, for Captain Wentworth, Charlotte, Maria, the Crofts and Jane Austen would return to Hampshire. There, Charlotte and Wentworth would announce their engagement while the Crofts would settle into Aginfield.

The rest of our company, consisting of Kitty, Colonel Fitzwilliam, Jane, Georgiana, Jason, Darcy, the Bingleys, our sons, and I would leave with our servants for Rosings Park.

Though we had received permission to go to Rosings, I still was worried about our reception. Yet it was a bridge that needed to be crossed—or rather a barrier that needed to be broken down.

Before our company had officially parted, Mrs. Croft took me aside, giving us one last moment of being in each other's confidence.

"It is all so amazing," she began, "for when we had come to the party, I was worried that my brother would be in danger of making a foolish match, but I never had expected that this would be the outcome. Is it not all amazing?"

"It is." I smiled.

"And it cannot ever be anything otherwise. And to think, the house that we rent now is in the same village as the location where his future wife lives."

"Is it enough to make you believe in destiny?"

"Oh," she chuckled, "I already believed in it."

"I hope you enjoy your stay in Aginfield," I said. "Yet I feel very certain that we shall see each other again."

"That much is very certain," she said, then nodded her farewell to me and joined her husband.

OUR CARRIAGES WERE SET, our luggage packed away, with Lucy had my sons stored securely in the last carriage with Jefferson to remain with her. We all assembled and were off.

As we rode on, our conversation was very idle and some of us fell asleep. In our carriage, which held Mr. Darcy, Jane, Mr. Bingley, Miriam and me, after two hours' time, only Fitzwilliam and I were awake.

"This is the closest we shall get to being alone." I leaned against his shoulder.

"Yes, it is."

"I confess myself a little unsettled at how it shall be for us to go to Rosings. Do you think Lady Catherine shall learn to like me?"

"She has no choice, for I shall give her none. You need not worry, my love, in remembering Rosings, all I can say is that her house makes her a better person. In Rosings Park, my aunt loves to talk, and is dominant, but never will her unpleasantness lead to her slighting someone to such an extent that she would have them desire to be rid of her company. No Lizzy, the very best part of my aunt's personality is in Rosings Park."

✺ 8 ✺

A FAVORABLE IMPRESSION

Samuel Lucas and Deborah Darcy remained with their gazes fixed upon one another, so much so that they forgot they were in the company of her mother, brother and sister-in-law.

Not fully enjoying the way Samuel Lucas eyed his little sister, Henry Darcy cleared his throat loudly, and that was enough to break the spell of wonderment.

"Oh, forgive me!" Samuel Lucas blurted out. "I forgot myself."

"Oh, it is quite all right," Deborah Darcy muttered, "It is all so... I never—I never thought I would see you again."

"I know, and I with you. Forgive me for my sudden appearance."

"Yes," she gasped, feeling out of breath. "It has indeed taken me by surprise. And as you might recall, surprises always lead to being at a loss of what to say. I am never up for the task of it."

"I can understand that."

"That does not... it does not mean that I am not happy to see you. Oh, Samuel, I can scarce believe that you are before me now."

"Nor I with you, and I could not help it. Forgive me for my abrupt arrival, Sister Ignatius, yet I had to see you once more."

"Oh, why are you apologizing?" She smiled, overcoming her nerves and approaching him with energy. "There is no need for you to do so. Oh Samuel!"

She opened her arms and placed her hands on his cheeks. The touch of her hands upon his face startled him and he shivered.

"Oh dear, you are blushing!" She laughed. "And you must call me Deborah, for I never forsook my name. It still is within me."

"Deborah..." he sighed, forgetting himself, then he realized that Emilia and Henry were watching them, so he took Deborah's hands from his face, but would not relinquish them just yet, and held them within his own.

"I..." he said, at a loss. "We..."

Lydia stood up with alacrity and smiled knowingly.

"You two obviously have much to speak of, and if my husband and wonderful mother-in-law would not mind taking a turn with me around the grounds of the convent, I would greatly love their company."

"Of course, my dear," Emilia said, standing up, "I too would like to take a walk."

"But..." Henry objected, looking at Samuel with distrust. "I do not..."

"Oh, Deborah is fine, Henry," Emilia said with an edge to her voice, which made her strong and determined son ready to comply. For even he was a man who understood the obligation to fear his own mother. The three of them stood up and left Deborah and Samuel to enjoy one another's company.

When seeing the look on Samuel's face, Deborah smiled.

"Are they not the best family ever?"

❦

"I confess," Samuel said, smiling at her, "that I have never met a family quite like this one!"

"And you never will, I bet, now come and walk with me."

"Of course."

In seeing that she was as he remembered her to be, Samuel felt his mood lighten as he walked alongside her. He was content in seeing that he had been in error to think the woman he knew was only a figment of his imagination, and that there could not be a woman of such vitality, optimism and good-natured frankness. Oh no, Deborah Darcy, in life, did find union with all those qualities, and she had not changed for the worse, but remained as the better.

"You received my letter with favor, then," she smiled, "for if not, then you never would have come."

"I am amazed, Deborah," he said, "at your courage."

"My courage?" She laughed. "What courage do I possess?"

"Much."

"How did you arrive at that conclusion?"

"Because you wrote to me. I could very well have rebuked you or found your daring to send me a letter as nothing less than scandalous."

"Yet I knew you would not."

"How did you know?"

"Because that is not in your nature."

"To think things scandalous?"

"No, to rebuke someone who needed to speak her mind, and speak she would."

"You think me having that much nerve?"

"You did have that much nerve. You do not become shocked so easily, Samuel. That was what I always liked about you."

"You did?"

"Yes. And you see whatever courage I have, you must have as much clearly."

"Now I know why I was amazed by you when we first met."

Deborah blushed and looked down at the footpath as they walked.

"You were never afraid to speak your mind to me."

"I never saw the fear of it, tis true," she said. "I am surprised that I never got into more trouble when I was young."

"As am I, for the world has a way of punishing such innocent courage. Yet I am also not surprised, for how can the world ever despise a creature like you? You shine like the sun, you know."

"I would say this is too much praise!" she exclaimed. "Yet I shall always love a compliment."

"You always did."

"As long as it seemed sincere."

"And I was always sincere."

"Yes, you were. That is what made Samuel Lucas special, I daresay."

"Deborah, you are not unhappy at all at my coming?"

"Why should I be?"

"I don't know. I just wished to make certain that you were not."

"As you can see from my eagerness to have seen you again, no I am not."

"That is very good. For I did not want you to be."

"Yet why did you risk so much? To come here now, when it is so late into our lives just to see me?"

"Curiosity is a strange thing. A powerful thing. And we are not always best at keeping it in check."

"Not all people are. And you could not school yours?" She gave him a subtle glance.

"No, I could not. At least, not in this case. I usually have held it in check with stern discipline."

"Then I am special?"

"Yes," he laughed, "you very much are."

"I like that I am so."

"And still so honest?"

"I am a nun. Our constant worries about death and preparing

many for salvation has taught me not to fear life and telling the truth while one has it."

"You would approach life in a convent differently than others. Deborah, you never did believe in being the same."

"It is never easy to believe in something that is so foreign to you. I once thought myself to be a wild beast."

"How so?"

"I loved to laugh."

"Many women do."

"I loved to laugh at those who took matters too seriously. I loved to be mad. This was before I met you."

"Did you often get censured for it?"

She nodded. "Yes. And I did not care."

Samuel stopped their walking and turned her toward him.

"Deborah?"

"Yes."

"What is it that fuels you?"

"I do not know."

"Surely you must."

"Perhaps it is my faith."

"Many of us have faith, but very rarely does it have the effect that it has upon you."

"Because very often people have the wrong sort of faith. And they call it otherwise."

৩৵ৎ৩

SAMUEL STOOD MORE ERECT, wondering at her comment.

"What do you mean by 'the wrong sort of faith'?"

"They look at it as only a set of rules and regulations, restricting us from many things. Yes, it is a code for morality and principles, but they treat morality as if it is a noose that we ought to hang ourselves with. They do not see what faith is meant to be. It is supposed to teach us morality, yes, but it is also meant to bring us joy, laughter, and acceptance."

She looked at him. "Most of all, it is meant to offer forgiveness for those who actually seek it. Do you know how many often forsake people for small mistakes and call themselves pious? It is too much to be born. Do you also know how many people find dancing to be a wicked practice? And yet they forget that the book of our Lord had dancing as a wholesome pastime. Many people enter this world with the right sort of mind, and are given the right sort of principles, but are taught to practice them in the wrong sort of ways. They label anyone who tries to change the world, for the better and the more tolerant, as a heretic or a menace, and yet they forget that our lord was also called every sort of name because he refused to submit to hypocrisy and injustice. They forget that he laughed, believed in joyous events and mirth. They forget what true love is. They speak one thing and act upon another. That is the wrong sort of faith. And I may be flawed, yet I do have it... oh dear, am I preaching again?"

"Yes," he said with a warm smile.

"I do that a lot, don't I?"

"Yes, but because you have something to say. It makes up for the fact that I have little to talk about myself."

"You are an odd sort of creature."

He cocked his head. "I am the odd one?"

"Yes, for how many men like for a woman to always wish to speak?"

"The right sort do. I never understood why men treasured silence with women—only through speaking can you begin to understand her."

She gave a wry smile. "Humanity is filled with those who only want to speak and not listen. Whenever two people marry, with the impulse to do so, they are committing a grave offense to their spouse."

"Indeed, they are, yet that is not a crime you shall ever have to suffer under. For you shall never marry."

"Yes, I shall never have to suffer under it."

At first, they walked in silence, understanding the implications of their speech.

"However," she continued, "I may not have to suffer it under a husband, but I do suffer it under the many prejudices here. You have no account, I can assure you, of how many nuns here are not easy to be amongst."

"Really?"

"I do not feel pain for saying it, because they have earned that title. They cling to ignorance of the world and still think they can preach of it. Some despise men—I know that men can be terrible, but so can we women. Humanity is a hard thing to be a part of, but we should never forsake the next person because of what the previous one did. Many come in here the best of women and some remain so, while others get destroyed by a crude system. Others come in here already wrong. They suffer the same weakness as the rest of us, having a hard time listening because they believe in their right to speak, but not be spoken to."

"Oh, so you exchanged one option of a husband for many wives?" Samuel laughed.

"Do not make such fun, however, now that I think on it...you are right!"

"I do not mean to offend my sisters," she amended, "nor my profession. I just simply—if it is the wickedness within me, then it is so. I cannot hold back what I feel and speak and only speak of the good. Sometimes what is not good to hear is what should be spoken off."

"Deborah?"

"Yes?"

"Why did you become a nun?"

Deborah was silent at first, for she did not know how to frame her argument, for it was more complicated than what she could put into her words.

"I have great faith, you know that."

"Yes, I do. But was that all?"

"I suppose that I could not see myself in any other fate that was before me. And I also wanted to change the world."

"Did you?"

"Yes. There are not many chances that a woman can do so, and I thought it would be this one. In truth, many women become nuns in hopes that this will be a chance to help the world, and to fight for it."

"Fight?"

"Yes, faith—or the right sort of it, is a war, in its own way. To protect those who cannot protect themselves, to fight against immorality, and to fight against those who use their notions of religion and wield it to do unspeakable acts. If people see us people of faith fight against injustice, then there is a chance that more will follow. Many who try fail though. I know I will fail as well, but I smile still because I still have hope that I may succeed."

"How strong are you?" he asked, amazed. "Deborah, could you suffer the burden of the world at its worst?"

"I already have," she said. "You haven't seen the fights I have undergone, both emotionally and physically."

"Physically?"

"Sometimes when you stand up for people, you are standing in the way of someone who wished to harm them. Samuel, do not ask me questions, but understand that I could not help but stand in their way."

"Deborah...you must never put yourself in harm's way."

"I must, if there is no one else to do it."

Samuel groaned inwardly, for he felt so helpless. Whatever

course Deborah would walk down, he could never be there to protect her, and it slowly ate away at him.

"I just want you to be safe," he said, "and I always want you to live."

"But what sort of life would it be if I did not live it with utter conviction?" she asked, her eyes wide in supplication. "Samuel, this is my life, and it can be no other. All I ask you now, after so long of us being apart, is to be proud of me."

"I am."

"Are you?"

"Yes, I just am not proud of myself."

"And why not?"

"Because I cannot protect you."

"It's best whether you are there or not. A man should always fight for a woman's life, but we must always fight for ourselves, and I will do so."

Samuel smiled gently, and he recalled all the conversations they both had in the past. Never did they ever go the way that regular conversations would between a man and a woman. And now it was the same as always. With any other woman, there would have been questions about the weather, state of the roads, and how was the news in England. But Deborah cared only for small talk when it was the only thing to talk about. Yet if she was acquainted with someone long enough to become comfortable, then she would never begin a conversation from the beginning but would proceed from the middle, or at the end and work her way backwards.

"Now," she said with finality, "we must conclude this interview because my Mother Superior will soon be getting vexed at the length of our meeting, and my family has walked around the garden five too many times."

"Of course."

"But you must come again in two days' time to see me."

"I love how you did not even ask me first."

"Would you have said no if I had asked?"

"No, I would not have."

"Precisely, then there was no need to ask or entreat you."

"You know me that well?"

"No, not really. I was just hoping for the best. And deliberately chose not to think of the worst. I would like you to stay in Philadelphia for at least two weeks, if you do not mind, and see me every other day. I know that staying that long might be dangerous for you, but I know that you are brave."

"I am getting brave."

"Good, continue to do so. Oh, and where are you staying?"

"At the Society Hill Inn."

"I shall speak to my mother, and she can ask father to have you remain at Canterbury."

"Oh, no you do not need to do that," he said. "I could not impose upon them."

She shook her head and smiled. "Oh, that is so courteous of you, because you only say that to be polite. And while being polite is always a necessity, I am not in the mood for you to be inconvenienced because I wish for you to remain here long. Samuel, please be guided by me now. Besides, staying with them is the best thing that you could do."

"How so?"

"I want my family to like you, Samuel. And if you remain in the inn, then how will they ever be able to do so? Even if you go there for luncheon invites, you will still only feel like a distant guest. But if you remain there, then my family shall get to know you well."

"Then I should be delighted."

"I knew you would be."

"But Deborah?"

"Yes?"

"Why do you wish for them to like me?"

"Because I was once in love with you."

Samuel halted once more, amazed at her frankness.

"And," she continued, "I want them to get to know the man who I had once felt so deeply for."

"Then...if you will appeal to them, I should very much like to stay at Canterbury."

"Then let us go back to my family and they will escort you to the inn so that you may retrieve your luggage."

"Splendid."

"And remember one very important thing."

"Yes?"

"I know you are brought up to be reserved, and that is well for society. Yet in Canterbury, find your voice, Samuel, and never be afraid to speak up and let everyone know the sort of man that you are. My family will love you very much if you open yourself to them."

"When I saw your mother first, I grew to understand where you learned how to be so liberal in your manner."

"My mother is an exemplary woman."

"Yes, she seems to be the sort that is made to deserve happy endings."

"I never knew there was a sort, but I am glad to know now."

"You must be."

⚜

WHEN THEY RE-MET THEIR COMPANY, Deborah requested Samuel to remain at Canterbury. Emilia readily agreed, not afraid to speak for her husband and all the plans were made posthaste.

They drove Samuel to Society Hill Inn, he collected his belongings, checked out, and they journeyed to Canterbury Park.

While doing so, Samuel began to inquire to Emilia about her family and acknowledged that he would be delighted to learn about them. Happy with his curiosity about something she never ceased to enjoy speaking about, Emilia began to regale him with many stories, every now and again making Henry add an anecdote of his own.

During her narration, Samuel Lucas listened attentively, most desiring to give a favorable impression, as Deborah had requested him to do.

For upon his arrival, all he had were hopes. Now, with his first day of seeing her once more, he felt it well within his rights to have expectations, be they little or great.

BE THEY GREAT OR LITTLE

Our journey felt surprisingly short and very soon we had arrived onto the estate of Rosings. We first drove past the parsonage at Hunsford, and it was quite surreal to see the very same house that Mr. Collins and Charlotte lived in as man and wife. It was also not surprising to see that the beehives were all removed, for if I was a reverend and had learned that the previous parson before me had died from drowning in honey, I would not think it a wise hobby to take up. To our surprise, whoever the reverend was had exited the house upon our arrival, went to the edge of his lawn, took off his hat and bowed to us slightly.

"He must have seen us from one of his windows," I said, by way of explanation.

"And it frightens me."

"Does it?" Jane asked. "Why so?"

"Because that reminds me of how Mr. Collins used to act."

"Darcy," Mr. Bingley said, "we must give him the benefit of the doubt before we get to know him."

"Very well. I just hope that my inner instincts about him are wrong."

"We'll see, my dear. After all, I believe that we shall eventually meet him."

"Oh, we shall. My Aunt Catherine will see to it."

As we drove along the lanes toward the center of the estate, Rosings Park House came into view. It was large, exquisite to the eye and was impressive, to the point of imposing.

"It is very grand indeed," Jane said. "Yet from all that Mr. Collins had always spoken of, I should not be surprised at its regal appearance."

"Yes, we should not be, but no words can ever fully be the same as seeing the sight. He spoke of it often to our Aunt Philips, and he found an attentive audience through her. Our mother also listened to him with eagerness, until he proposed to Charlotte, and then afterwards, she stopped listening to anything he said."

"Ah, that would be enough for her to stop caring about his conversation," Darcy said as we rolled down the lane.

Upon our arrival, we were immediately met by the steward, who ushered us inside, and organized our luggage to be brought to certain rooms. We made sure to know where Lucy would take Caiden and William, and then he began to tell us that we would be brought to Lady Catherine when a door opened and a young woman entered—it was Mary!

"Elizabeth, Kitty, Jane!" she called out.

"Mary!" we all said in return. With an energy that was quite unlike her, she came bounding up to us and we all embraced her. When we parted, she smiled warmly, and I saw that she was in good health and looks. Her attire was also slightly improved, which would make sense, for being Anne De Bourgh's companion would require her to look fashionable enough while still also appearing of lesser rank. Mary did look better, yet her look was also still practical and comfortable.

"I can scarce believe it," she began. "I thought you would never come, and finally you are here."

"Yes, we are," Jane said. "Oh, Mary, you look quite lovely."

"Oh, no I do not."

"Yes, you do," I concurred. "You do look greatly improved."

"And happy," Kitty added. "I never knew having an occupation would suit you so well, but apparently it does wonders."

"I suppose it has," she affirmed, "for it is nice to have a sense of purpose. And Mr. Darcy, Mr. and Mrs. Bingley, Colonel Fitzwilliam, Miss Darcy and..." she trailed off, for she still had never met Jason.

"Oh, if you will allow me," Georgiana said. "Mary, this is my fiancé, Mr. Jason Whitfield. Jason, this is my sister-in-law, Miss Mary Bennet."

Mary and Jason offered their hellos to each other. Mary turned to the steward and told him that she would lead us into the sitting room where Lady Catherine De Bourgh and her daughter Anne awaited us.

The steward acquiesced to this scheme most readily and our company was then following Mary along the grand estate of Rosings. It was so interesting to watch her as she led us, for it was quite ironic. Mary always kept to plainness and simplicity before, yet now she was altering to a whole new lifestyle and adjusting to it well.

"Well," she began, "all the reports really are true. And yes, the chimney piece alone truly did cost 800 pounds."

"Really?" Miriam asked lightly.

"Oh, yes, the butler himself has told me so on more than one occasion." Mary laughed gently. "It seems as if he wanted me to know that especially. But how have you all been?"

"We have been very well," Kitty said, "and we have some news for you."

"Is the news good or bad?"

"Good, and it will surprise you."

"Then what is it? Pray do not leave me in suspense any longer."

I chuckled. "You have learned how to be curious and that is most refreshing."

"I have Miss De Bourgh to thank for that. She has taught me the benefits of having a curiosity about things."

"Then you both are good friends?"

"I want to believe that I am doing my duty well and that she likes me," Mary said bashfully, "yet only she can say so, and I say nothing for myself. But what is this news?"

"We shall tell you when we are assembled with Aunt Catherine," Mr. Darcy said, speaking to her for the first time. "For the news affects all of you."

"It does?" Mary asked, still a little awed with my husband.

"Yes, it does."

"Well then, I have no choice but to wait, therefore tell me how my two nephews are?"

"Oh, William and Caiden are quite well, healthy and they are now beginning to walk!"

"Really? You did bring them, did you not? So that I can see them at last."

"Yes, we have, they are simply tired and their nanny, Lucy, is putting them to bed. You shall see them before we retire to bed, for I can show you them after we all sit to dinner."

"That will be very nice. I hope they like me."

"Don't worry," Mr. Darcy said, "they are at that age where they will like anyone who will choose to like them."

"A golden age," Mary acknowledged. "For only when we get older that we do not accept others as easily as we ought to."

"Yes, the innocence that comes with childhood is unparalleled. And all too brief."

Finally, we arrived at the sitting room, and to the sofa that was facing us, Anne De Bourgh was seated on. She was as I remembered her: thin, meek, dressed incredibly well but too well, and the clothing did not necessarily flatter her. Yet she smiled when seeing us and I knew we would find a sturdy ally, for what she lacked in physical abilities, she made up for with her resilient nature.

At last, I glanced to the left of her and sitting on the most luxurious sofa in the room was Lady Catherine De Bourgh herself.

I could not fully recall when the last time was that I had seen her, however my memory was still one that was filled with mixed emotions. She was the sort of woman who you impulsively cannot like, but also one that must be withstood—and even exonerated. She said and did much that I did not agree with, yet because she was family to us, I felt compelled to always give her one more chance.

We entered, we all stood before her and bowed and curtsied when our time came. As we all stood in a line before her, she looked us all over.

"So," Lady Catherine said, looking at Jason and Georgiana, "Georgiana you really are engaged?"

"Yes, I am Aunt Catherine."

"And you are so to this Mr. Whitfield?"

"Yes, she is your ladyship," Jason said.

"Upon my word, you do speak your words up sharp, sir."

He smiled. "I have no choice but to do so always, for it is a side effect to my occupation."

"Your occupation?" Lady Catherine said, leaning forward, "You are a man of profession?"

"Yes, I am your ladyship. I come from the Whitfield family of Errodin Abbey."

"Errodin Abbey?" Lady Catherine said, leaning forward, "I have heard of that great estate."

"Yes, we are a family of attorneys," Jason said.

"Are you to inherit the estate?"

"No, that honor goes to my older brother, Victor, for he is the oldest in the male line."

"Was the estate entailed away to the male line?"

"Yes, but there was no need to fear in my generation, for my parents only had sons."

"That reminds me of Longbourn," Lady Catherine said, "for the late Mr. Collins's sake, god rest him, I was glad of it. But otherwise, I see no occasion for entailing estates from the female line—it was not thought necessary in Sir Lewis De Bourgh's family. And is your older brother married, Mr. Whitfield?"

"No, he is still living the life of a dedicated bachelor, Lady Catherine."

"Well then, that makes you his heir, and until he produces a child himself, you may still be lucky."

"And unlucky equally, for if I was to gain an estate, then that would mean that my brother would be deceased. So, while I would gain a house, it would not be to my liking, for I would lose a brother."

"Well," she said, not replying to the question and then turning to the rest of us, "welcome you all to Rosings Park."

We all thanked her in turn.

As we all sat down to coffee, Lady Catherine began what she might have called a discussion, when it was really one long monologue. There was little to be done but hear Lady Catherine talk, which she did without any intermission, delivering her opinion on every subject in so decisive a manner as proved that she was not used to having her judgment contradicted. After she talked of many things, she then turned her attention to Miriam.

"Do you play and sing Mrs. Bingley?"

"A little," Miriam replied.

"Oh! Then some time or other we shall be happy to hear you. Our instrument is a capital one, probably superior to—you shall try it someday. Do your sisters or brothers play and sing?"

"One of them does."

"Why did not you all learn? You ought all to have learned. The

Miss Mills in this county all play, and I am quite sure their father has not so good an income as yours...do you draw?"

"No, not at all."

"What, none of you?"

"Not one."

"That is very strange. But I suppose you had no opportunity. Your mother should have taken you to learn from the masters."

"I'm sure that my mother would not have minded it, but my father did not think it beneficial to our education."

"Oh, he did not?"

"No, he did not."

Mr. Bingley was beginning to get unnerved and a little vexed at the pointed questions toward his wife and began to shift uncomfortably. But Lady Catherine did not notice, for she turned her attention suddenly to Jane, Kitty and I, which indicated that it was now our turn to be the object of her scrutiny.

"And yet," Lady Catherine began, "I never have asked Miss Mary here, but you are all assembled now, minus one"—and here she sneered a bit, remembering Lydia's infamous elopement—"therefore I may make proper inquiries. How many governesses did your parents employ to teach you?"

Jane, Kitty, Mary and I looked between each other, but it was Mary who had spoken up first.

"We never had any governess," she replied.

"No governess? How was that possible? Five daughters brought up at home without a governess! I never heard of such a thing. Your mother must have been quite a slave to your education."

"Not at all, Lady Catherine," Jane answered with a smile.

"Then who taught you? Who attended you? Without a governess you must have been neglected."

"Compared with some families," I said, "I believe we were, but such of us as wished to learn never wanted the means."

"Indeed," Kitty said. "Though sometimes we did not appreciate the opportunity, we were always encouraged to read, and had all the masters that were necessary. Those who chose to be idle certainly might. But that is the choice of the will, and that will varies per person."

"Aye, no doubt," Lady Catherine said, "but that is what a governess will prevent, and if I had known your mother sooner"— and here she flinched, for she must have recalled how our mother and her first met— "I should have advised her most strenuously to engage one. I always say that nothing is to be done in education without steady and regular instruction, and nobody but a governess can give it. It is wonderful how many families I have been the means of supplying in that way."

"Indeed, you have been very beneficial and charitable to many in this county, your Ladyship," Mary said with grace and ease. "And it puts me in mind to recall the four nieces of Mrs. Harper who are delightfully situated through your means."

"Oh yes," Lady Catherine said. "Mrs. Darcy, as you can see, your sister has proven a very good addition to our conversation here at Rosings."

"I am happy that she is so."

"Yes, and as she has said, I did find good situations for Mrs. Harper's children. I am always glad to get a young person well placed out. And it was but the other day that I recommended another young person, who was merely accidentally mentioned to me, and the family is quite delighted with her. Miss Bennet, did I tell you of Mrs. Prill's calling yesterday to thank me? She finds the governess I recommended to be a splendid find. 'Lady Catherine,' said she, 'you have given me a treasure'."

Lady Catherine continued in this vein for quite some time and every now and again I looked on Mary and she suppressed a smile. It became clear that Mary had also not only learned purpose in coming here, but she also learned cleverness. She knew that if she had steered the conversation toward education in another light, Lady Catherine would cease to question all of us in so direct a manner.

✠

WE ALL CHANGED FOR DINNER, then went down to the drawing-room for supper, and while we all sat in our proper seating, Lady Catherine began to question us once more.

"So, I know that Mary plays the pianoforte quite well, but do any of you other Bennet sisters play?"

"I play as well," I said, "but only a mere little."

"And what of the rest of you?"

"I was humble enough to understand that I never possessed the talent," Jane said.

"And I never possessed the self-discipline," Kitty admitted.

"A great pity, for my dear nephew here, the Colonel loves to hear a truly accomplished musician."

"It is all very well, Aunt Catherine," Colonel Fitzwilliam said, "for we have many other things to occupy us rather than hearing her play at the instrument. Besides, if I ever desired music, then I could always play myself."

"You play the pianoforte?" I asked, surprised.

"Yes, he does." Kitty gave him a tender smile. "And he is quite proficient at it."

"I merely play a little," Colonel Fitzwilliam said.

"More than a little, my love."

"I had the gift in my hands, but my talent is not greater than Darcy's over there."

"What?" I asked, turning to Fitzwilliam.

"Yes, I was the musician, and Darcy was the singer."

"You can sing, Fitzwilliam?" I gasped, overwhelmed by such knowledge.

"You did not know your husband's talent?" Lady Catherine sneered. "That is quite unobservant."

"It is not unobservant to not know something that you were never told, Aunt Catherine," Darcy cut in, in my defense. "Yes, my love... I, um... I was trained to sing."

"And you neglected to tell me?" I asked, critically.

"I, well, forgive me, but I was always a little shy about it. When I would sing, I would always be worried to the point where I would feel sick. I simply never wished to embarrass myself in front of you."

"Oh, Fitzwilliam!" I sighed, my heart reaching out to him. "I did not mean to press the matter, but you need never think I would be disappointed in you."

"And your insecurity, Fitz," Colonel Fitzwilliam said, "was always one found on virtue, but wholly unnecessary. I would play the pianoforte while he accompanied me with his baritone voice, and we amazed many a woman with our duo."

"Oh, Richard!" Kitty laughed.

"This was before I met you, I swear," he chuckled.

"This is most obscene talk for the dinner table," Lady Catherine reprimanded.

"Forgive me, Aunt Catherine," Colonel Fitzwilliam said, smothering a grin.

"Yes, apologies Aunt," Darcy echoed, taking another spoonful of food.

"Well then," Lady Catherine ordered, "since we have so many in the house who have musical understanding, I think it is safe to say that we may have a miniature concert. This shall be the lineup for this evening. Miss Darcy shall play, for she is the most proficient, then Mary shall play us a few pieces that she has been working on, and the last shall be Richard and Fitzwilliam shall sing for his accompaniment."

"Oh, but Lady Catherine," Mr. Darcy began to object, "I really am out of practice."

"Oh, yes, yes, yes!" she countered. "You always say so, but you have the voice of an angel, Fitzwilliam—well if any angel is allowed to be a baritone that is. And I will brook no refusal. The next evening Mrs. Darcy shall play, as will Mrs. Bingley, and if Georgiana shall play again, that will be lovely. Have you heard your fiancée play yet, Mr. Whitfield?"

"Indeed, I have, Lady Catherine," Jason replied, "but I have heard her impeccable skills enough to want more."

"Ah then, you sir, are in for a treat."

Georgiana sat at the pianoforte first, and we heard her play, which was quite masterful. As I looked around, I rested my eyes on Jason, who stared at her, mesmerized. When playing, Georgiana was quite a wonder to behold, and with such a sight mingled with his pure adoration of her, naturally his heart must have been affected.

Next to play was Mary, who I had heard so often that I could recognize every piece that she played after the first couple of notes. She actually began with a couple of Irish melodies, but her playing had actually improved, for there seemed to be more than just technique to it, but now there was emotion involved. When Mary used to play at Longbourn and Lucas Lodge, her style was always practiced, but she never really felt anything about what she was playing before. I suppose, now that she had a larger acquaintance with the ways of the world, she had earned a point of view, and her playing showed it.

However, what was most incredible and would mark the evening for me as a most memorable one, was the last set. Colonel Fitzwilliam and Darcy took to the instrument. Richard sat at the piano bench and Darcy stood over him. I did not recall ever seeing two men do a duet together, and I did not believe that it was orthodox, but orthodox would not have sufficed in that moment. Even before they played, they looked mesmerizing to me, for Richard looked confident as ever and Darcy looked too bashful for anything. Indeed, I wanted to go up and hold him, to tell him that he need fear nothing. But all I could do was sit there, willing and waiting to watch this spectacle.

Richard began to play, and to my utter amazement, he was quite accomplished! A man of such strength and a soldier, and he played with pure grace. I turned to Kitty, and she smiled at him with satisfaction mingled with passion. The image of him at the pianoforte must have been ideal to her.

I turned back to the duo. After a couple more bars of music, Fitzwilliam opened his mouth and began to sing.

Can you define a moment in time that feels indefinable, for it is so wholly unexpected and more perfect than you could have ever imagined something to be?

Darcy's voice, deep and resounding, was impeccable—it was timeless, smooth, masculine, and it said much. It contained his grace, elegance, musk, manliness and the passion that always lurked beneath the scowl that he had perfected.

All the rest of the room faded away, it seemed, when I looked upon him and heard his voice. Nothing so beautiful would ever come from me. Therefore, in that manner, his talents would have to be enough for the both of us.

At the conclusion of their duet, I felt a tear roll down my cheek, for I did not even know that I was crying, and I was the first to clap. When looking upon me, Darcy's face grew red from blushing, and I had to mouth the words 'You were brilliant' before his face turned its normal hue.

⚜

WHEN ALLOWED to retire to our bedroom, I waited for Fitzwilliam. As he entered, I threw one of my stockings at him.

"And what was that for?" he asked.

"Why did you never tell me that you were gifted?" I gasped.

"Because I was shy about it. And I am a little petrified of singing in public."

"But...Fitzwilliam, you sounded wonderful. Your voice is amazing."

"Thank you, Lizzy. I am happy that you liked it."

"It made me think you even more beautiful—do not misunderstand me, I always did so, even when I did not know you possessed such talent, and this only augments it."

"Then you still love me for who I am?"

"Of course," I said, approaching him and wrapping my fingers within his own. "Fitzwilliam, you could not have any talent, and very well could fail at many things, and I would still think you are wonderful."

"Thank you, Lizzy. You have no notion of how much that means to me."

"Yes, I do. I always have."

Fitzwilliam leaned down and we kissed.

It is a wonderful thing, generally not known or recognized, that an idea of love is often mistaken for love itself. Love, in all essentials, is not adoring someone for all their talents, but is loving them even when they might have none. So many equate success, popularity, appearances, or talent with what is beautiful and what is worthy of love—however those qualities are only a plus. True love is not dependent on an outside source of that person's natural state of being. If you love them when they fail, embarrass themselves unknowingly, or did not possess the qualities that lend itself towards being distinguished, then you know that you love them.

Not all of us are born to be great, but all have the right to be granted having a great love in our lives. Or at least, I had faith that it was so.

Darcy loved me, even though I did not excel at anything other than spirit.

And, I suppose, that he wished of me to love him for his essentials, and no more or less. His singing voice enhanced the man within, but did not define him.

Yet it was still nice to know that he was marvelous to hear—indeed, my husband was a great beauty, for I believed that my entire life would be spent always finding something new within him that I did not know the day before.

⚜

THE NEXT DAY, we presented Caiden and William to her Ladyship, and despite her proud manner, she could not help but lean forward and touch their little hands, amazed by the sight of them. Caiden, who was born to be a charmer clearly, clapped his hands together and extended his arms toward her, in hopes that she would embrace him.

Lady Catherine may have been made of staunch character, but even she was not made of stone. As he took a few steps toward her, she softened and allowed him to sit on her lap and then proceeded to lecture Fitzwilliam and me on how best to raise them, feed them and nurture. Fitzwilliam and I listened most attentively, but knew that in our hearts, we would still go our own way.

After they remained with us for an hour, I took them back to their rooms and told Fitzwilliam to inform Lady Catherine that I would remain in the nursery for a while with our sons. Naturally she would be vexed with me, but I cared little on the matter.

In the nursery, Lucy sat down, waiting to be needed but also happy in knowing that she could recline, which I allowed her to do most readily. I crawled around the room with Caiden and William, marveling at how they had evolved since they were first born.

In truth, I never thought that I would have ever had children. I often had believed Jane would be the one to get married, and I would live in her home with her, teaching her ten children how to play the pianoforte and sew cushions very ill. It all seemed so ironic now, in our present state. Jane had her children to teach, and I had mine to raise. And they both brought us equal amounts of vexation and peace—but the peace was the best parts. William and Caiden, without a doubt, were all that was best in me. And all that was best in Fitzwilliam. And I daresay that I was ready to have another child. Indeed, Darcy would get his wish; he would have another child and another and another, until either we were satisfied or until I got too old for it to be safe.

Truly... I was ready for a daughter.

After a while, the door opened, and Miriam entered along with Mary. Miriam, who was now five months pregnant, was growing large herself, but still moved with ease. How she had willingly jumped into the water at Lyme was still amazing, however clearly her exertion did not harm her child so, for he or she was clearly growing in size.

They sat down with me, enjoying the peace of being in a smaller company and with more to talk about that gave me my opportunity to inquire more about Mary's time at Rosings.

"I enjoy my time often," Mary said, "and Anne has greatly improved her autonomy."

"Has she? She did not speak much when we first arrived."

"Oh, she did not because she knew that her mother would wish to do all the talking. However we ride out together to visit all the neighbors in the county, we visit the sick and also supply some of the lesser fortunate with provisions."

"But you are maintaining your own health, are you not?" I asked, worried. "Mary, you know that you have not the strongest constitution."

"You still worry over me?" Mary laughed. "Do not, for I am not nearly as sickly as I once was when we were children. I am much stronger now and I can weather much."

"I hope so," I said, dubious.

"And I know so." She gave me a saucy smile.

When Mary was young, she was sick quite often. She and Jane actually proved to be the least robust out of all of us. While Jane was the only one who had ever neared death from pneumonia when we were children, Mary was the one who suffered earaches periodically when she was a child. To this day, I still remembered how in pain she once was. Yet she was correct, and I was being paranoid. For she had been healthy as a horse these last four years together, and only at her referencing visiting others who were sickly did my mind begin to recall her past ailments. Therefore, I let my worry subside, for it was quite ill-founded. Mary was as strong as the rest of us, and she had proven so on many occasions.

"But it is a great pleasure, Lizzy and Mrs. Bingley, to be seeing Anne evolve so. She has even begun to consider courtships with her peers."

"She has never had any prior suitors?" Miriam asked.

"She was often too sickly and therefore always had to remain at home," Mary explained. "Therefore, it led to her never being presented at court until recently."

"She has been so?" I asked.

"Yes, she has, and I am surprised that Lady Catherine did not mention it, or rather she was waiting for the proper moment. Therefore, if she mentions it, act as if I did not say anything to you."

"Will do, but how is she able to be presented if she is so sickly?"

"She is no longer as bad, as you have seen. Yes, she has greatly improved, and I think it has to do with the lesser medicines that she takes."

"She takes less medication now?"

"Yes, and I do not know why Lady Catherine suddenly came upon the notion so. But sometimes taking too much medicine can lead to one developing an immunity to it and it ceases to do its job correctly. She has taken less. Lady Catherine has changed doctors, and this new doctor prescribes less medicine and more natural remedies, as well as a change in diet. Now Anne is greatly improved."

"Yet if she gets married, you shall return to Longbourn."

"Perhaps," Mary said, "but I do not fear my future now. Also, since Anne and I have become good friends, she might wish to keep me on as a companion. Her husband cannot always be present, and it is best to always have a friend. If she does, then I shall look on it as the best of gifts, for it will enhance my circles. I am in my late 20s now, Lizzy, and I feel that there is a slight change in me. I believe that I am ready to enter the world now, for I have more confidence in me. And books could not contain me forever. It is pleasing to read about others, but I had not much to call my own in regards to activity. And if I go home, then I shall do something I never thought that I would do."

"And what is that?"

"I shall do my best to dance every dance there, provided that there will be a man who will stand up with me."

"Oh, Mary, that is wonderful, and I think that you will be just splendid."

"Thank you, Lizzy. Yet enough of me, let us talk of my two nephews. Truly William and Caiden are beauties, Lizzy."

"Yes, I am quite proud of them, and Mary, when you do get a moment to be amongst them for a long duration of time, you shall love being around them, for they always lift the spirits."

"And they are the perfect olive branch."

"Pardon?"

"Lizzy, you are no fool, and you know that Lady Catherine was not fully disposed to liking your coming, but upon seeing her great-nephews, now she will have altered completely and will see your union as the best of things. Children are perfect at establishing disorder one moment, but peace and prosperity in another. Children are innocent and makes us adults wish to be so. Therefore, William and Caiden have given you a great victory, for they have won you

Lady Catherine as a great ally—little soldiers they are, be they great or little."

"Oh, they are great."

"Yes, I am certain they are."

Miriam chuckled, holding her belly.

"Sisterly affection—now that is beautiful. Especially since it was rare in my household."

❧ 10 ❧

A SERIES OF DREAMS

When the Crofts arrived in Hampshire, along with Jane Austen, the Lucas sisters and Captain Wentworth, they all had felt quite exhausted from their journey. But upon arriving at Aginfield, Captain Wentworth wished to travel with Charlotte immediately to Lucas Lodge where he would declare his engagement. However, Charlotte wished to speak with her mother first, to convince her of the illegibility of the match, and the Crofts urged him to remain at Aginfield, for a day before he were to declare himself.

"I wonder if I should remain here at Aginfield," Wentworth said, "for perhaps my sister and brother-in-law would like the house to their own for a while."

"You need not do that," Charlotte said, "for believe me, the estate is large enough that if they want some solitude, you can disappear from them and still be in the same house. But if you are so eager to be alone, there are two inns here in Hampshire and they are The Dancing Prince Inn, and The Drunken Prince Inn."

"They are honestly called that?" He laughed.

"Yes, they are. Ironically, I've found The Drunken Prince Inn to be the cleaner one."

While Captain Wentworth enjoyed the idea of staying in an inn with either of those names, the Crofts would not hear of him not coming to their large new home that was made specifically for guests.

Thus, the company was separated and the Crofts settled into Aginfield along with Mrs. Croft's brother, Wentworth. Charlotte, Maria and Jane Austen traveled onward. The Austen home was along the way to Lucas Lodge and therefore she was the first to be dropped off.

They were immediately greeted by Cassandra Austen and the rest of the family, who inquired of their journey, helped Jane pull down her luggage. Charlotte informed them that she would tell them everything if they could come to Lucas Lodge for the dinner in four days' time. This was readily agreed to and before Jane went inside with her family, she turned to Charlotte.

"What shall you tell your mother?" she asked Charlotte.

"I do not know," Charlotte replied. "For I am quite making up my life as I go now."

"I see. Sometimes that is all that one can do."

Jane Austen said farewell to Charlotte and Maria, then entered to tell Cassandra all that had occurred in Lyme—excluding Charlotte's engagement to Captain Wentworth.

⚜

THE CARRIAGE ARRIVED at Lucas Lodge and Sir William Lucas, Lady Lucas and the rest of the family, with the exclusion of Samuel, were there to welcome them. There was much talking at once, for no one else in the family had ever gone to Lyme before and her father, desiring to know about how it all went, asked the only question that he knew to relate back to himself.

"Well then," Sir William boomed, "to be among such illustrious company, have any of them been presented at Saint James Court?"

Charlotte chuckled silently while Maria responded for them both.

"We did not ask them if they had been, Father. But I am sure that a great deal of them were, for you must recall, that the host of the engagement party was Lady Russell."

"Ah, capitol! Most capitol! And was she mannerly?"

"She was a very gracious host," Maria continued, "and a most open one, but would you believe that there was an elopement at the party?"

"Maria!" Charlotte gasped.

"Oh, there is no use in not talking about it," Maria retaliated, "as long as I do not say the names."

"But who eloped?" Lady Lucas asked.

"And as I said, I am not telling," Maria said, "though it shall spread easily in London, I suppose that is one secret I can keep."

"Oh, but we shall find out who," Sir William said. "You know this is true."

"They do have a point," Maria said to Charlotte.

"Which is why we should have never spoken," Charlotte said. "But very well...a friend of Admiral Croft's named Captain Benwick, eloped with a gentleman's daughter named Miss Crawford."

"Oh, that is awful and that must have been to the eternal upset of Lady Russell," their mother said. "Eloping is always a terrible business. I wonder how the Bennets felt about Miss Crawford's plight. For it must have reminded them of when Lydia ran off."

"Oh, there is no need to talk of that," Charlotte said sharply.

"They were lucky that their ending was happy, is all that I can say."

"Just as I was fortunate in that my match did not lead to a more prosperous outcome."

"Charlotte, what are you—"

"I am simply acknowledging that my actions were truly no less mercenary than many others, and it was an error on my part."

Sir William and Lady Lucas looked at each other with apprehension, not knowing why Charlotte was speaking so. Charlotte stood up and smiled down upon them.

"Mother and Father, I would like to speak to you both in father's study, and I shall like to do it immediately. If you do not mind."

"I hope the matter is not serious," Sir William said, "yes, Charlotte."

"It is serious, but not of gravity, now if you please, Mother and Father, I truly am wishing to tell you."

Sir William and Lady Lucas submitted, and Charlotte followed them to the study, leaving the rest of the family to wonder at them.

❧

"IMPOSSIBLE!" Sir William gasped after Charlotte had told them the news of her engagement to Captain Wentworth. "You have made another match already?"

"Yes, Father, only this match is nothing new, but very old. Captain Wentworth had courted me before when we had gone on holiday in Brighton."

"Yet I was not told of it."

"Because I had refused his proposal," Charlotte said evenly. "I had loved him, but due to his lack of fortune and with no monetary gain in sight, I was persuaded by others to reject his suit, which I have been regretting ever since. My marriage to Mr. Collins was one of necessity and out of gratitude to finally have an illegible match, but this one shall be one of love. He has already asked for my hand, I have accepted, and even though there should be no objection to his hand on your side due to his brighter prospects, I shall brook no refusal from you," she said, looking directly at her mother. "I shall marry him, yet I do not ask for your permission, only your blessing."

"My dear Charlotte," Sir William Lucas exclaimed. "What has occurred within you? What is this new tone in you, that is so headstrong?"

"The change that comes with resolution," Charlotte replied. "With having faith in one's own voice, views and determination. Father, one time, in the past, I listened to the wrong person, and I was wrong in turn for doing so. I will only be right in my ways now. Please, Father, when Captain Wentworth comes to announce our engagement, give your consent."

"Of course I shall," Sir William said, "for he is the sort of man who I could refuse nothing, but Charlotte?"

"Yes."

"Do you really love him?" he asked gently, to which Charlotte turned towards her father, startled by his sincere but vulnerable address.

"Yes, Father, I really do."

"I wish I had always known of this. You must tell me everything —yes, I give my consent, but still, you must tell me everything. For in moments such as these, I feel as if I have been left in the dark, and I do not wish to remain there."

"Very well." Let us begin then."

Charlotte proceeded to tell Sir William everything about her history with the gallant Captain Wentworth. Her mother listened politely, but held her tongue all the while, dwelling in between the realm of wounded pride and humbling guilt.

When she finished her narrative, Sir William awaited the Captain's arrival the next day with anticipation. He was happy once more to know that the daughter he feared would fall back into spinsterhood, that she had narrowly avoided once before, now wouldn't.

Charlotte excused herself to unload her luggage and rest so that she could receive Frederick with favorable looks the next day. While she was waiting for her bath to be drawn by their main servant, Bella, there was a knock on her door.

"Is that you, Maria?" Charlotte laughed, removing her shoes, "You know you need not knock!"

The door opened and Charlotte sat up in alarm as she saw her mother's reflection in her mirror as her mother stood in the doorway.

"Hello Charlotte."

"Mother."

"I—I wished to talk with you before you had bathed."

"If you are planning on telling me to refuse Frederick because of your pride, then you must know that I will not listen."

"That is not what I come to do, Charlotte. Surely you must know that."

"No, Mother I don't know that. How can I know anything of you anymore?"

"You have lost faith in me?" she asked.

"I wish to say that I have not, but I do not know what to say now."

"Captain Wentworth certainly always had a talent for discomposing you, that much I can say."

"And you have had the power to influence me, ma'am, and I feel sorry for it."

"Charlotte, I am your mother!"

"And you were wrong!"

Charlotte blushed at her exclamation but could not deny the necessity of voicing her feelings.

"Mother," she began, more gently, "I understood your views when you told me to refuse him, but you did not ever look into my heart, or his. You did not see clearly."

"Oh, but I did," Lady Lucas replied. "You think I have never been in love?"

"Well, of course you are...with Father."

"I grew to love him, Charlotte, but I was not in love with your father at first."

Startled, Charlotte blurted, "What?"

"Yes. Before I met your father, I had once been in love with a farmer."

"You were?"

"Yes," Lady Lucas whispered, wistful. She sat down on her daughter's bed and therefore began the story that she ought to have told Charlotte years ago. "And he was something that was beyond anything I have ever seen. He was not perfect, but he was beautiful, and he thought I was as well—and we were terribly in love. Never had I felt anything like it before. At first my parents would not allow a courtship, but we had decided to elope."

"You did!"

"We had thought to do it, but then my parents found out about it. My mother sat me down, as I had done with you, and painted the worst portrait of men she could. She convinced me that he was just using me for monetary gain, that he only thought he loved me now, yet when the love wore off, he would mistreat me. It very well could have been so, or not, however I grew to believe her, and I told him that I would no longer indulge our love and that I released him, to find someone who he could have an easier chance of love with. I wrote to him, telling him that I was not worth the trouble, scandal and degradation that he would endure. He tried to contact me, but eventually he ceased when he saw that his efforts were fruitless."

"Did you never see him again?" Charlotte asked, greatly distressed by this revelation.

"Yes. Many times."

"You did?"

"Yes, for I knew where he lived. I would sometimes have my coachman ride me out to his farm, and I would just watch him. He got older, got married, had children and I saw how happy they were. I saw age take away his beauty in the eyes of some, but never in mine. My mother was in error. He never wanted me for anything else but me. Would I have been ridiculed? Yes. Would I have had to work on a farm even in my old age? Yes. Would I have been the butt of jokes? Perhaps. But he might have been worth it all. He showed his wife that he was."

Lady Lucas covered her mouth, trying to suppress her emotion, though the tears trickled down her face slightly. Charlotte wished to hold her mother, but she was at a loss of what to do.

"You would think that I'd hate myself for choosing a different fate than him," she continued. "And I did at first, but then the most wonderful thing happened."

"What?"

"I grew to love your father, and he gave me children. He gave me you. Now look upon yourself, Charlotte? How can I regret my decision when you are the product of it? That is why I told you to deny your love for him, because that same denial ruled my fate. That same denial was all that I had ever known. And whether you were happy or not, you would have your children eventually, and you would find the same peace I found."

"Mother... I am so sorry."

"It is not your fault for hating me. I just want—I think it is better that you should know me now. All I had ever wanted was your good fortune. And to not live your life for one mistake."

"I understand now, and I cannot hate you. I never could, but I must rule my life now. Even if my life would have been harder, he would have been beside me. And all the rest be damned. Love out of convenience will no longer be my fate. Either I will have him, or I will have no one. Spinsterhood does not frighten me any longer— only living with the false sort of love does."

Lady Lucas stood up and kissed her daughter on her cheek.

"Then be happy, Charlotte. Amazing it is! Samuel has rushed into danger in Philadelphia for a love that will never be reciprocated, and you walked toward love in Lyme. Then... here is your second chance. A rare thing it is, second chances, for I had only been given one."

Smiling gently, she left the room, and Charlotte was left in wonder, amazed at how all her life, she had never fully known the woman who gave birth to her until that moment.

THE NEXT DAY brought Captain Wentworth to Lucas Lodge where his confident air and strong frame made him naturally impressive to Sir William.

He announced his proposal for Charlotte's hand, added that Charlotte had given her consent and therefore most humbly wished to set a date. He needed the wedding to be rather sooner than later, for he knew that he would soon be called to war once more.

Sir William was happy to offer a date in a month's time, and Lady Lucas replied boldly that she would be able to supply all the proper decorations in that period. Captain Wentworth at first was cold toward Lady Lucas, only offering pleasantries when it was required. For he could not tear his mind from the fact that she had been the means of almost destroying his happiness. But over the length of his visit, Charlotte helped his mind toward ease and forgiveness, and his resentfulness gave way to acceptance.

The Crofts also paid their respects, inviting the Lucases to Agin-field, and there was much interaction between both estates over the fortnight. The Admiral and Mrs. Croft had always liked Sir William. While Mrs. Croft had originally found Lady Lucas a bit stiff when they first met, eventually time allowed comfort in between them.

True to her word, Lady Russell sent a letter to the Lucases, offering congratulations to the happy couple, who she would always boast of being the means through which they became united. It should go without saying that the letter had the desired effect and cemented even more so the fortune of the match. And while Sir

William would grow to boast of it to his friends, Lady Lucas would display it to her companions, including Mrs. Philips, Mrs. Long, and eventually Mrs. Bennet.

News was spread very quickly through Hampshire as well about their engagement, and Mr. and Mrs. Bennet paid their respects.

ONE DAY, as Mrs. Bennet sat in the parlor of Lucas Lodge, in paying a visit to Lady Lucas, both older women sat there and exchanged pleasantries on their children's fate.

"I must congratulate you," Mrs. Bennet said, after reading Lady Russell's letter, "for Charlotte's splendid second conquest."

"Thank you, Mrs. Bennet. We had thought her fortunate to have made one illegible match, but for her to be offered a second chance is most miraculous."

"I must confess to liking this second match more."

"As you should." Lady Lucas sighed. "I can see how you would view Charlotte's first marriage as mercenary and also insensitive to your bad fortune in Longbourn being entailed away to Mr. Collins."

"For it was," Mrs. Bennet said, not afraid to be direct with the woman who had once rivaled her happiness. "I shall not deny it, Lady Lucas."

"I can see what you are feeling, and perhaps I would have felt the same thing in your case. We are not so different in the end, are we?"

"I cannot determine if so or not."

"We are, and you are aware of it. We love our children and will do anything to secure their happiness."

"I sometimes made mistakes on that score," Mrs. Bennet admitted. "My intentions were well, but that did not justify my errors."

"Then I was correct, we are similar, for my good intentions did not justify my errors as well. And they were many. Mrs. Bennet, I never meant to hurt you in my daughter marrying Mr. Collins, and she did not either. It does not make up for our doing so, for it was cold and insensitive. All we can therefore do is apologize."

"Well," Mrs. Bennet answered, "we all wish to live. And that is all that we can fight for, therefore I understand Charlotte's actions. You need have no fear of me remaining angry. Our children have found their paths, despite our machinations and schemes, they each found the correct ones."

"Yes, they have. It is all well, but what do we do now?"

"What do you mean?"

"I mean that what use do we have now? My children are all leaving."

"This I cannot tell you. For I am still learning that myself."

⚜

AT AGINFIELD, Charlotte had visited for her daily meeting with Captain Wentworth. They both were walking along the grounds of the estate, walking far enough that they were allowed to hold one another's hand and be unobserved.

"I do so wonder," she began, "how shall we make up for all this lost time spent?"

"Oh, that is simple," Captain Wentworth said.

"I cannot see it so easily. Therefore, what could it be?"

"We shall have to promise to never stop loving one another."

"Oh, is that all?" She laughed. "I believe that shall be quite simple."

"Oh, I do not know. I have many flaws to get used to."

"You cannot frighten me so easily with your flaws, Frederick. I have seen them all and they are marvelous—and nothing compared to my own."

"Then it is quite clear that it is our flaws that make us the most suitable for one another."

"That is one thing that links us, but there is another."

"Such as?"

"I never forgot you, as you never forgot me. I never released you from my hopes, and here you are. Perhaps it is a series of dreams that we have both had that links us, for we never stopped having them."

Captain Wentworth stopped their walking, wrapped his arms around her waist and pulled her in closer.

"Yes, perhaps we do both hold that."

He closed the gap between them, and they kissed.

NO MORE ROADS TO TRAVEL

O ur stay at Rosings Park went by leisurely, but not too soon, for though Lady Catherine had softened over time, nothing could replace the comfort that came with being home once more.

The day before our leaving, Lady Catherine had demanded that we remain for another month complete. Yet we informed her that it was best for us to leave as planned for we had to make necessary arrangements for Georgiana's wedding, which I was sure Jason Whitfield was getting angry at it taking so long to obtain.

On our last day, while we had all sat down in the drawing room, playing a round of cards after our supper, I had favored a round of backgammon. Anne De Bourgh was the first to challenge me. At first our game denied us the ability to speak lightly, but once we had fell into the method of it, our conversation grew organically.

"You shall be happy to return to Pemberley?" Anne asked.

"How could I not? Nothing is greater than home, as you must feel in being at Rosings. I believe that when we leave, you shall be happy to have your house to yourself again."

"While such peace is always wonderful, I shall admit to missing the sound of you all. And my mother has grown to love William and Caiden especially."

"Yes, it has always quite amazed me how she has taken to them so."

"I am not surprised really. In truth, I know that in her heart, she always wanted a son as well."

"Oh, well that is a natural impulse."

"And all the gladder I am that my mother did not have one. If she had, she would have spoiled him and therefore would have ruined him in the process. Also, as for myself, I would have been pushed to the wayside and she would never have noticed me, thereby ruining me."

I looked at her pointedly. "Oh, there is no way of knowing that."

"I know my mother and that is natural for her. While being under her constant attention is sometimes irksome, it is better than never being seen at all."

"Then I am happy that you escaped that fate."

"And with Mary here now with me it is more pleasant for my mother also pays her much attention and we are now kindred spirits."

"Mary and you seem to understand each other and get along very well."

"Yes, she does her job well."

"It is not only that, Anne, she has taken a liking to you truly."

"She has?" Anne asked eagerly.

"Yes. You are therefore a good lady, for Mary does not like everyone and anyone so easily."

"That... that is nice to know. Thank you, I do feel a little better."

"You ought to. Anne, would you mind if I asked you a personal query?"

"It depends. But do so, and I shall choose to answer or not."

"Well, you are looking much better of late, more robust and healthier. Is it because you are mixing more in society? Mary hinted at other possibilities, but did not know fully at how you are so greatly improved."

"Oh," Anne chuckled gently. "It is more than that. I have been improving since we had come from America. Apparently, when we were at Canterbury, Thomas Darcy exchanged a few words with my mother on how to treat me, and for some reason, he had this strange power over her. She took heed to his advice. Upon our return, she hired new physicians who prescribe a lot less medicine and more natural remedies, and they also recommend more physical activity. It turns out that my main sickness was inactivity. Yes, I had a sickly constitution, but exercise is enough to strengthen anyone, and now I walk and ride horses more—sometimes Mary and I even run together for a short duration. It feels wonderful, I can assure you."

"Oh, I run sometimes as well, and yes, it does possess a small kind of accomplishment."

"It does, and...because Mary is here, I am less lonely. I daresay, I smile more. And as you can see, having something to smile about provides a strength in its own right."

"Yes, I suppose it does. Anne?"

"Yes?"

"I think you shall get on just splendidly."

"Thank you, Elizabeth. I believe that I shall."

⁂

THE DAY of our departure from Rosings Park finally came and Lady Catherine offered us a polite enough farewell, which was suitable for her style. Anne was pleasant, but I felt that I would miss Mary. It was odd how being away from her for so long seemed to improve our connection as opposed to dissolving it. We offered them the chance to come to Pemberley for when Georgiana and Jason would wed, and this was met with eagerness.

Therefore, as we all departed, there was nothing but well wishes all around, and for once there were no feelings of disquiet between Lady Catherine and myself; it was so rare that it almost frightened me.

On the road back to Kent, Miriam grew sick a couple of times, and her appetite could not be ever fully satisfied. It was nice to see her in the throes of full pregnancy, but I pitied the constant agony she was in.

As for herself, despite all the drawbacks that arrive from the pregnant state, she only had one real complaint.

"I hate not being able to see my own feet," she groaned, "for I have quite forgotten what they look like."

❧

EVENTUALLY WE WERE HOME! And Kent seemed to fold its arms around us like a large parent that had missed its children.

Mrs. Reynolds was happy to see us once more, Lucy and Jefferson were happy to be home as well, and we all settled in comfortably.

After a couple of days, however, Mr. and Mrs. Bingley retired to Allenwell, where they would finally settle into their new home and Miriam would begin her laying in. Mr. Bingley had sent word that Caroline and the Hursts would be visiting Allenwell to 'be present to assist Miriam', but we all knew that they just wished to visit for the sake of doing so.

As for the rest of us, we all settled back into our old ways with great ease. Jane began to teach the children of Pemberley's farms once more, and they had all missed her terribly. I continued to serve them food in between their lessons, which broke up my day quite nicely.

Georgiana and Jason would visit the families of Kent together, in hopes of helping the people of Kent to grow fond of him.

Kitty and the Colonel were another matter entirely. They would often ride along the grounds and the Colonel was teaching her as much as he could about horses, for they both held them in fascination and wonder. They would remain with us at Pemberley until after Georgiana's wedding, and then they would journey to Longbourn where our father would begin to teach the Colonel how to run the estate.

There they would henceforth live and when our parents passed away, they would then become the sole owners. I dreaded the expected day of their departure for they had been living with us for so long that it would seem strange when they would leave. However, it was only natural that family was meant to separate in such a way, therefore it was something that I had to adjust to.

As for Caiden and William, it was even more of a constant source of joy for me, because they had begun to start learning how to speak. They had first learned the words dada, which was their form of 'dad', but I was not jealous for I knew that they knew me, and 'mama' was much harder to form in a baby's tongue.

Thus, our days continued. Peace reigned over Pemberley, and we spent it all in camaraderie, peaceful contemplation and the joys of being at home, for at the present there were no more roads to travel.

𝕊 12 𝕊

INTO THE UNKNOWN

On a clear day, Samuel Lucas and Deborah Darcy were walking along the grounds of the convent in Philadelphia.

"So," Deborah began, "you have been living with my family for almost a fortnight now. How have you found it?"

"Surprisingly easy!" Samuel smiled. "At first I was stiff, but two things came in the form of a godsend."

"And what is that?"

"The first is Lydia, who despite everyone's constant censure of her in Hampshire, always had a way of making one feel comfortable and at ease. In truth, some of us people are too reserved and need a little drawing out, and like you, she is very good at that."

"Except for Jane, all the Bennet girls are good at it. And I am not censuring Jane by any means, but her strength is that of a different kind. Kitty, Elizabeth and Lydia are the sort to draw warmth from coldness and Jane is the sort of woman who brings calmness to the hotheaded."

"Did you meet Mary yet?"

"I did, for she was at Lydia and Henry's wedding. However, I did not meet her long enough to gather a ready opinion. What is she like?"

"Bookish, but I have not seen her of late, and she could be greatly changed."

"All too true. We humans change so often that it makes constantly loving some hard, and also sometimes makes constantly despising those who have wronged us even harder."

Samuel chuckled. "Oh, does the nun beside me acknowledge that she sometimes despises people?"

"I'm a nun, not a saint," Deborah corrected him.

"On the contrary, Deborah, or Sister Ignatius, you have more sanctity in you than any other saint that I have read of."

"You praise me."

"Yes, I do."

"How lovely," Deborah cooed. "I do not fear compliments."

"Why should you?"

"Because they feel expensive to receive. One has no way of paying them back often. It took me well into my twenties to figure out what would be the proper recompense."

"And what is the proper payment for a compliment?"

"Simple. If someone pays you a compliment, the only way to pay them back is to pay attention to what they say afterwards. Giving someone the right to be heard is the best of payments. And then if they ever say something idiotic, forget that they said it by the next day."

"Oh, that can be hard to do."

"So was their compliment in being given."

"In some cases, you are correct that it is true."

They walked on a little further, in comfortable silence, and Samuel Lucas began to grow nervous.

"But you mentioned," Deborah said, "that there were two things that made it easier for you to live at Canterbury."

"Oh, yes! The second one is your sister Helena."

"Oh, Helena speaks to you?"

"Yes. I know that she is mentally ill, but she fights it clearly and she fights it well. I like her immensely. She reminds me of you, actually."

"Yes, I am mentally unsound myself sometimes."

"Indeed, you are," Samuel joked, resulting in Deborah pushing him away from her playfully.

"Oh, you have resorted to pushing now?"

"I find it to be one of my better weapons, Mr. Lucas."

"Are you trying to annoy me?"

"Yes. Is it working?"

"Not at all. It is adorable and nothing more."

"I must change tactics then."

"Oh, you are free to try, and equally free to fail."

She gave him a sidelong glance. "I see that my family has had some influence on you."

"Yes, they have, and I am afraid to return to Britain for the fear that I shall not fit. I have been quite spoiled here."

"How so?"

"At Canterbury, all is different than anywhere else. People prefer to speak there, as if were they to stop, they will all lose the gift of speech."

Deborah laughed.

"Oh, indeed I am in earnest," Samuel said. "There is liberty in your home. The likes of which I have never seen before. I do enjoy that freedom. And your parents are eager to accept those who show themselves to be acceptable. They seem to..."

"Enjoy life."

"Precisely. And those who have it in them as well. Though the fact that you are so closely connected to Mr. Darcy of Pemberley is even more of an amazement to me."

"How small the world is and it frightens you, doesn't it?"

"Yes. Yes, it does. It makes one feel as if one will eventually walk back to the same place over and over."

"Because one does. We are all on the same path, aren't we?"

"Yes, yes, we are. And I would sound hypocritical to say otherwise, for here I am, covering my own past footsteps."

Deborah smiled at him, then leaned down and picked up a flower, twirling it in her hands.

"Deborah?"

"Yes?"

Samuel breathed in and out heavily, then gathered his courage and proceeded.

"I must away back to England tomorrow."

"Yes, I know," she whispered. "We quite stole a bit of happiness in these last two weeks, did we not?"

"Yes, I suppose we did. And nothing about these last moments are easy. All I can say, Deborah..."

"Yes?"

"Is that these last weeks with you have been some of the best in my life."

"I know... for I have felt the same way."

Not caring for decorum or the repercussions of her actions, Deborah placed her hand in Samuel's, and he squeezed it gently in response.

"When you go back to England," she began, "you will live and find your happiness, but you must never forget me."

"No, I never shall. Never in all my years."

Growing wistful, he raised her hand to his lips and kissed it.

"Deborah, I was in love with you."

"As I was with you."

"And I was a fool."

"Yes," she laughed, "you were. But an honest and good fool you remain."

"What goodness do I have?"

"You came back to see me one last time. It is not the goodness of a man who never made a mistake, but rather it is the goodness of a man who returned to right a wrong, which takes all the courage in the world."

"Deborah, I am sorry, but I must..."

Grabbing her suddenly and giving her no chance to resist, he pulled her to him, and they kissed.

When they finally released, Samuel looked at her sheepishly.

"Will you get in trouble for my indiscretion?"

"No, for I have organized it with my other sisters that they distract our mother superior while I am with you."

"Oh, that is splendid, I just..." Samuel Lucas then almost broke down, fighting back his tears. "If I had a chance to undo all that I had done, I would have done differently. I would have never forsaken you. I promise, I will always love you."

"And you shall always be in my heart. Take comfort Samuel, to have the heart of a nun is to know that you are the only man that she loves. And always will."

❧

PARTING from Deborah had been the most difficult thing Samuel Lucas had ever done. As the carriage that transported him from the convent rolled on, Deborah watched him as he left, and he rested his eyes upon her still form. Further and further the carriage went until it turned the corner, and she disappeared.

Happiness was what Samuel found in being alone in the carriage, for alone was what he had needed as he began to silently weep. Tears rolled down his cheeks in slow succession as he realized that he may never see her again.

As his eyes closed, trying to end the fall of his tears, his mind swept over every aspect of Deborah Darcy's face.

First, he recalled her eyes that were a deep brown.

Then her cheeks.

Her lips.

Chin, nose and delicate neck.

Her hair was always hidden under the black cloth of her uniform, but he had remembered it from when they first met. It was a rich blonde that was thick with curls. Very much he had wanted to pull off her veil to see it once more, but all he had was his imagination.

In that moment, he cursed the man that he once was; the foolish weakling who thought it prudent to walk away from the greatest woman that walked the earth. He was the heir to Lucas Lodge, and she would have been the ideal mistress to it.

He could walk up and down every inch of Britain and never find a woman to equal her, as Darcy would have walked up and down America and all of Europe and never have met another woman like Elizabeth Bennet. Yet Darcy had made the right decision in the end, while Samuel had done the wrong thing in the beginning. And the beginning was all that he had. That was where their paths altered.

Upon returning to Canterbury, the occupants were sad to see him leave, and that was the night that one of Thomas and Emilia's daughters, named Victoria, had come to meet him with her husband.

Being amongst them all one last time made Samuel Lucas even more wistful, for their domestic joy reminded him of his singular position.

As the night drew on, Helena joined the group, and she sat with him.

"This..." she began slowly.

"Do not fear," Samuel said. "Remember to take your time and understand that I am not going anywhere."

"This is your last—night here?"

"Yes, yes, it is."

"And you, you saw Deborah! You saw Deborah today."

His smile was warm. "Yes, yes I did."

"Was it true?"

"Was what true?"

Helena then leaned her head in to his closely, whispering like a child.

"Was it true that you were in love with her? Hen—Henry told me so, so."

Samuel chuckled and pulled one of her curls playfully.

"Yes, but not only was. I still am."

"Did you know that...that my mother was hoping you both would fall back in love?"

"What do you mean?"

"I mean that she—she had had hopes... that Deborah would fall back in lo—love with you so much that she would want to leave the convent. She hoped you both would marry."

"While I like that idea, your sister has her goodness, her stubbornness, and I shall not take it from her this day. Or the next."

"Then don't," Helena sighed, looking suddenly intelligent. "And just let us feel sorry for you both."

"Thank you, Helena."

"You...you are good too."

"Am I?"

"Yes. Or at least, I think so."

Samuel playfully poked her nose, and she screeched happily then rushed away from him.

THE NEXT DAY, the occupants of Canterbury escorted Samuel Lucas to Penn's Landing where he boarded the ship called The Rosetta. He beheld them from the deck of his ship as it took off. They waved to him, he did so in return and as the ship sailed away, they grew smaller and smaller until they all but disappeared.

Samuel Lucas turned his attention to the wide body of water ahead, knowing that in heading back to Britain, he would be returning home... and yet, it felt as if he was sailing into the unknown.

For behind him was a destiny that would never be seized, a path he did not walk down, and the memory that could never leave him and nor did he want it to.

She was Deborah Darcy, and she was a true heroine of his.

❦ 13 ❦

MANY MEETINGS

At Pemberley, we all had fallen back into the ways of domestic joy very easily. But a date had been set for Georgiana's wedding and thus began all the events that led up to it.

With family, duty is as duty always will be, and when one is getting married, it cannot be achieved without much of the family still not meeting one another. Therefore, first and foremost, invitations were sent to Errodin Abbey for Jason's older brother, Victor, to come to Pemberley to meet his future sister-in-law. Having already met Jeffrey, it was suitable for him to remain in London, but Victor's arrival was most pressing.

Yet in sending the oldest Whitfield brother an invitation, we also were in the way of receiving an invitation from Matlock, the seat of Earl and Lady Fitzwilliam, who wished to meet the fiancé of their niece. Thus, the plan was laid bare that Victor would arrive at Pemberley and then we all would proceed to Matlock.

However, what would happen next would be a wonderful mixture of parts to our plan that would be both a blessing and equally grievous.

In that time, I had asked Darcy if I could invite the Gardiners to Pemberley, so that they could visit Matlock with us. He thought it a marvelous idea, however only half would be able to attend. My Aunt Gardiner and Issy—or Isabella—were eager to join us. Although the rest would have to remain in Cheapside, for my uncle's business would not allow him time away to leave, at the moment, and Harriet was engaged! We did not know how this had come about and who the lucky man was, but we were sure to be told all the details about it upon our aunt's arrival. However, her fiancé was in London, and she did not wish to be away from him for long. So she would remain in Gracechurch Street with my uncle and the rest of my cousins while only Aunt Gardiner and Isabella came. When it came time for Georgiana's wedding, then they would travel to Kent for the happy event and return straight away back to London.

And then there was the last element to the mixture; the Hursts and Caroline Bingley were now at Allenwell.

✖✖✖

WHEN THEY HAD ARRIVED at Allenwell, Bingley had sent word, and we all went to pay our respects.

Miriam had to remain in her room upon our visit, for she had grown too large, making Georgiana wishing to alter her wedding plans.

When we had visited Miriam in her bedroom chambers, Georgiana brought up the topic of a lengthier engagement.

"Oh no, Georgiana!" Miriam had objected. "I do not wish for you to delay your wedding all because of me. I would feel most guilty, especially since I know that you wish to marry."

"I do," Georgiana confessed. "Yet it will not do to do so while you are confined to your bedroom and having no attention on you when it ought to be. You are expected to have a child, Miriam, and this is your time. Besides, I would like you and Charles to be at my wedding. You surely cannot do it when you cannot even stand, now can you?"

"No," Miriam laughed, "for I am a walrus."

"Oh, indeed," Jane said, smiling at her. "Elizabeth, remember when you were this size?"

I exhaled sharply. "I do, every moment of it, and I truly don't miss the extra load to carry."

"And you had twins," Miriam said. "How were you possible?"

"A question I ask myself often."

"Now we have no choice but to go back downstairs, don't we?" Georgiana groaned.

"Yes," Miriam answered, "there is nothing for it. Yet you shall find Louisa fully agreeable now, and as for Caroline... well, she is more tolerable than usual."

"Indeed, is she?" I asked. "And pray, may I ask? Is it in address that she improves? Has she deigned to add ought of civility to her original style? For I dare not hope that she is improved in essentials."

"Oh, no! In essentials, I believe, she is very much what she ever was. When I said that she improved, I did not mean that her mind or manners were in a state of improvement, but that from knowing her better, her disposition is better understood."

I was slightly alarmed at Miriam's kinder words of Caroline, for it can sometimes be hard losing an ally who also has the same enemy as you. One feels less great in numbers that way.

"Then you and she are now beginning to become friends at last?" I said, "That is very well."

"Oh, no we are not there yet!" Miriam said with a dry chuckle. "For I still cannot forget everything she has done to me, and therefore forgiveness shall not come easily. Also, she still can be her snippy and prudish self when she forgets to check her manners. All I can say now is that she is trying."

"Why do you think she is, though?" Kitty asked. "For I am

wondering if her efforts of improvement are genuine or simply are because she finds she might have something to gain in it."

"And you hit the nail right on the head," Miriam exclaimed. "Her actions at self-improvement are noble, if they are in the right place. Yet I fear that it is not so, and that she has some other scheme afoot. Or is it my paranoia that is clouding my judgment? And my pregnancy?"

"It is not your judgment being misplaced," I said, "or your maternal state. No, it is because Caroline has made herself unable to be trusted at best. I shall do my best to judge for myself, but I admit to being dubious as well."

"Don't be any other way," Miriam warned. "Give her a chance but also given her your skepticism. She is deserving of both."

When we had rejoined the group, Mr. Hurst was as to be expected, gruff in manner and often not speaking. All that we got from him was a greeting, a brief inquiry about our health and that was the end of his exertions. He sat on the sofa and removed himself from the rest of the discussion.

Mrs. Hurst, to my happiness, decided to take the reins of the conversation and inquire much on our time at Lyme.

"We have wonderful news on that score," Jane said to her.

"Oh, I always love news," Mrs. Hurst said. "Don't you as well, Caroline?"

We all turned to Caroline, who was startled by her sister's sudden attack on her, and then she recovered, smiling forcefully.

"Of course, news is always welcome."

"Well," Jane continued, "one of our dear friends, Charlotte Collins."

"Charlotte Collins?" Caroline Bingley interrupted. "That clergyman's wife on Rosings Estate."

"Yes."

"Was it not true that he died by drowning in bee honey?"

"Yes, it was most tragic, was it not?"

"How is it possible to do such a thing?" she exclaimed, half-laughing. Everyone looked on her censure however, and she quieted her girdle and asked Jane to continue.

"Yes, that is the same Mrs. Collins. Well, she came to Lyme with us as Miss Austen's companion, and while there, she met an old acquaintance of hers, named Captain Frederick Wentworth."

"Oh, I have heard of him," Mrs. Hurst replied.

"Have you?" Kitty asked.

"Yes, in London, he moved in our circles, and we attended some dinners where he was present."

"Indeed, we did," Caroline added, trying to contribute something positive to the discussion. "He had much conversation and a very definitive air about him."

"Did you all enjoy his company?" I asked.

"Yes, we did. And I liked him immensely, for he was quite charming."

"Well," Jane continued, "then with your permission, I shall write to his fiancée that you have complimented her beau."

"His fiancée?" Caroline blurted out, "but I recall that he was still single."

"And that is where our dear Charlotte Collins comes in. They had long since known each other, to our surprise, for years, and they had once carried quite a strong affection for one another. Now that both were free of any restraints, they re-met at Lyme and little by little, fell in love once more. Before leaving Lyme, Captain Wentworth proposed to Mrs. Collins, and now they are engaged."

"Oh, that is most delightful!" Mrs. Hurst said, and then she turned to Mr. Hurst to confirm her proclamation.

"Oh, yes," he said, "Wonderful."

Mrs. Hurst could not help but roll her eyes at his lackluster response but did her best to smoothen his obvious indifference.

Caroline Bingley was another matter entirely.

Her expression was livid to say the least, and what could be the reason for it? I did not know her full acquaintance with Captain Wentworth, however surely it could not have been much at all. Yet she had not even met Henry Darcy before she developed a desire to captivate him, so small acquaintances never really affected her designs on people.

She quickly masked her expression with one of surprise.

"How fascinating!" she announced. "And most astonishing. I offer my congratulations to her."

"And I as well," Mrs. Hurst added.

"Well then," Jane continued, "when we next write to her, we shall tell her of so."

"Thank you," Mrs. Hurst said. "Oh, but I heard the most alarming news as well about the Cumberland Company. I heard that Miss Fanny Crawford eloped with a Captain Benwick."

"Oh, yes that did occur," Colonel Fitzwilliam said. "However, it was not a cowardly act, but one done out of necessity really. They are not villains."

"And from the reports we have heard in town, you are correct, Colonel. The couple did make it successfully to Gretna Green, they wed, and when they returned, it was at the very time when Captain Benwick was invited by royal decree to be presented at court for his receiving a high position in our new armada in the war."

"What?" Jason asked. "Is that true?"

"Yes, he returned to England with being anticipated a hero. He has not left for the war yet, but he was the main Captain who was recommended by an Admiral in the navy."

"Perhaps it was Admiral Croft," Darcy said.

"Yes, perhaps it might have been. Either way, all came to a good end for them, because his being distinguished at court and being given such a high position has made Mr. and Mrs. Crawford quite forgive him and their daughter, and they have welcomed them back with open arms."

"Then fortune gave them a good turn?" Kitty asked. "That is delightful."

"Yes," Mr. Hurst groaned. "They have been rewarded for their reckless nerve."

"And you forget, Mr. Hurst," Jason said, "the immortal words of the Roman poet, Virgil. 'Fortune favors the bold'."

"I thought he was a Greek."

"No, my dear," Mrs. Hurst said, a little embarrassed, "Remember, he was the one who wrote 'The Aeneid'."

"Oh, right. They all seemed the same to me."

Everyone looked away and groaned at Mr. Hurst's willingness to cling to ignorance.

Mrs. Hurst continued to dominate the conversation on their side, and I welcomed it. From what I recalled, while Mrs. Hurst did sometimes side with Caroline, she still always had a more open nature and was less willing to cling too hard to her prejudices.

Caroline Bingley on the other hand, was a different matter entirely. She spent the rest of the visit speaking when needed and seeming to attempt to choose her words wisely, in hopes of being kind. It was nice to see her attempting to improve her manners and desire for civility in her address, but I did not forget her cold words about Mr. Collins. While one might think the death of Mr. Collins was a strange way to meet one's maker, you do not scoff at it out loud! Openness of words is one thing, but with the freedom of speech still comes the need to choose one's words wisely and know when to conceal what one feels.

And then there was her initial reaction to the announcing of Charlotte Collins to Captain Wentworth. While I thought on how she could have formed an attachment to him, when he did not even think much of her to have mentioned his acquaintance with her, made me draw a possible conclusion to her nature. At first Caroline had developed a fascination with the men in the Darcy family, undoubtedly. Yet over time her needs worsened.

Caroline Bingley was a beautiful woman who was now seeing everyone else receive a proposal but herself. She must have been filled with puzzlement over how such a thing could continually occur, and it must therefore be a blow to her ego every time.

In short, she now had a jealousy that was indiscriminate and knew no bounds. She might be jealous of any woman who had found her happiness in a fate with any gentleman who Caroline would have found suitable. It would not matter that she had never cared for the man initially. Yet once another woman obtained him, she would grow envious. Therefore, perhaps it was not the man and his name that Caroline craved for, but the idea of love that she obsessed over. With her jealousy so unfocused and willing to be ignited at random, I doubted that she would ever be a woman who could find satisfaction—and it would take a very strange sort of man to do the duty with success.

Our visit soon came to an end, and we left for Pemberley, under the express desire to have them for dinner once my Aunt Gardiner and Cousin Isabella arrived, which the Bingleys agreed to, thus ending our rounds of many meetings of our families once again.

✣ 14 ✣

FOOLISH FEELINGS

After the Pemberley Company left to return home, Caroline sought isolation and told her brother and sister that she would be walking along the paths of Allenwell for some exercise.

Louisa offered to escort her sister, but Caroline declined it, telling her that she requested the peace that came from being alone.

"But it might rain soon," Louisa said.

"It shall not rain."

"The last time you said that it would not rain when you went for a walk, it did rain."

"Oh, for goodness sakes, Louisa! That was only one time!"

Caroline retrieved her bonnet and rushed out of Allenwell, going along a popular walk around the house.

At one time she would have said that it was a sufficient house but was not nearly as incredible as Pemberley. Yet now she never wished to see Pemberley again, she thought rashly. The sight of it might overwhelm her, and therefore Allenwell was all that was good in her eyes, except that it was so close to the estate that she wished not to behold at this moment.

She once dreamed to be mistress of Pemberley, but she was not. She thought it would be suitable to be the wife of Colonel Fitzwilliam, who was the son of an Earl, but it was not to be. She then thought the idea of being mistress of Canterbury would make do, but another Bennet had snatched up her chance. For a time, she had thought to pursue Henry Fitzwilliam, but he never seemed to want to be in her company. And then there was Captain Wentworth who, though charming, never took an interest in her.

And what did all these women possess that she did not?!

It was all too nonsensical in her eyes.

And heartbreaking.

Yet with this list of men who had all walked past her without offering her their careful consideration, it now began to occur to her of why did she relentlessly pursue them?

Why did she feel an attachment to Henry Darcy when she had never met him before?

Why was she jealous of Charlotte Collins for winning Captain Wentworth when she had only met him a couple of times and then forgot him afterwards until his engagement was announced?

Why did she desire Colonel Fitzwilliam just because Kitty had enthralled him?

With Mr. Darcy, her obsession had made sense, for they had been well-acquainted before. She had thought him handsome and a splendid conquest. And therefore, when Elizabeth Bennet began to find her way into Darcy's heart, naturally Caroline had become possessive.

Only Henry Fitzwilliam was the one who she had the restraint to not fancy, and that was because she had never heard of him ever pursuing a love.

Yet therein was the problem.

Was it the men she fell in love with?

Or was it the anger that the men had chosen other women besides herself? For if they continued to do so, then there might have been truth in what Louisa had once said: perhaps Caroline made herself not likable. And because she was not likable, she perhaps was also not lovable.

Walking back and forth, lost in her daydreams, she then realized that within her was a great need: she needed to be loved, and felt that she had the right to be.

Therefore, the fact that she was not was beginning to destroy her inside, and it brought out the worst in her. Or did it? Was there really great evil in her?

No, surely there was not. She acted as many women did in the ton. But they had husbands, they had distinction, prestige and all the decided attractions that a socially successful match would give her. Therefore, she would not give up, and was content in believing that she would only try harder.

And to all who were not her, only they saw the flaw of her plan. For a woman who already tried too much, regarding romance, was her flaw, and to try even harder would make her become even worse.

Thus, ridding her mind of her foolish feelings of regret, Caroline looked to her future with optimism mingled with hubris. She would have her moment or fall down trying.

15

A STRANGE SORT OF MAN

The arrival of Aunt Gardiner and Isabella to Pemberley was a welcome addition to our party. For while Aunt Gardiner was always much loved by Fitzwilliam, Isabella was also growing to become a favorite of his. Her simple and artless manner put him greatly at ease and even she could see it.

When they arrived, they entered with much lack of ceremony and much calm filled our company.

"Oh, to be in Kent again!" Aunt Gardiner said. "Did I ever forget to mention to you, Mr. Darcy, that I spent some of my childhood here?"

"No, Aunt Gardiner," he answered, while all except Jane, were assembled. "You did not."

"I used to have family who lived here in Kent," she continued, "and they would invite me here in the summer. Many a happy time I spent in enjoying the beauties of the Kent countryside in my youth."

"And for a place that you have much fond memories of, Mother." Isabella laughed. "It is strange that I am now twenty years old and have only now just come and seen the place for the first time."

"Yes, life can be ironic in that way," Mr. Darcy acknowledged, "but how are you, Isabella?"

"Decaying I suppose," she joked, and we all laughed in turn.

"And what does that even mean?" Aunt Gardiner said.

"Mother, it means that I have been stuck in a house where my older sister is getting married. I have therefore been so confined in a place where I hear of married-this and married-that, and I am quite out of my element on the matter. Having never been married and not likely to be so, I do not know what to speak of on the subject, therefore I always feel as if I am wasting away, for I have nothing to contribute."

"Your support," Georgiana said. "I believe is all that is required. And I believe Harriet shall love you for that alone."

"She would if I was any good at talking about weddings. Indeed, I do not even know what the proper sort of fabric for a wedding gown is. I do the duty of being a woman very ill."

"Oh, do not fear, Issy," I said, "for there are many definitions to being a woman."

"And I shall fight to find mine," she said resolutely, "but still there is no excuse for me, for my father runs a textile factory."

Kitty laughed. "Oh, yes that is true! Fabric is in your blood."

"But not in my heart," Isabella continued, "or my mind."

"And what is in your mind?" Colonel Fitzwilliam asked.

"In truth, I believe I am only good at one thing."

"And what is that?"

"Eating."

"And how are you even good at that?" Kitty laughed. "You are plump, very lovely, and well-made, but not fat. Therefore, are you certain that you are an expert at it?"

"It is not my fault that my body will not gain more mass."

"Oh, Isabella," Mr. Darcy chuckled.

"Do not forget, you have my permission to call me Issy or Isa."

"I like Issy more."

"Of course you do. Everyone does."

"But where is Jane?" Aunt Gardiner asked.

"Oh, she is here, but only she is teaching her lessons to the children," I said, "and I was hoping that tomorrow, you might observe her as she does so."

"Then she is quite good at it?"

"Very good," Kitty said. "Indeed, I never would have thought she was made for such a fate, but she has proven to be the sort to have confounded us all."

"That is marvelous."

"And," I continued, "she has gotten so well at it, that I might even allow her to teach William and Caiden when they get older rather than hiring a governess."

"You ought to. For it will show much confidence in your sister's talents."

"And our sons shall grow to learn with children who are not as fortunate as them," Mr. Darcy said, "which will be an education in itself that cannot be taught, but only experienced."

"Indeed, that is a noble view."

"Now," Isabella said, "forgive me for sounding too eager, but how long till I am allowed to see my cousins again? For I miss those two boys."

Caiden and William were quickly sent for and brought in by Lucy. They had remembered their Great Aunt Gardiner and favorite cousin Issy and were all smiles.

To add to their charm, they had now also learned how to say 'mama' and they called me so often in their presence, making me even more prodigiously proud of them.

Eventually Jane had finished her lessons and joined us with

relish, and we were all a merry company, who had only one more visitor to fulfill our circle.

"Aunt and Issy," I said as I was leading them to their rooms, "I'd hate to spring another acquaintance on you so soon into your arrival, but in two days' time, we expect an addition to our family party."

"And who will that be, my dear?"

"Victor Whitfield, who is Jason's older brother."

"Oh, we should be delighted to meet him."

"Thank you, and to add to this all, Georgiana and Jason's wedding has been pushed back, to accommodate Mrs. Bingley's laying in."

"That is very considerate."

"Then you do not mind having to remain at Pemberley a little longer than what was expected?"

"Of course we mind, Lizzy!" Isabella said, rolling her eyes with sarcasm. "For how could we love being here? After all, it is not as if Pemberley is a nice house, richly furnished and quite comfortable. And just to tell you, we do not really like you all here either!"

"You and your jokes."

She gave me a quirky grin. "Where do you think I learned it from? Oh Lizzy, we shall be very happy to be here longer, won't we Mama?"

"Of course we shall," Aunt Gardiner said. "For there was never any doubt, was there?"

"No," I replied happily, "there never was."

"But I am curious, what sort of man is this Mr. Victor Whitfield."

"I cannot tell you, Aunt, for this will be my first time in meeting him as well, and therefore we might all be in for a surprise."

THE ARRIVAL of Victor Whitfield was, as to be expected, if it weren't for one small detail: it was not at all what we expected.

For one, he arrived a day early, and two, he arrived not in a coach, but on horseback, only carrying enough change of clothes to last four days at a time.

When he had arrived suddenly, requesting entry, I was sedate, but Mr. Darcy was irate.

"What the devil is he about, coming a day early?"

"I do not know, let us see."

When we all had arranged ourselves, we entered to find him waiting by himself in the sitting room of Pemberley, standing by the fireplace. When he turned to us, he smiled wickedly.

"Well, I daresay that I have already begun by making a bad impression."

"You bet you have, Victor," Jason said, coming forward. "What the devil are you about arriving a day early when nothing is prepared? That sort of behavior is acceptable between families, but not when you are meeting someone new."

"Oh, so serious, younger brother. You always had the best manners, but my early arrival is by sheer accident."

"Really? So, you did not deliberately choose to act on your wild ways?"

"You would teach this company not to believe a word I say or think me rash and reckless, Jason," he said with a hint of wickedness to his address, then he turned to the rest of us. "That is monstrously ungenerous of him, is it not?"

Turning back to Jason before anyone could respond, however, he clapped his hands together.

"But before I give my explanation to why I am remiss in following my own word, I should like to become acquainted with my hosts and company. And Jason, tell me, who is the lady who was so kind as to accept your mediocre hand in marriage?"

"That would be me," Georgiana said, coming forward rather than waiting to be introduced. "And you are to be my new brother."

"I am." Victor Whitfield smiled, approaching her. "And you, Miss Darcy, are clearly too good for my brother."

"Oh, am I?"

"Yes, for you have spirit to you. He knows that I like spirit."

"Clearly," Mr. Darcy said, annoyed.

"And judging by your reaction to my cheek, you must be her brother, the illustrious Mr. Darcy."

"Mr. Whitfield," Mr. Darcy said curtly, nodding his head, "I shall begin with proper introductions. This is my wife, Mrs. Elizabeth Darcy, my cousin, Colonel Fitzwilliam, his wife Mrs. Kitty, then Miss Jane Bennet, my wife's and sisters-in-law, Aunt Gardiner and her daughter, Miss Isabella Gardiner."

"Well, it is pleasing to meet you all," Victor said, bowing with ease.

"And welcome to Pemberley, sir," I said, and then I ordered the tea to be brought while inviting him to sit down.

"So, now that we are introduced," I said, smiling warmly, "tell us this mysterious reason for why you are arrived so much earlier than you had proclaimed initially, sir."

"Right to the point, Mrs. Darcy, I see?"

Fitzwilliam grumbled while I felt all too ready to arrive at the challenge Mr. Whitfield set.

"What would be the reason in dawdling? Especially when you have offered a fun tale to tell."

"You think it was fun?"

"You smile in a way that determines it to be so. Therefore, am I wrong?"

"And now you are procrastinating," Isabella added.

"Isabella," Aunt Gardiner reprimanded under her breath.

"Oh, ma'am!" Victor said. "Why do you reprimand her, when she is correct? I am the one who is procrastinating, as well as being a little crass, therefore," and here he winked at Isabella, "she and Mrs. Darcy are fully within their rights to reply in equal measure. And indeed, I will have no inequality when in my company. If I am spicy, then let a woman meet my sauciness with her own."

"Oh, Victor," Jason said, "whatever wickedness I have, you have too much of it."

"Indeed, I do. Now, onto my tale."

Victor leaned back and unfolded his story.

"It is the story of a man who does not like to wait, you see," Victor began. "I was riding along in my chaise and four when our carriage was overturned on the road."

"Oh dear," Jane said. "You were in an accident?"

"Yes, but I still have my limbs, so you need not worry over me. Luckily my coachmen were not harmed as well, and the horses were too strong to be injured by the accident. It turns out that one of the wheels to my coach had broken and it would take a few days to be fixed. I therefore took the strongest horse from the chaise and four, named Xerxes, took the smallest of my luggage and told my men to take the coach to the nearest blacksmith to be repaired. I gave them sufficient money for the repairs and continued on my own at that place. I know that I could have gone to the closest inn and remained there, writing to you of my delay, yet it seemed to be more agreeable to me to be a day early with my speed rather than be four days late."

"Well then," Aunt Gardiner said, "you are not at all to blame."

"No, I am not."

"Poor Mr. Whitfield," Jane said.

"Oh, there is no cause for that, though I must say that I enjoy your concern for me, Miss Bennet. At present I have every cause for cheer, for now I find myself a day earlier in a society that is very pleasing and as good as I can find anywhere. So, I absolutely forbid you to feel sorry for me. Yet now that I am here, I do so wish to know you all quite well."

"You shall have plenty of time for that, I assure you," I said, "too much time, I dare say."

"Too much time?"

"You shall stay for a fortnight. It will be long enough for you to know every part of our personalities."

"Life has taught me that people are too complicated to be figured out so easily."

"You claim to be a studier of humanity?"

"I claim to only like to observe. Now, am I forgiven for being early?"

"Your room is already prepared for you, therefore, we feel no sense of being slighted."

"Thank you, and I daresay that I have given you a service."

"And how so?" Kitty asked.

"You have all gotten the chance to know me under abnormal circumstances," he said with a smirk, "and as you can see, I am no good at doing things the normal way, therefore I have shown you how to adapt to my nature most easily by throwing you headlong into it."

"But can you adapt to ours?" Mr. Darcy asked, critically.

"That I hope I can do well enough."

Looking between my husband and Victor, I could sense a rivalry beginning to erupt, and I did not want it to be so. Therefore, I felt it wise to change the subject.

"Mr. Whitfield," I began gently, "did your enigmatic brother tell you how he and Georgiana met?"

"Oh dear," Jason said, looking at his hands.

"What sort of a response is that?" Victor said to Jason. "You look panicked, brother, which means this story is about something that you do not wish me to know. And therefore, I must know it. Mrs. Darcy, Miss Darcy or Miss Bennet, you three have proven to care for my company the most, so who wishes to begin this tale?"

"I am his fiancée," Georgiana said, "therefore I and I alone have the right."

"I was correct," he said. "You are too good for Jason. Well, Miss Darcy, please begin to tell me how my brother worked his way into your heart."

"Stealthily, Mr. Whitfield. He did it most stealthily."

At the end of her story, Victor chuckled, turned to Jason and clapped his hands in mock applause.

"I give you much credit Jason, for that is a brilliant story—one right out of a novel."

"I did not mean to be deceptive," Jason groaned.

"No, you just accidentally did it. And thank you Miss Darcy, for now I have a story to always hold over his head."

"I have many more to hold over you."

"True, but it shall always be so that it ought to be known; while I am the one who speaks with trickery, you are the one who acts on it."

"My intentions were noble," Jason said, "and I was fighting for many causes. Which do you fight for, Victor?"

"I am working on which cause to favor, for there are so many."

"That is just your way of saying that you are being idle," Jason said with a harsh laugh.

"No, that is me showing my bravery."

"How so?" Isabella asked innocently.

"Because a person can always take a stand, but some of us are plagued, always thinking of both sides of the argument, to the point where we get accused of being indecisive. It is not easy to look a standpoint in the eye and accept seeing the sides of both. Have you ever seen two sides of an argument?"

"I have often, for it comes with the territory of having siblings."

"Precisely. Were you a coward to do so, or were you brave and compassionate for doing so?"

"I am sorry, I do not have a ready opinion. I am... indecisive on the matter of being brave or being indecisive."

"Ah, how interesting. Now, I shall be the perfect guest."

"Do you know how to do that?" I laughed.

"I can, when I put my mind to it."

"You are about to put your mind to it?"

"I have my moments."

"Do you?" Kitty asked. "How many do you have per hour?"

"At least sixty."

"That is better than me, for I can only have a moment per day. I am not as unique as you."

"You are, my dear," Colonel Fitzwilliam said. "Your moments are just not nearly as bold. But they are very worthwhile to observe."

"Then, it follows," Kitty answered, "that love can offer one such uniqueness. I would like to believe it to be so." Then she turned back to Victor. "Forgive me for being so far behind you in the race of always standing out and having prolific memories, yet I daresay that I like the ones I do make."

"I would not have you do otherwise. Now that I have met you all, I am desirous of being the one to do the listening as opposed to being the one who speaks always."

"Is that your way of saying that we are making you tired?" Jane laughed.

"No, that is simply me beginning to try and be the perfect houseguest."

"Well," I said, "in that case, we are all happy to oblige you with our histories."

"I am not afraid to start first," Georgiana said.

"Perfect," Victor said, "let us begin with you."

We all then began to tell Victor a little bit about ourselves while we all ate some cakes and drank our tea. All the while I looked between Jason and Victor.

As for looks, they could not have been more different. Jason was very short, being no more than a couple inches taller than Georgiana. While Victor was not especially tall, he was roughly four inches taller than Jason, and had curly hair as opposed to Jason's straight one.

Like Jason, he could not be described as a great beauty by any means, but nor was he ugly. Neither handsome, ugly, nor even plain. He was simply what he was, quite indescribable. I suppose that my judgment on his looks was greatly impaired by his personality. While Jason had charm, there was much sincerity behind it that could cool any attraction a woman might feel for him.

Yet with Victor, he had charisma as well as charm and it was a most dangerous thing. Not only did it perhaps make him look more appealing in the eyes of others, but it made me wonder if he was a bit of a dedicated rake. Also in his favor was age, for Victor was in his late forties, and he had earned all the confidence that comes with being a man of experience that was enhanced by natural selection. He was born with charm, perhaps, but the ease of manner that he acquired over time increased his powers. I was wary of him, because while my love for Fitzwilliam made me immune to any other man, Isabella and Jane were single, and I worried about what effect he could have over them. Yet I schooled my worries, for surely Victor Whitfield would do nothing to hinder the relationships between himself and the family who his brother was marrying into.

By the end of his first day at Pemberley, Victor had proven to be a strange sort of man with a strange set of powers. The most potent of them however was that, despite perhaps being a bad influence, he was undeniably lovable.

✣ 16 ✣

THE WORST WAY OF MEETING

On a warm day, Caroline decided to go for a long walk through the meadows that bordered Allenwell. The days went by steadily there and Miriam had been the center of everyone's attention. Though she had grown large from being pregnant, Charles was the loving and expectant husband who doted on her.

She was still far enough away from her expected due date that she still had one more month, but she was so much in size that she was bedridden.

A couple of days before, Charles announced that the Pemberley company would be leaving for Matlock, the estate of the Fitzwilliams. While Mr. Bingley and Miriam could not attend, the Hursts and her were to attend in their stead.

It was the strangest thing, but she was actually quite annoyed with the news. At one time, she would have loved being a part of a company who was visiting the house of an Earl, but now she had felt as if no decisions were her own. Yes, she very much was like a pawn that got moved about, her destiny uncertain.

She did not deserve to feel sorry for herself, but she did anyway, and whether it was her own bitterness or her idleness, she allowed herself to feel greatly ill-used, and not seeing any of the luxuries that her life afforded.

It is true to say that none of us could really feel sorry for Caroline Bingley, who always had a way of making herself the object of scorn and turning into a character that one could never fully understand. But when being in her position, with her mindset, one perhaps did not, nor could not, see the errors of ones' own nature.

And so it went, that as she walked, she was filled with such thoughts so much, that as she approached a stream, bending down to take some water, she did not take heed to the horse and rider until they were almost upon her.

When she finally did hear the noise, she turned to see the horse rear on its hind legs suddenly and the rider fell off and into the water.

"Oh, good god!" she cried. "What were you about, riding your horse into me? You could have killed me!"

"Oh, of course!" he cried, soaking wet, "I am the one who should offer you my pity! I am the one who is fallen from my horse and is drenched in freezing water."

"I cannot feel sorry for you," Caroline replied, "for while you had fallen, I would have been run over and crushed."

"And you did not even offer to help me up!" he cried, standing up in the water. "And what the devil were you about bending down like that?"

"I did not hear you approach, and the reason I did not help you is because we have not been introduced. I should not even be speaking with you."

"Are you in earnest? At a time like this, where I could be hurt terribly, you are caring about decorum?"

"Well I..."

"You foolish woman!"

"I..."

It was all too amazing, for in that moment Caroline would surprise all who knew her, or all of us who thought that we did. For a split moment, Caroline did see the ridiculousness of what she had just said. The man could have killed her, but he did attempt to stop his horse at the last moment, and he did succeed! At the expense of falling off his horse into the water and almost hurting himself.

"I..." Caroline said, at a loss.

"Yes, I know," the man said. "You are very good at saying I. I wonder now if that is all that you think of."

Caroline opened her mouth and then closed it once more. At a loss of what to do, she felt herself unable to speak, so she looked around and saw that the man's riding crop whip was laying on the ground, where he must have dropped it during his fall.

Acting on an impulse that she did not know the origin of, she walked over to the whip, picked it up, walked back over to the man and handed it to him.

He looked down at her outstretched hand, holding his crop, and then he sneered and seized it from her. Without looking at her, he got back on his horse and looked down at her.

"I am not going to ask your name," he said, "for as you have said, we have not been introduced. And perhaps I do not wish to know it anyway. I hope your devotion to primness was worth it, good lady."

He tipped his hat to her and rode off.

As his horse rushed across the stream and across the fields, Caroline stood there, feeling as if she had been slapped.

Why did he walk away feeling so bitter, for she had at least handed him his riding crop. Was that not a gesture of good will? And surely, she should be the one who was the most put out!

As she thought to walk away, she then remembered suddenly a mistake on her part. She had never asked him if he had been alright. She had not been injured, but he might have been, and she never even asked him if he was well.

Most unlike her usual nature, she was struck with a sense of rudeness on her part, or inconsideration, and realized that it made her appear cold. He could not be fully blamed for their near collision, for it was an accident and neither was at fault, but she had been the first to be rude.

Of course, however, he was very rude as well.

Suddenly filled with remorse for her ill-refined manner, she turned back to see the man riding away and she began to rush forward.

"I am sorry!" she cried. "Understand, I am sorry!"

Yet the man did not turn as he rode off, for he was too far ahead to have heard her.

THE NEXT DAY, they had all been prepared and Charles saw off the Hursts and Caroline.

They were to journey to Pemberley first, join their company and together they would all begin the trip to Matlock. With Allenwell being so close to Pemberley, they reached the estate in no more than half an hour's time, and they were met by the Pemberley Company, save one.

"You must forgive our brief delay," Jason Whitfield said, "For my brother is late in returning from the fields. He always enjoys a morning ride and knowing that he would be cooped up in a carriage for hours with others, he felt that he needed his morning exercise."

Caroline sighed inwardly at this but was not overtly angry. She only worried that their company would cause a bad impression on the Fitzwilliams if they would be late. Therefore, they all entered Pemberley, walking around the sitting room to stretch their legs before they would have to remain in their coaches for a long duration.

The rest of the company was present in their waiting. Jason

looked ashamed, but their wait could not have been more than a quarter of an hour. In that time, Caroline allowed her mind to wonder, and as she walked alone, her thoughts rested on a memory of when she had asked Elizabeth to take a turn about the room with her at Aginfield, in hopes of getting Mr. Darcy to pay attention to her. In looking back upon it, her reflection was one of embarrassment.

What had she been in hopes of achieving with that action? It was foolish and counterproductive. Was Louisa, in all essentials, correct? Had she been trying too hard, and as a result, succeeded too little?

There were the sound of footsteps and she was torn from contemplation as she looked up to behold the man who entered the room.

"Forgive me for my lack of presence of mind," Victor Whitfield had said, upon seeing all eyes upon him. "But I trust that you had not been waiting long and—"

His eyes fell on Caroline Bingley, and they widened with as much alarm as hers had.

For there she was, the woman who he had almost hit at the stream, and there he was, the man who she had been terribly rude to, making it a painful sight for them both, for their acquaintance had been already established in the worst way of meeting.

17

THE SAVIOR OF CAROLINE BINGLEY

When both seeing one another, their bodies froze as well as their gazes. On one side was the tendency to always lean toward inconsideration for how his actions were viewed by others, and on the other was her not in the habit of knowing how to react after receiving a shock.

Jason Whitfield and a few others, however, did observe their preoccupation. Therefore, he decided that it would be best to put an end to it. For when it came to his brother, this moment could lead to nothing but trouble.

"Mr. Hurst, Mrs. Hurst and Miss Bingley, allow me to introduce you to my elder brother, Mr. Victor Whitfield."

At hearing her name, Caroline flinched, then remembered herself, and moved to be introduced.

Louisa and Mr. Hurst approached him while Caroline remained rooted to the spot, transfixed.

After Mrs. Hurst had said her piece and expressed herself most eloquently, Victor had no choice but to turn to Caroline Bingley and bow.

"Hello, Miss Bingley."

"Mr. Whitfield," she whispered. "It is a pleasure to meet you."

"Thank you, but that pleasure must be swift for I have made us late in our departure long enough."

Caroline knew very well that he must have wanted to be as little near her as possible, and therefore she did not take any steps forward and make any more gesture than simply to smile. Yet even she could feel how forced the smile was.

Everyone began to put on their bonnets, and the day proved to be a most wonderful one to take a journey. Georgiana professed her hopes that the days to and at Matlock would be so nice and the rest echoed her sentiments.

The carriages were arranged, so were those who sat in it, and the five carriages were off, headed for Matlock.

As they rode onward, Caroline sat with the Hursts and Jane Bennet, who was not only one of the other single women in the company besides Caroline but was the only one kind enough to always give Caroline a second chance.

They made very quaint small talk, both relying upon old nostalgia to carry them through, along with Mrs. Hurst who always regarded Jane as a favorite.

"Do you not recall?" Louisa said. "Of when we had first come into Hampshire with our brother, Jane, and we first met at the Assembly at the Red Lion?'"

"Indeed, I could never forget it," Jane said. "You were the talk of the assembly."

"Yes," Caroline added. "And it was there that you became a great favorite of ours most quickly. Do you not recall, Louisa, that Jane was called the beauty of the county?"

"Oh, I remember it very well," Louisa said.

Blushing, Jane murmured, "Oh, I was no such thing."

"You were and are my dear," Louisa continued, "and in truth, it always makes me wonder at your single state."

"You forget," Caroline said, "Jane here was on her way to happiness, but her beau was stricken with a bad fate."

"Oh, yes he was, was he not?" Louisa said. "Your fiancé died, didn't he?"

"Yes, he did," Jane said, looking out of the window, avoiding their eyes.

"That still must weigh on you heavily, my poor Jane."

"Thank you for your kind words," Jane answered, "but I am well now and... though this may sound harsh of me, try to understand—I do not wish to speak of him. For it always hurts to do so."

"Of course," Louisa said. Caroline beheld Jane, who had suffered a great loss, and bore it like a saint. If she, Caroline, had lost someone in such a way, would she carry it with such fortitude and silence?

"And yet," Caroline added, feeling as if maybe she might have found a kindred spirit in Jane Bennet, "it must have been such a shock for you to discover that your sister's fate would result in catching Mr. Darcy."

Jane eyed Caroline demurely, but her expression masked her incredible suspicion. She had done all in her power to like Caroline Bingley once, but even she had learned her lesson on that score. She would always be kind to Caroline now, but that was all that she could offer—and all that she owed to the woman who tried to wound her sisters who she had always devoted herself to looking after.

"Yes, it was, but it was a welcome surprise," Jane said with a smile. "And her path had led to be more prosperous than the original scheme others thought."

"What was the previous scheme?"

"Oh, there was much talk in Hampshire that my sister and your brother were to be the perfect pair."

"What!" Caroline exclaimed, surprised beyond all belief.

"Indeed!" Louisa echoed, "What do you mean?"

"Oh," Jane said, happy to use amazement to confound Caroline and wound her by the simple truth. "Yes, I can see how you were ignorant of it. Yet when your company first arrived in Steventon, it appeared as if Mr. Bingley and Elizabeth were to be the perfect match."

Caroline Bingley felt as if she could have been knocked down and therefore was happy in remaining seated in a carriage where her words and reactions would not be observed by a multitude of people.

"And when you had invited me to Aginfield," Jane continued, "well, I was quite happy for I wished to become further acquainted with you both, and also hoped to bring your brother and my sister together. Therefore, you may imagine my surprise when I had done well, but I had been focusing on the wrong aim. And to think, all the while, I had hopes of Mr. Bingley and Elizabeth, when in the end I had been bringing her close to Mr. Darcy."

"Miss Bennet," Louisa gasped, "you have us in much alarm."

Jane chuckled. "I can very well believe so. But in the realm of sisterhood, what sister would not do so for another? Yet I was happy to have been in error, for Mr. Bingley and my sister, as you know, are friends, but never had any affection for each other beyond camaraderie. It does indeed go to warn one against matchmaking, does it not? Imagine if I had been bent on telling Elizabeth to set her sights on another path other than Mr. Darcy. I would have driven her from true love. Therefore, that moment had taught me to not take to matchmaking, for I would do it most ill. Though we sisters often make the mistake of taking an idea and running wild with it. And yet, with my thoughts not coming to pass, my sister fell in love with a man who loved her, and your brother fell in love with the perfect match for him. Oh, the beauties of being wrong!" She chuckled at herself. "For imagine if all that I had hoped had come to pass. Your brother and my sister would be married, and Mr. Darcy would be single to be free to pursue another path, and that would not be wise!"

At the end of Jane's confession, Caroline Bingley felt as if she wanted to punch the window.

Originally all had thought that her brother and Elizabeth were meant to fall in love?

Yes, there had been some hint of this before, but Caroline had never taken it seriously. While Caroline would have once thought it outrageous ultimately, she now would have regarded it as a blessing in immense disguise. Yes Mr. Darcy was still engaged to Anne De Bourgh at the time, yet as time showed it, the engagement was a flimsy one that fell apart as easily as it had been formed.

It was Elizabeth Bennet who had been the true obstacle for Caroline, and to think that the obstacle could have never occurred if only Charles and Elizabeth had fallen in love with each other.

Machinations can often lead to immense speculation and internal occupation, and this was a revelation that put her and Louisa's mind to work.

What if Mr. Bingley and Elizabeth Bennet would have fallen in love?

The whole story of their lives would unwind utterly and be changed!

And Mr. Darcy would have been changed as well, for his heartache at possibly seeing Elizabeth in the arms of his friend would naturally have made him either bitter, or desirous of overcoming his disappointment—and Caroline would have been there for him. It would have been all too easy in fact. With many compliments offered on her side and weakness from emotional frustration on his, she would have appeared as a friend, a constant companion, and Anne De Bourgh would have fallen to the wayside while she had been the one Mr. Darcy had fought for.

Everyone's roles would be reversed if that were how the story had ended—yes it could have all turned out differently, she supposed. But it didn't.

For reality had been reality. Elizabeth and Charles had never fallen in love with each other. Mr. Darcy had stepped in, forgetting Caroline, risked everything for his love for Elizabeth, and now they were all where they were, travelling to Matlock because of who married who.

As for Jane Bennet, her sudden slip of the tongue was not out of pure malignance or ill-intent actually. Oh no! Rather she was filled with an objective, a desire to teach a lesson, as teachers often are in the habit of doing, even when they have quite left their classroom.

"Indeed," Jane continued, deliberately avoiding Caroline's gaze. "This all does go to teach one that all we can do is be happy for those when destiny finds them, accept the things that cannot be changed, only change the things that ought to be, and have the ability to see the difference between each of those things."

"Does it?" Mr. Hurst said suddenly, engaged in the discussion for the first time. They all turned to him, surprised that he was even listening.

"What?! I have ears as well. And does it?"

"Yes, it does," Jane replied evenly.

"So, you are truly happy with your sister's fate?" Caroline asked, a little bitter in seeing that she would not ever find a like-minded person in Jane Bennet, "You never find yourself to be... jealous of her? For she is wed, and you are still single?"

"Singularity of situation is not the curse or bane that people label it to be," Jane replied lightly, "for I have family and that quite destroys any feelings of loneliness. Oh no, Miss Bingley, I am lucky enough not to look at it in such a way. And as for jealousy, one should never be envious of another's good fortune if that good fortune was well-deserved, and my sister deserved it. For when one does begin to feel jealousy, it has catastrophic effects. Mostly one should never feel jealousy to the point where they hurt those they envy, be it through thought, word or action. For the minute you do, you become a villain. So never will I indulge the green-eyed monster; I have seen the damage it has done to many a woman's soul."

Caroline bit her lip and coldly looked out of the window of the carriage.

As for Jane Bennet, she knew very well that she might have lost a friend in Caroline, despite trying to be as nice as she could. However, she did not fear the reaction or the repercussions of her words. For she had learned a most valuable lesson: sometimes telling a truth was worth the cost of gaining an enemy.

Caroline Bingley needed to change, and it may not be through Jane's influence, but she could at least plant some seeds of doubt within her.

Whoever would be the savior of Caroline Bingley would have to do the rest.

18

UNCOMFORTABLE COMPANIONS

Matlock was not close enough to reach in one day, therefore they would have to stop at an inn.

Along the road, they came upon a very large establishment called *The Conquering King*. Their horses were taken to the inn's stables, overseen by Nicholson while Jefferson requested the rooms, spoke to the innkeeper, offered him the payments that Mr. Darcy, Mr. Bingley and Victor Whitfield gave him, and inspected the layout of the inn.

Caroline and Jane Bennet were to share a room to save money. While Caroline was secretly apprehensive to do it, Jane was so compliant to the idea that she knew she would have appeared callous for changing the scheme. A couple doors down from their room, Jason and Victor were sharing a compartment. Yet Caroline did not fear it, for they would only be there for one evening.

Thus, when it was time to go into dinner, Caroline had to linger in her room to fix her hair while Jane left and assured her that she would tell their party where she was.

Looking in the mirror at herself while she re-pinned some loose curls, Caroline sighed, wondering how she arrived where she did.

How did she get there? In an inn, going to Matlock while accompanying a group of people who perhaps did not desire her company.

It all became quite clear now to her then.

They did not like her!

For surely, she could not continue to lie to herself and act as if Jane's subtle hints of jealousy were not aimed toward her. They were indeed, and Elizabeth and her had once argued, Mr. Darcy naturally would know of it, Kitty naturally would not like her, the Colonel would have regarded her as a pathetic woman who once found him attractive as well but he did not regard, Georgiana always sided with her sisters-in-laws on everything, Jason was Victor's younger brother —and then there was Mr. Whitfield!

Ah yes, Victor Whitfield, who she had given a terrible first impression to, and surely would not forgive her. She had placed herself in a nest full of her own enemies, and now, she had to admit, she brought it on herself.

Sitting there, she realized that there was only one thing to do. Never had she gone to Matlock and met the whole of the Fitzwilliam family. Perhaps, if she was on her best behavior, she could impress the Earl of Matlock and his wife, along with the remaining sons. And how had she not thought of it before? There was Henry Fitzwilliam, the heir to Matlock, and Acton, the youngest son. How had she forgotten them? She brightened immediately, realizing that her prospects were still very much open. For Henry Fitzwilliam was the heir and must therefore be a splendid chap to set her sights on. And if he still would not care for her, then surely her dowry could attract the youngest son, Acton, who would require a woman with a bit of a fortune to her. Yes, with her looks and pocketbook, surely, she must do for one of them.

And there, at Matlock, Caroline Bingley would turn over a new leaf. She would begin to be nice to the hosts of the estate and gradually show her better sides to those who were used to seeing her worst. Maybe, in moderation, she would change what the world thought of her.

Her hair was finally finished, she smiled at her reflection, convincing herself that she could withstand one evening with a group of people who might not regard her in the best sense, stood up and walked out of her room.

However, what could be more disconcerting to her present confidence than a quick trial to her resolve? For as she had stepped out of her room, someone exited from a few doors down, and it was none other than Victor Whitfield.

⬥

As he closed his door, Caroline had the quick impulse to rush back into hers, which she began to do. Stealth, however, was not a habit of hers, and she therefore made a bit of sound in her efforts.

"Oh," she heard his voice exclaim from where he stood. "Do you care so little for my feelings that you wish to avoid me so?"

Caroline closed her eyes, feeling the pain of the moment all the more. Turning to him, she did her best to appear calm, but she knew that she clearly looked flustered.

"I was not wishing to do any such thing. I had only realized that I had forgotten something in my room and that I wished to retrieve it."

"And now you are lying to me," he said, standing there.

"I am not lying."

"And now you are lying about lying," he said, folding his arms.

Caroline clenched her fist. She had been wishing to appear polite and be mannerly, but it was as if Victor was wishing to ignore all social etiquette and wanted to see her at her worst.

"And what makes it worse," he said, approaching her, "is that you are not lying to spare my feelings, but to gratify your own."

"I do not know what you are talking about."

"Yes, you do. You offered that excuse not because you care that you insulted me, but rather because you just don't wish to experience any unpleasantness."

"You are doing your best to offer me unpleasantness," she retorted.

"You act one way, and therefore I respond in kind."

"Do you not recall that you almost ran over me with your horse?" she spat. "Does it not occur to you that I could have died?"

"Yes, and I feel most sorry for it," he said, his voice so final and stern that Caroline was forced to take heed. "Until you showed me that you cared nothing for what happened to me in turn."

"I..."

"You what?"

"I am a woman here now, being spoken to with much callousness. You sir may have the title of gentleman, but you are not acting like one."

"The word gentleman is often given to men who only know how to appear as so, which are those who flatter and deceive when they would sell you down the river if it was in their best interests. Therefore, if I am not your idea of a gentleman, then I take that as the highest compliment."

"It is not the highest."

"In your eyes, no it isn't. And yet your eyes are not ones that I wish to look through."

Caroline's face reddened. "How dare you?"

"How dare I cast aspersions at the woman who is trying to avoid me?"

"Yes!" Caroline confessed. "I did try to avoid you, because I worried that this would happen, and it has! You are vulgar, base and conceited."

"Then you were wrong. Clearly, I am a gentleman."

Caroline was at a loss of how to speak to Victor, because she had never recalled having such a conversation in the course of her life.

How was such a man to be worked on? She could not even begin to understand...

"Now," he continued, "As you are. Go and retrieve whatever it was that you left, and I shall wait to escort you down the stairs."

"You don't need to do that."

"It is what a *gentleman* would do."

"Or rather I do not want you to."

"Well, you have no choice," he said, concealing his hurt feelings. "For I must do so, and I would not forgive myself if I did otherwise."

"Never mind then. Whatever I was going to get I now see that I do not need."

"You do not need it because you never were in search of it, rather."

Caroline found herself heated at their discussion and wished to be free from it, and as a result, used the practical approach.

"You do realize that we have to go down to dinner."

"I am not stopping you."

"Yes, you are."

"No, I am not. I am simply offering to escort you, and you are the one trying to give me the slip."

"And you wonder why."

"No, I do not wonder. Then shall we go?" he asked, challenging.

"Yes, let us go."

Victor offered Caroline his arm, and she eyed it with distaste, but took it out of obligation and they walked down the hallway.

"Is this how we are to spend our time when we are in each other's company?" Victor asked.

"I did my best to be polite," Caroline persisted, "but you would not let me."

"Because your manners do not impress me, for I have seen what you are like when your regular manner is revealed."

"And what did you see?"

"It is best not to say."

"Then you should not have begun."

"But I did begin, and now I shall put an end to it."

"Fine by me."

"Is it?"

"No, it is not. I am simply saying that to find a platform of peace."

"Not peace, Miss Bingley. You just want the appearance of it."

"Is there a difference?"

Victor eyed her with distaste.

"That was the wrong thing to say," he replied boldly. Caroline started at his reply, for she could not see what he had meant by that. But the whole conversation was the most provoking she had ever had, and it was not till they had reached the dining hall and separated did she have time to reflect and feel the full effects of it. How had that conversation even come about? It was too absurd!

Victor had specifically sought war between them, and she would therefore respond in kind. Amongst the set of uncomfortable companions she had, he would be the worst, but whatever provocation he could concoct, he would find her a formidable foe.

❦ 19 ❧

MATLOCK

The entrance of Caroline Bingley and Victor to our dinner did not escape my notice. While they both had come in with their arms linked, I saw how their eyes held much contempt, and they separated as soon as they had entered. The separation was almost too swift, and I had also noted the look they had given each other at Pemberley.

Not thinking it would hurt to consult Darcy on the matter, I sat next to him and began to whisper in confidence.

"Fitzwilliam, did you notice anything peculiar about Caroline Bingley and Victor Whitfield?"

"Oh, you mean that strange look they gave each other when they first met at Pemberley, and also how they enter together now."

"Yes," I said, not surprised at the notice he took, for in truth, he noticed everything, and it was the gift often given for those who were observers. "What do you make of it?"

"There is something between them that they are not telling us," he stated. "They have met before today."

"You think so?"

"Yes, for theirs was a look of familiarity."

"But it does not seem like there is affection between them."

"Yes, I do not believe so. Wherever they had met before, it is clear that it did not begin well."

"Do you think we have to worry?"

"About them?"

"Yes... and about any surprises."

"I hope not. Yet there is never any way of knowing."

THE NEXT DAY, we left early in the morning, and by 12 in the afternoon, we had entered the grounds of Matlock, where at the center, was the Matlock House in all its grandeur.

Large and exquisite, Matlock was the proper seat for an Earl of such prestige, but it looked a little too imposing to me—and though not gothic, it still held a tint of baroque to it. When our carriages arrived at the front steps, the whole Fitzwilliam household came out to greet us. First and most prominent were Earl and Lady Fitzwilliam, and then behind them were Henry and Acton Fitzwilliam.

All were as I remembered them, but Acton was the most voluble. Knowing his role as the younger brother most well, he made himself quite agreeable.

"How are you, Mrs. Darcy?" Acton said as he stood beside me when we entered.

"I am well, Acton," I said, "and I am very happy to be finally seeing Matlock."

"Yes, our home is one of the better parts of us."

"But not the best." I smiled and added, "I dare say your personalities suffice—but only a mere little."

"You still love a good joke," he laughed.

"Yes, I do."

"And it is nice to see all you Bennet girls together, except for two that are missing."

"Yes, Lydia, as you know shall be estranged to us for quite some time due to living in America, and Mary has to tend to Anne De Bourgh. But she did wish to be here."

"Oh, how is Mary?"

"She is well and is very happy at Rosings."

"How rare to hear such a thing." He chuckled.

"It is indeed, yet Mary has always been the sort to require structure and occupation, therefore she does not mind the rigidity of Lady Catherine."

"When I met her at Kitty's wedding, she did appear to have those elements to her nature. But once we danced for longer, I did feel her spirit give way to amusement and levity."

"Oh, yes," I said, remembering when they danced at the wedding. "She did enjoy dancing with you. And I thank you for that, for it takes much to pull her out of her shell, and she found ease in doing it with you."

"Then I am much obliged. But while we are here, please kindly tell Fitzwilliam that I did not mean to encourage her—that is to say, I had no designs nor was meaning to flirt. I was just wishing to make her feel a part of the family."

"And you did it well, as it was an honorable objective, Acton. You may set your heart at rest, for Fitzwilliam was going through a phase where he was overprotective because he needed to be. He now knows that you meant only good and no harm."

"Thank you, now, help me to get acquainted with your cousin here and your aunt."

"Oh." I smiled, happy that he took notice of them. "Aunt Gardiner and Issy, Mr. Acton here would like to get further acquainted with you."

"And he is not the only one who wishes to do so," Henry Fitzwilliam said with emphasis. His efforts were plain to all who knew the impulse behind them; he was trying to follow Acton's lead and gather a favorable impression with those who were new to him. "I too should like to know more of the new people in our company. For you have brought many smiling faces with you," he said, looking around from Isabella to Miss Bingley and the Whitfield brothers.

"Well, sir," Aunt Gardiner said, "we thank you for wishing to be so agreeable upon first introductions."

"But what more could be expected of the Fitzwilliams," Caroline said, "for your very title commands excellence it seems, and very good breeding."

"Thank you, Miss Bingley," Henry Fitzwilliam said, smiling warmly at her.

"Then I suppose I am the only one who is frightened," Isabella said, smiling bashfully.

"And how so?" Henry asked, turning to her. "Or why so?"

"Because you frighten me."

Everyone turned and looked on Isabella with curiosity, and Aunt Gardiner looked pale in the face.

"Isabella!" she whispered desperately.

"And how could it be?" Lady Fitzwilliam said. "That my son would be frightening?"

"And this is where the conversation gets interesting," Lord Fitzwilliam said, "and I shine in such times."

"How could you think so of our gracious host?" Caroline asked, with alarm.

"Do you not believe I have the right to say why?" Isabella asked.

"Yes, I suppose so," Henry Fitzwilliam said slowly, feeling his warm welcome to have backfired in the worst sort of way. "How do I frighten you?"

"Because you are happy to meet us and therefore wish for us to make a favorable impression. Well, sir," Isabella chuckled, playful, "that is the best of hopes that leads to the worst of outcomes."

"How so?" Henry Fitzwilliam said, feeling lighter in seeing that she was toying with him playfully.

"Because I have no choice but to perform terribly. Have you, sir, never walked into a room and were expected to say everything perfectly? Yes, I am sure you have. And it was the most frightening thing in the world, was it not? Because it made you so nervous, that all your good qualities gave way to doubt, uncertainty and forgetting how to speak to the point where you stutter. And now, I am frightened, because I am nervous!"

Now that we all heard Isabella's explanation, we laughed.

"Well, I hope I do not make you nervous," Henry said with a smile.

"It is not your fault," she sighed, "nor is it mine. I am merely telling you this now because I want to warn you."

"Warn me? How?"

"Because now you know that whenever I begin to lose my wording, it is not because I have no respect, but because I am simply trying to offer you a favorable impression of me. And I failed, because I am a terrible actress."

He studied her. "Then have no fear. I am not the best actor as well, and I certainly have not the talent which some people possess of conversing easily with those I have never seen before. I cannot always catch their tone of conversation, or appear interested in their concerns, as I often see done."

"It is hard, is it not?" Isabella asked. "To not hold that sort of skill? I, as you have seen, have a hard time when it comes to the art of dissembling, and so I have quite given up. But if conversation was an instrument, such as the pianoforte, I could only say that my fingers do not move over this instrument in the masterly manner which I see so many women's do. They have not the same force or rapidity, and do not produce the same expression. But then I have always supposed it to be my own fault—because I would not take the trouble of practicing. It is not that I do not believe my fingers as capable as any other woman's of superior execution. Therefore, in the instrument that is the gift of tongue, I suppose I should just learn the art of proper etiquette."

"Precisely," Caroline Bingley said, adding her input into something that was not meant for her to. "There is a proper method to speaking to a host when you first meet them, and with strong application to it, it can be learned and perfected."

"And yet I find it not unsuitable to break from the standard of things every now and again," Henry Fitzwilliam objected, "for I do not claim to be one who always acts perfectly oneself, and Miss Isabella, you are perfectly right. You have employed your time much better, for no one admitted to the privilege of hearing you speak just now can think anything wanting in regards to honest truth. And it is clear we neither of us perform to strangers."

"Oh dear, what are you both truly talking of?" Lady Fitzwilliam laughed. "Henry, you know I must have my share in the conversation!"

And thus, everyone laughed even more.

"See," Isabella said, "my sauciness was not for nothing."

"And how do you see that?" Lord Fitzwilliam asked.

"You must forgive my daughter, Lord Fitzwilliam," Aunt Gardiner began. "She can be wonderfully pertinent—"

"No, it is quite all right. I get quite bored with standard pleasantries, so I am enjoying myself as of now. Miss Isabella, how do you account for your sauciness being for nothing?"

"Oh, because its aim has now struck true," she replied. "I worried that we would be uncomfortable around each other, now we shall not be."

I couldn't help but laugh. "Upon my honor, Issy, you truly have no fear."

"I know that I should," she began, "but I do not."

"It is all well," Acton said. "For I do feel us less likely to sink into uncomfortable silences, because we now know we have the right to say anything."

"Yes," Victor said, "Miss Isabella, you did free us, and for that, we are glad."

Lord Fitzwilliam turned to me and he chuckled.

"And I thought having one of you in my family was enough, but now I have two."

"Be careful," I said, "for if Fitzwilliam and I are allowed to have another child, I shall welcome giving you a third one."

"You would!"

"Yes, Lord Fitzwilliam, I very much would. And will!"

At the suggestion of our children, Lord Fitzwilliam asked to see our sons, and William and Caiden were brought to be put on display. Lady Fitzwilliam, who loved children, picked up Caiden and twirled him around, exclaiming that he looked exactly like his father, and then she kissed William on the cheek.

After they amused us all, Lucy took them away once they began to grow restless and wished to enjoy the toys in their nursery.

As they left, Lord Fitzwilliam turned to Georgiana and Jason.

"Now that I am not distracted by Miss Isabella's wit, I have time to direct my attention to the newly engaged."

"Oh, it is not so new, uncle," Georgiana said, "but rather it is as if we have been engaged for years!"

"Spoken like a proper fiancée." Jason smiled, then he turned to the rest of us. "Oh, sorry for my impertinence."

"Not at all," Lady Fitzwilliam said. "It is nice to see a healthy affection displayed between two people who are intended for each other. Now tell us everything about you all, and your family."

"Victor?" Jason said, turning to him playfully. "You are the oldest and therefore are the best at giving histories."

"A painful duty it is," Victor groaned, "in being the oldest. We have to answer all the questions of expositions in times like this, while the younger brothers can sit back and enjoy their great passions."

"Oh, your sacrifice is so terrible," Jason scoffed, "because it is not easy to be the oldest and the heir to our father's estate and most of his wealth."

"Precisely!" Acton exclaimed, looking at Henry. "What is with you oldest brothers always complaining of your lot? Or finding some way to appear as the wounded ones?"

"Indeed," Colonel Fitzwilliam agreed. "Henry, you and Victor here sound as if you are identical to each other."

"It is the painful habit of being human, I suppose," Victor said, "to not appreciate what one has, and then for it to be enhanced by another habit we have, which is the right to complain because at the moment in time, there is nothing else to do."

"That can be true," Henry agreed. "And it very well may turn out that we are no more a black-hearted villain than other rich men who are used to getting their way. When you are used to not having a problem, the smallest thing can easily become a problem."

"And then we obsess and fixate upon it," Victor said, "because it is the closest thing that we can find that all of us need: an obsession."

"Are you trying to make us feel sorry for you?" I asked. "For I shall not give in so easily."

Henry laughed. "We do not ask you to, we only show you the defects of being spoiled."

"But nor should we give in with such difficulty," Kitty argued, "for as Issy said before, we all must practice. And to make you feel better about yourselves, Mr. Whitfield and Henry, every sister in a family has to school herself not to flirt."

"Do you?" Henry asked, happy to see that Kitty was not afraid to talk to him, even after their turbulent past.

"Yes, for flirting is often regarded as a woman's trade, that we should always keep in practice. But then extremity becomes its resting place, and we do it too brown, and our efforts give way to either exposing us to vulgarity of manners or showing more than we feel and not less. Flirtations are useful to a point, as is everything, but sometimes it becomes harmful. And so, you see, older brothers," she said with a smile as she leaned toward Victor and Henry, "You are not worse than the rest of us."

"Well then," Henry answered, "Victor shall tell the story of what it means to be an older brother, for we are similar in having two younger brothers. Let us see if you are right, my sister, or if you have given us too much credit."

"Yes," Victor said, "let us see if so."

Victor then began to tell us all about their growing up at Errodin Abbey, how they were a family of attorneys and what it was like to be the oldest brother of three.

"Each station of sibling position has its own benefits and negatives," Victor said, coming to the end of his narrative. "For us older ones are given all that is best in regards to legacy, but we are also meant to watch over the youngest ones and have them learn from our examples. I therefore confess that I quite have failed them in that regard."

"No. I will not allow that," Jason said. "For though we quarrel often, Victor, you still are a good sort of older brother."

"Oh, my dear Jason flatters me."

"But I still cannot feel any pity for you. For it is we middle brothers who have the worst fate."

"Here here!" Colonel Fitzwilliam saluted.

"Oh, I have a kindred spirit in you, Colonel?"

"Very much so," Colonel Fitzwilliam said. "For we are the least special it appears, unless one parent chooses to be kind and have mercy on us." He smiled at his mother.

"Precisely," Jason said. "We have not only the bad fortune of not being the one to inherit the fortune or the estate, but we also have to find some way to show ourselves unique in some way. When we are not special, and have no talent at all, we can easily fall into the trap of being a disappointment."

"You middle siblings use that excuse for your pains too often," Acton said, "and therefore I must rebel against it."

"You are about to declare that you youngest brothers are the least fortunate, aren't you?" Colonel Fitzwilliam scoffed.

"Of course I am Richard, of course I am. For you all often believe that we younger brothers are spoilt, that we are the babies and therefore we must be the favorites. Well, sometimes it may be so. But Victor, if your younger brother Jeffrey were here, he would support me in this; **you older** brothers think we are the favorites, but we are not always. Our mothers and fathers love us no more than you all, and treat us no better, and it is all in your head."

"There is but one claim that younger brothers do have," Louisa Hurst said, "for I have learned this just by observing the way it was with Charles. I know that you shall say that he was the favorite because he was our parents' only son, but that was not what I found. By the time that our mother and father had my baby brother, they had learned from their mistakes. I was their first time at being parents, and I was the means through which they tested the waters. Then Caroline came along, and I thought her to receive special attention, but then I grew to learn that the things my parents did simply were from the lessons they learned from me. Thus, when Charles was born, they had perfected their roles as parents, and it was his privilege to have them at their best."

"Well said," Lady Fitzwilliam added, "for it is often the case. Acton, with Henry, he was the first and heir, therefore special attention was paid to him. With Richard, he was the one who most reminded me of myself, and therefore he was saved from falling into the generality of all middle siblings being forgotten. With you, you were our third one, and your father and I found how to be the best of parents to you. Thus, you all were luckier than most, for you all got something good out of us."

"Yes, Mother, we did," Colonel Fitzwilliam agreed.

❧

"AND YOU ARE all forgetting those of us who have it the worst then," Caroline Bingley said suddenly.

"Why?" Isabella asked. "What was your burden, Miss Bingley?"

"That of being the middle child, and a woman," she said, avoiding looking Isabella in the face, for reasons that I knew why. "For Louisa was the eldest and she took superiority. Charles is the youngest and a male, so he had the luxuries of being the baby and a boy, thus being the heir of our father. If Charles had come out second, then he would still be special for inheriting the legacy, and if I were the youngest, then I may be another daughter, but I would still be the baby, and therefore still be special."

"Oh, Caroline, that is too cruel," Louisa said. "Our parents did dote on you often."

"Often enough because it was an obligation, but not to the rate of you and Charles. And therefore, nothing could be worse than being the second daughter in a family, for we are both the middle child and the one who are not needed."

"That can be quite true, but you are too hard upon the full definition of us," I said. "For while we are not a particular favorite often, we are still needed by someone, and when we reflect on it, it is often our older sister or brother who needs us most."

"Indeed," Jane said. "My mother showered me with praise often and gave me attentions that were too much. I had Lizzy to confide in. Every older sister needs a younger one to save her from the pressures of being the oldest who is required to marry first and save the family."

"And in regards to myself," Kitty added, "every younger sister requires an older one. For it was through Lizzy that I was able to accompany her to places which changed my life. You see, second daughters can have a place to their siblings."

"Yes," Isabella said, "for I have often found so in my own life. I'm the second daughter to a family of four and my brothers are the younger, but while I am fortunate to have parents who still treat me quite special, it was Harriet who always relied on me."

"Indeed," Louisa concurred. "Caroline, remember when we grew up, I quite relied on your admiration of me?"

"Oh, then I was to be regarded as special because I built up others with my admiration?" Caroline laughed. "That is my lot? To be worthy of only being the person who makes someone else look better by comparison?"

"That is not what your sister meant," Victor said directly, to which Caroline looked at him coldly. "Are you being younger sister-like and doing your best to misunderstand her?"

"No, I was merely being lighthearted."

"Oh, that is what you were doing?" He asked with a hint of sarcasm.

"Yes, that is what I was doing. And I was being younger sister-like in the sense that I was trying to be funny by being a pain."

"Then you must forgive me," Victor said, taking a sip from his tea. "For not having a little sister of my own, it is hard for me to understand when little sisters are being playful."

"Ignorance has no choice but to be forgiven—if the apology was heartfelt."

"What is your definition of being heartfelt?" he asked.

"What everyone else's definition of it is."

"You lean toward objectivity over the subjective concept of truth?"

"There is a time and place for both," Caroline responded.

"But that is where the confusion lies, when and where those times are."

Caroline sighed, feeling very much out of her element, clearly, for she grew nervous. "These are philosophic and cosmic queries that lie beyond my knowledge."

Victor said, not looking away from her. "They are beyond your knowledge."

"And beyond anyone here or in the world."

"Yes, and most of us are aware of that."

Victor's gaze was firm and set. Though I did not know him well, I could sense that he was looking to intimidate Caroline, and though she was hiding her true feelings behind a mask of indifference, her resolve was slipping. We were in a room of two people who did clearly have a past—and now I knew more than ever that it was a volatile one.

Suddenly Victor laughed and he did his best to have it appear organic.

"I do so love a good philosophical debate at the beginning of an engagement party. For nothing says 'congratulations on getting wed' than a discussion of the cosmos and how we are so small within it!"

Everyone laughed, and ironically the loudest was Mr. Hurst, who had surprisingly remained attentive for this whole interaction. In truth, I think the man was under-stimulated by boredom all the time, and he liked a good disagreement in company.

"And we are taking attention away from the time of Georgiana and my brother here," Victor concluded, "therefore I shall yield the floor to them."

☙❧

"IT IS ALL VERY WELL, VICTOR," Jason said, "for taking the floor was always your skill, and while I am the attorney, I spend too much time speaking. So I am happy to hand the duty over to others every once in a while. And being the middle son, if you recall, I always had to do all the talking, or no one would have taken notice of me."

"Oh, Jason, stop lying."

"Indeed, I do not, you large oaf."

"I am not so large."

"But my brother is," Georgiana said. "I suppose Fitzwilliam and I were lucky then. For with him being the eldest and a male, he gained our parents love for being the heir, and with me being the youngest and a woman, they gained their younger child and a female. Thus, we were both special."

"Perhaps that is where our luck does lie," Darcy said. "Two can be a better number than three."

"Perhaps," Isabella said, "for between two parents are two hearts, and with two children it is easier for the love to be evenly divided."

"But I had four and your father and I love you all equally," Aunt Gardiner said.

"Very well then, Mother. It can be safe to say that regarding children that it is best to have two children, or more than three. Does this all sound irrational?"

"A mere little," Henry Fitzwilliam said. "For there are no set rules to such things. But if you are taking a generality, then at least you know it has many flaws within it."

"Yes, and in time, if it is my fate to be a mother—which I still am not certain on—I shall put my theory to the test. One child is dangerous, for if something happens to them, then you are at a loss, but with three, one will always feel left out, but with two, there is room for one, or with four or more, there is too many for one parent to bind themselves fully. Oh yes, my thoughts are very foolish, but there is something amusing about them."

"But you must not take what you say as serious," Caroline said, "for it is not sound."

"Do not worry, for she was not doing so," I said. "And that is the meaning behind her theory. It is an observation that may end in a joke."

"An observation that may end in a joke?" Lord Fitzwilliam said. "I do so like that phrase."

"But since we are speaking of our stories as siblings," Jason said, "and three of the Bennet women are here, you must tell us what life living with five sisters was like."

"Oh, the stories are endless!" I said.

"It cannot be summed up in a few words!" Jane said.

"You will die of fatigue before we finish!" Kitty exclaimed.

"Well," Victor said, sitting down, "that is the wonderful thing about being wealthy and living in this time period. We have nothing to do—and therefore we have a lot of time."

We went to the dining hall to eat and while there, Jane, Kitty and I told them much about what life was like on Longbourn. It was so strange that everyone paid close attention, for I thought we would have bored them. But we did not. What also helped was that Aunt Gardiner added to our narratives with little anecdotes about what we were like as children.

For one, everyone was amazed that when little, Jane was quite the prankster, that I was very shy at times, and that Kitty was often afraid to speak—the times had changed us, for age had more in store for us, we would come to find out.

Before our supper ended, Lord Fitzwilliam stood up to make a toast. He congratulated Georgiana and Jason on their engagement, Fitzwilliam and I on our two sons, and he also was grateful that so much of his family had come.

"Age makes a man softer, perhaps," Lord Fitzwilliam said, "for when young, I cared little for family, but now at my age, I am quite obsessed with it. Therefore, I shall cease my cynical ways for a moment and announce what is within my heart.

"Old family and new friends, you all know me to be a crass man sometimes, but never does it mean that I do not care deeply. For you all to be here now, well... it makes me sentimental, and allows me to see all the ties and bonds this family has. We are always growing, and we also never seem to forget each other, which is a great blessing. We are a set of people with profound feelings, and those feelings are what drive us. Georgiana and Jason, you are proof of this family's strength, and I welcome the future, for I know that you all are within it. So here to my family, which is one for the ages!"

Stirred by his words, we all raised our glasses and drank. Lord Fitzwilliam was never a man who displayed his emotion and therefore, when the time came to show it, it was all the more impressive and awe-inspiring.

We cheered for him as well, then he sat down, and Lady Fitzwilliam took his hand.

It proved to be the most wonderful way to conclude our dinner, but we all were in for another surprise.

"Father," Colonel Fitzwilliam said, "better words could never have been spoken and if you will not mind, I shall like to add to your wonderful speech with one of my own."

"Of course, son, you were always the orator."

"Thank you, Father," Colonel Fitzwilliam said, standing up with his glass. He looked upon Kitty with affection and she smiled up at him as he raised his wine.

"Friends, Romans, countrymen, lend me your ears!" He boomed and we all chuckled.[1] "Well, as you say Father, you are happy for your family to be growing ever more. And my dear Kitty and I are happy to add to your happiness. She has waited to be sure, but we have spoken with the doctor and all signs have proven to be true. My lovely Kitty is with child."

I felt as if the wind was knocked out of me. My younger sister was with child, and I had not even seen it!

There were many cries of congratulations and amazement at the

---

1. This line is from Shakespeare's play *Julius Caesar*, and the line was spoken by the character Mark Anthony.

news, but nothing could have been more amusing than Lady Fitzwilliam's reaction.

"Oh, my goodness, about time!" she cried. "Have you any idea how long I have wanted to be a grandmother? Honestly, I worried that I would never see this day."

"Well, you have," Kitty laughed. "And we are happy to oblige you."

I offered my wishes of joy as well, but Lord and Lady Fitzwilliam were quite beside themselves.

"In truth," Kitty said after all the excitement died down, "we had a few close happenings before, but it kept on not coming to pass, so I hope this one grows and lives."

"We all do," I said, "Oh, Kitty, it is wonderful, but I confess that seeing you as my little sister for so long has disarmed me from understanding the vision of you as a mother."

"I have had the role of little sister, daughter and niece for so long, that I can understand how this changed state will overwhelm anyone. But perhaps being a mother will be another title I bear proudly."

"Do not doubt yourself at all," Aunt Gardiner said, "for Kitty I know you will be just splendid."

"And it gives me more cause for celebration," Lord Fitzwilliam said. "And thus we conclude with our last announcement."

"Another one?" Acton asked. "This is very interesting!"

"Yes, and I cannot take credit, for it is all Lady Fitzwilliam's scheme. In honor of Georgiana and Mr. Whitfield's engagement, we have decided to give a ball!"

And if there was one thing that could set off the table for effusions of joy, that would be the news. Georgiana was all aflutter, and Jason looked forward to the chance to dance with her again.

"And now," Lord Fitzwilliam said, "we can send letters to the neighboring families that the celebration shall be expanded to include the joy of my son and Kitty beginning a family of their own."

"Thank you, Father," Colonel Fitzwilliam said.

"Then you must give up your living in the army," Lady Fitzwilliam said. "Richard, I cannot bear the concept of you falling in war and your son never getting the chance to know you."

"You need not worry on that score, Mother. For I have already sold it."

"Have you?" Lady Fitzwilliam asked. "That is wonderful."

"But I waited to do so until I had a firm ground to place my feet on, and now I do. Mother and Father, I waited to tell you this wonderful news, but Darcy and our sisters all know this already. I have been adopted as the heir to Longbourn."

"Longbourn?" Acton asked. "Isn't that the home of Kitty's father?"

"Yes, and it is a lovely and quaint home. The grounds are lovely, but not so large that a one-time soldier cannot learn to run it. It can comfortably hold a nicely sized family, as the lovely Bennet sisters have shown."

"Then you shall be a man of property?" Lord Fitzwilliam said.

"Yes."

"And with no inconvenience to myself?" He sighed. "For I admit that I was considering buying you a home for a late wedding present once I found an available one."

"You did?" Kitty cried. "Oh, that was very considerate."

"Yes, and now I am not needed in that way. But I shall do my duty as a father and give you a large sum to make sure you are comfortable, and that way I shall be content."

"Thank you, Father."

"Well," Lady Fitzwilliam said, "it turns out, Kitty, that you were the perfect choice of wife for my fighting son."

"I hope that I shall always be so," Kitty blushed.

"You always will be, my love," Colonel Fitzwilliam said.

I looked at Henry Fitzwilliam to witness his reaction to this interaction and he looked down slightly, but there was no malice or resentment in his look. If there was anger at still losing Kitty, he masked it really well. Though, for the sake of hope, I wished to believe that he was overcoming his love for her.

While it would make sense for him to have changed his mind toward Jane, I knew that it would not be so. For their spirits had not matched up at all, and Jane was quite altered. Marriage did not suit her ambitions any longer, and therefore her manner never leaned herself toward attracting anyone.

And then there was the obvious intent of Caroline Bingley, who I saw as clearly trying to impress Henry Fitzwilliam and gain his attention. But her manner, as usual, proved to be too obvious and therefore she left nothing to the imagination. For most men in the ton, her obvious manners would work naturally, but she still did not learn that the Fitzwilliam and Darcy men were so very different. What had fascinated Henry about Kitty was that she seemed very multi-dimensional in nature, and therefore, upon first meeting her, he still knew there was more to her than what appeared at first. Therefore, Caroline's simple tactics were not challenging enough for him. And therein also lay another flaw within her: she was never challenging enough. I did not know what it was about Darcy's family that they all secretly adored the complex, but it was so.

And then, as it was my desire to observe, I saw Henry Fitzwilliam run his gaze down the table... and they rested on Issy!

I looked at her as she laughed at something Acton had told her, for they sat next to each other. Then I turned back to Henry, who did not look away. His expression turned slightly sour in looking at Acton, and it could very well be the hints of jealousy again.

Could it have been? Could Henry Fitzwilliam just be at the beginnings of an attraction to my cousin, Isabella? Indeed, it very well could have been, for surely the sort of woman that Kitty was did align with Isabella's. Also, in being cousins, Issy did look similar to Kitty, Jane and me. So well enough that the similarity must be keenly felt.

If it was so, then knowing that Caroline Bingley liked Henry Fitzwilliam, and then knowing that he might like Isabella was too much for me to think on. For it would cause many problems, and that was not how I wished to remember my first night in Matlock.

✣ 20 ✣

THE WOES OF A WORRIED MAN

That evening, Fitzwilliam and I lay in bed, our bodies spent after having made love to one another.

"That was a brilliant round," I said. "And you were at your best, Mr. Darcy."

"Do you think me a piece of bread, my love, that I need to be buttered so easily?" He smiled, running his hands over my breasts and down my stomach.

"Fitzwilliam, I know you are a piece of bread!"

"Oh, cheeky!" he said, rolling me over, getting on top of me and caressing me in between my thighs while I clung to his shoulders out of ecstasy.

"Tell me that you love it when I do this!" He cried.

"Of course I do." I squirmed with pleasure as he touched me.

"Very well," he said, running his hands even faster while he kissed me tenderly, "Is it so strange that every time we make love, it feels so..."

"New?" I finished for him with a little gasp. "As if we are just doing it for the first time?"

"Yes."

"No, it is not strange."

With affection, Fitzwilliam lay on top of me while I ran my hands gently down his back and massaged his shoulders.

"Fitzwilliam, I know you don't wish to speak now, but I have much on my mind."

"Do not worry, I am not fully exhausted," he said, rolling off me. "What does my wife wish to speak of?"

"I wish to know your mind, my love. And you have a gift of perception, as well as much intuition."

"Yes, I am bread, for I do love being buttered by your compliments so."

"I know my love. Thank you for no longer acting coy about it. And now I want you to dissemble your gift to me. Did you observe anything suspicious tonight?"

"And by that you mean Miss Bingley's apparent setting her sights on my cousin, Henry?"

"Yes. Precisely. I cannot blame her for doing so, for there is never any error on a woman's part for setting her sights on a worthy gentleman, but there is the problem of—"

"Of her irrational jealousy awakening inside of her towards your cousin, Isabella."

"Yes, so you have seen that as well? I am not being generous in thinking it so?"

"No, you are not. Isabella intrigues Henry, and it makes sense. After Kitty, Isabella would be the next best option. She is witty, vivacious, and is almost as lovely as you."

"But Issy should not be considered because he reminds her of Kitty. That is a poor way of gathering feelings for a woman, because the woman has no choice but to slip."

"Indeed, but Henry is still wounded perhaps, and if Issy does in fact help his wound close, then I shall say it is all for the better. For from the little I have seen, Isabella is capable of not only taking care of herself, but also of living up to the image many place on her. She is like you in that way."

"Now you treat me like a piece of bread."

"This is not buttering, but pure fact. When a man first meets you, you are the same woman he sees on the first day as he will see on the hundredth. Your nature never falters, and Issy seems to be the same in that way. Also, there is not so much danger if Henry does cling to her, as long as she does not know his past obsession with Kitty. If we are right on this score and Henry has begun to find Issy attractive, which I believe us to be so, then as long as she does not learn of his past, she will never feel as if she is being compared to anything."

"You propose that ignorance is bliss. Perhaps you are right. And that is a good plan."

"But as for Miss Bingley, there was a time where I would have been worried over her, but now I am not."

"You are no longer afraid of the fruits that her jealousy can bring?"

"No, for we have one thing that clearly will always stop her from getting her way."

"And what is that?"

"Victor Whitfield."

"Oh!" I realized, closing my eyes. "Yes, I see what you mean."

"You were right, Lizzy," he said. "Something happened between them. They have in some way met before and there was clearly discord between them."

"Yes, and I wonder what it could be?"

"We might learn of it in time, but while I was at first hesitant about liking Victor Whitfield, I must now be glad he is among us. He seems to lack any tact with her, making any effort she gives on causing trouble impossible."

"You think him a formidable foe?"

"In her regards, yes I do."

"He seems to also frighten her. This suggests that he knows something that she does not wish to speak of."

"Anything is possible. But what is certain is that she does not frighten him. It is best that she has someone here who will thwart her at every turn."

"Indeed, she shall now know how it feels to have limits."

"I see that she is trying to change, but her original nature still wins out often."

"Yes, it does. Isabella is not the sort to intentionally establish an attachment to Henry, for she just looks to be pleasant, but not romantic. However, that may very well be what Henry needs right now. Whatever the situation, I just do not wish for her to be hurt and become a casualty in Caroline's wars of the heart."

"She will not be, I assure you. Victor shall keep Caroline too busy."

"Who would have thought it would be him to have that position in our company?"

"I would not have, and I enjoy it. Therefore, while I usually do wish to have much under my control, this situation does not need me, Lizzy, or the woes of a worried man. I now know that no matter what the outcome, our family shall survive anything, even a vexing love entanglement."

"Aye, we have had our share of those."

"Yes, too many," he said, kissing me gently before we both fell asleep in each other's arms.

21

ORIGINS AND ORIGINALITY

The next day, Lord and Lady Fitzwilliam hosted a picnic for us on the grounds of Matlock.

"Tomorrow," Lady Fitzwilliam said, "we have arranged for us all to travel to Blenheim, where you shall meet Mr. and Mrs. Shelby, who own that great estate. I hope we were not being presumptuous in planning ahead."

We all agreed that we would love to see Blenheim, which was an estate that I had often heard talk of but had never actually seen.

"It is good that you shall make the acquaintance of that family, for they are going to attend the ball. A few days from now, we also have arranged to travel to Chatsworth where you shall become acquainted with Sir and Lady Hughes. That will be most amusing, for they have seven children, and the eldest is married, but the others are still single and shall enjoy our large company."

"That many children?" Victor said. "Were they hoping to have made a miniature army?"

"Actually," Lord Fitzwilliam said, "that number was quite normal to have in previous generations. My grandfather came from a family of ten children."

"And I was told that my great-grandmother," Lady Fitzwilliam said, "had fifteen brothers and sisters."

"That is overwhelming," Isabella said. "Though perhaps, due to medicine back then being what it was, it was best to have that many."

"And while having that many children would seem alarming," I said, "I suppose at that state, the children would start to help raise each other, because the parents could not always do so with so large a number."

"One would never get any time alone," Georgiana said. "Would that not be hard, oh imagine Fitzwilliam, if you had to live such a way? Sorry, brother, but it is quite amusing a sight—you with that many brothers and sisters."

"It is hard to say," Fitzwilliam said, "for if I were the oldest, I could easily have hated it, but a part of me could have also loved it."

"Really?" Colonel Fitzwilliam asked, skeptical. "You sir, who love peace? No, Fitz, I cannot believe it."

"I do not love being confined," Mr. Darcy objected. "That is a big difference than having so many brothers and sisters. Having that many sisters and brothers to look after might have given me more of an occupation. I was left to be idle for too long and did not understand the joys of activity. I think the responsibility of looking after so many brothers and sisters would have been stressful, but it would have been fun. And it might have also given me a stronger sense of identity."

Acton chuckled. "Be careful, Elizabeth, for I think that this is a subtle indication to you that my cousin here wants many more children."

"Oh, he already told me the truth on that one," I retorted. "But I did not know, Fitzwilliam, that you might like that many!"

"Oh, do not worry my dear," Mr. Darcy answered, "I would not put you through that much pain. Though I am open to the number of four to five."

"Four to five?" I asked. "You wish to have the same household number of Longbourn."

"That would be a fun coincidence if we did."

"Yes, it would. Redundancy can be entertaining in a circumstance."

"Well," Lady Fitzwilliam asked, "if you had a say in the matter, which the Maker shall not give but it is still fun for us to talk of, what gender would you like those next three to be?"

"It is strange," I said, "but I would prefer the last three to be girls. And I know that Fitzwilliam wants the next one to very much be so. But with all girls, I think it would be best, for it will give Caiden and William the ability to be the older brothers that they ought to be to their baby sisters. But if it were a boy, he would have to suffer under the weight of being a male who was not a twin, like his brothers. No for me, three separate girls would be best."

"Well," Fitzwilliam said, "if you are so inclined to choose all their sexes, might I choose all their names?"

"Oh, come now," I answered. "You are my husband, and how dare you think you have rights?"

"Oh, I dare, beloved, I dare. But I shall still consider you this moment and think the name Helena to be a brilliant one, and then there is the name Josephine, which I have grown to like."

"Really? I had never known."

"From the name Josephine comes the nickname Jo, and I do so like that on a little girl. And lastly, there is... well, what about Hero?"

"The name Hero? Like Hero from *Much Ado About Nothing*?"

"Yes. And while I prefer the character of Beatrice, I cannot warm to that name unfortunately."

"Well," I said, "you have thought of this much?"

"I admit to it."

"Hero, Helena and Jo, short for Josephine. Yes, I quite like those." Then I turned to Kitty and the Colonel. "What name would you consider for your child?"

"If it is a girl, I do not want it to be named Catherine," Kitty said.

"Why not?" Jason asked.

"Because my name is too traditional, and it does not allow one the chance to be unique."

"And that is my reason for not choosing Richard if it is a boy," Colonel Fitzwilliam said. "I love it, but I want my son to have his own path, not mine. Or anyone else's."

"So, therein lies the conundrum," Kitty said with a smile. "What, oh what can we do! Let us see, for a girl, what of the name Diana, Psyche, or Io, or Leda?"

"Oh," Victor said, "So you favor the names of Greek mythology?"

"I am not good at being original, but I wish to still find something that is rare and beautiful. I think I might like the name Psyche the most, seconded by Leda."

"We might be able to use both," Colonel Fitzwilliam answered. "I should hope to have two of them. Two versions of you running around Longbourn, it would be a comfort to their old man of a father."

"And now, Richard, what for your sons?"

"I am not as unique as you, my dear, but what of the names Luke or Glenden."

"Glenden? Where did you hear of that name?"

"It was from an officer who once served under me in my regiment, and I quite liked it."

"Glenden Fitzwilliam," Kitty said thinking it over. "Yes, I quite love that. Luke and Glenden Fitzwilliam, handsome names."

As we sat at the picnic, eating, Henry Fitzwilliam sat near Isabella and Aunt Gardiner while they ate some salad. Being within such short proximity of each other, I was able to overhear their conversation quite easily.

"Since we are on the matter of names," Isabella said, "what family member did you get your name from, Mr. Fitzwilliam?"

"My grandfather," Henry said, "for there usually is a Henry in every generation of the Fitzwilliam line."

"Is there one in your father's generation?"

"Yes, one of my father's younger brothers, my Uncle Henry."

"So, there are a sea of Henrys in your family?"

"Yes. And what of your name? Are there a gaggle of Isabellas in the world of the Gardiners?"

"I am not the best person to ask that," Isabella said, and then she turned to my aunt. "Mama, what do you know of this? Does the name Isabella inundate our family line?"

"No, it does not," Aunt Gardiner said. "At least not to my knowledge, there are no Isabellas."

"Then was there a particular reason for why you named her so?" Henry asked.

"Yes, it is simply me living vicariously through my children." Aunt Gardiner laughed. "When growing up, I wanted to have the name Isabella, and naturally it did not happen. I had no control over my own fate regarding nomenclature, but I did with my children, which I used on you, Issy."

"Well," Isabella smiled, turning to Henry, "there you have it, Mr. Fitzwilliam, I was the product of disappointed hopes."

"But the nickname, Issy? That is most strange, for I have never heard that before. Usually, one just goes by Isabella...or Belle sometimes."

"I know, but I am so strange that way," Isabella said. "I have never favored Belle or Bella for some reason, and when growing up, my older sister Harriet just called me Issy one day, and I loved it. I daresay that was the only control that I had over my own name, and I felt that it captured my spirit most. If a name can capture a spirit, that is."

"It can. It is certainly better than Henry."

"It is not better, no more or less. It is simply different, and I'm happy that you approve, though to be honest with you, I was going to keep to it whether you liked it or not."

"Why, aren't you stubborn?"

"Yes, I am, I am, I am," she said, shaking her head and pursing her lips, being playful, to which Henry laughed.

"Thank you, by the way."

"How so?" Isabella asked. "What do you owe me?"

"You were correct, the day before, when you spoke your mind when we first met. I was nervous, and in my best efforts, I needed someone to tear down the wall of propriety and find the truth underneath, so that I was comfortable. How did you know to do that?"

"I didn't," Isabella said, becoming serious. "I just made a quick assumption, and began, in hopes that I was correct. And now I am happy that I could be of service. Believe it or not, to be of use to someone, whether it be personal or to the world, means a lot to us little folk."

"Yes, to be of use...that is something we all desire."

"I suppose that is why I like to be called Issy," Isabella said, looking ahead. "It does make me feel as if I have my own place amongst people, and it is the perfect mixture of origins and originality. I have a name that has a history, but I found a way to make it my own. Do I have that much?"

"I do not know. You tell me?"

"Yes," she chuckled, "yes, I do."

※ 22 ※

CHOICE AFTER CHOICE

T he next day, we all went to Blenheim, where we were greeted by Mr. and Mrs. Shelby, and their unmarried daughters!

They also had two sons, but they were married and lived in town. Their daughters however, named Julia, Maria, and Fanny, were in their late teens and early twenties, and were quickly showing themselves to be the sort who were ready to be fallen in love with. Thus, when we arrived, Mr. and Mrs. Shelby were most kind in receiving us. They allowed us into their home for a mid-day meal that was very much well displayed and presented.

However, while our company was very good at receiving us, and Mr. and Mrs. Shelby proved to be excellent hosts, the single men in our company naturally became the most popular. Victor, Acton and Henry were viewed as nothing short of dashing and a gallant set of men, and the fact that they were three in number was too much for the daughters' sensibilities! They did their best to act mannerly and refined, but their basic natures were too much for the coincidence— and it did not help that the men were all quite attractive in three different ways.

Victor, however, was the most popular with their set, for his sarcastic nature actually could be quite fascinating and allowed him to contain a mystery about himself. And thus, his conversation with them often went as follows:

"Blenheim is a wonderful establishment, and it makes Errodin Abbey seem like a prison."

"And how is it so?" Maria asked. "For I have heard everything pleasing about your seat at the abbey."

"Oh, a house is like any other house, no matter the size. But rather it is the company that makes it more agreeable, and how can I not find the company here more varied in society and more able to make me smile. I do not smile often."

"But we do smile here often," Julia added. "Therefore, I hope that it influences you to visit us again."

"Oh, I have talked my way into another invitation? Wait till you become better acquainted with me and then see if you still wish to see me a second time."

The three sisters laughed at that most readily, and I worried that Victor was doing his compliments too brown. But Henry was not being that attentive, for he was attempting to disentangle himself from their set and move more toward Isabella. However, he found himself thwarted by none other than Caroline Bingley, who placed herself next to him in a way that he had no choice but to remain at her side and offer her his arm.

"You are distracted, Mr. Fitzwilliam," she smiled up at him. "Are you so moved by the beauties of Blenheim as well?"

"It is an overpowering sight," he said, obliged to reply, and he smiled most forcefully, in hopes of hiding his impatience.

As we sat down to the luncheon, Caroline Bingley immersed herself with the Shelby sisters, and Maria, Julia and Fanny took to her very easily. Miss Bingley had always been the sort to adapt herself very easily amongst gentlewomen, if it suited her to exert herself. She was smooth in conversation, until she meant to offend, and it was clear that she was doing all in her power to make a good impression on the Shelbys. She was successful at it. Thus, since the Shelby sisters occupied most Victor, Acton and Henry's attention, Caroline was able to do so with ease and grace.

After our meal, Mr. and Mrs. Shelby proposed that we all would take a walk along the grounds. As could be expected, our company began as one, but the grounds were large, and we began to separate. Our company became split by accident. Some of the men, including Colonel Fitzwilliam, Mr. Hurst, Darcy and Lord Fitzwilliam, wished to remain in doors, playing billiards, while the rest of us went for our walk. Mr. Shelby remained with them to be their host.

Our company was even more broken up when Georgiana and Jason lost themselves most shrewdly. But Lady Fitzwilliam and Mrs. Shelby managed to shadow them, in hopes of giving them a chaperone. In the midst of the confusion, Jane, Kitty, Mrs. Hurst, Caroline, Aunt Gardiner, Isabella and I were left to wander along one path, for we had got separated from the Shelby Sisters and Victor, Henry and Acton.

"How could it be," Mrs. Hurst exclaimed, "that we were managed to be quite forgotten, and there is no host to lead us around?"

"Well, it is not so very hard," Jane said, "for we all know where the house is and can return anytime that we like."

"Yes," Caroline objected. "But it is still most ungenerous and inconsiderate!"

"Mrs. Shelby perhaps expected her daughters to remain with us," Kitty said, "but they were quite taken with our single men, that I am sure they were only oblivious and did not mean to forsake us on purpose."

"Yes," Aunt Gardiner said. "I know much how we women can be at that age. Being on an estate where there is usually not a beau for miles, and then to see one suddenly, it makes one quite forgetful of everything else but them."

"They are being flirts," Caroline said.

"Many are in their case."

"And I do see your point, Mrs. Gardiner," Louisa admitted. "I just do not see how this separation had ever come about."

"Oh, you do not recall? Many of us had stopped by to look at the pond, some had continued, and we did not notice they had until we all were alone in the clearing."

"Well, I cannot help but feel ill-used. But as you say, I am taking this all too personally and I do understand their mistake. Young attraction does tend to overpower one," she said. "I recall doing some foolish things to ensnare Mr. Hurst when I first met him as well, to be truthful."

"Such as?" Kitty asked.

"Oh, you will think me vulgar to admit it."

"We are all fools in love," Kitty replied. "Your actions are perhaps no more scandalous than anyone else's, I deem."

"Oh, thank you my dear, well I let him kiss me a couple of times before we wed."

Jane, Kitty and I looked at each other and we wanted to burst out laughing, for that was tame compared to what our family had done.

"Oh, truly?" Isabella asked. "What is it like to kiss someone for the first time?"

"Isabella," Aunt Gardiner said, "do not worry, you shall find out one day, and in truth it is different for each woman, I believe."

"Yes, it is," Louisa continued, "and I will not deny that I woke up the next day, and the whole world seemed different. I cannot say that I handled myself well either, for when you first kiss, you become bashful, you feel regret, guilt for some pathetic reason, and you do not wish to speak to the man—it is not that you hate him... but—you just never wish to see him again for a while. Even though you also wish to see him again terribly."

"Yes, physical stimulus can be so confusing to one's reason,"

Aunt Gardiner admitted. "It hurts often to know that love can make things all the more complicated."

As we walked on, we came upon our party of people that consisted of the Shelby sisters, who linked arms with Acton, Henry and Victor.

"Oh, there you are!" Caroline cried, rushing forward and linking her arms immediately with Henry, who looked on Isabella with embarrassment. "You used us abominably ill, in running away while we all were looking upon the pond with fascination."

"We did not even know that we had separated from you before we had already gone," Henry said hurriedly, only looking at Isabella. "Indeed, we have been looking for you ever since."

"Well," Caroline said, "now you have found us, and I shall not let you go so easily."

When looking upon the sight, the walkway that they had walked down only held room for their company and the rest of us would have had to follow behind. Victor looked around at both groups and felt the rudeness of them continuing to walk immediately, so he began to object.

"This walk is not wide enough for our party. We had better go into the avenue."

"Oh, no," Isabella said for the rest of us. "No, no, stay where you are. You are charmingly grouped and appear to uncommon advantage. The picturesque would be spoilt by admitting us all. We shall walk back to the house."

"I insist on accompanying you then," Victor said, removing his arm from Julia's and wrapping hers in Acton's. "He shall have to do for you both, Miss Shelbys, and please do not devour him. For duty calls and I must protect this second set of ours from any gnomes that would attack them along the walk back.

"But," Henry tried to object, but Caroline thus attempted to take his attention again.

"Well," I whispered to Isabella, "might you tell me what your reasoning for us not joining them was, Issy?"

"It was clear that we would have gotten in the way, in their eyes. They are our hosts, and I do not want them to view us as competition of any kind. Let them have the men's attention for now and know that we allowed it. For if they do, then that will make it all the pleasanter when they come to the ball."

"When did you develop a gift for diplomacy?"

"When I learned that I would never be good at conversation. After that, I learned that I had to be able to compromise and bow out sometimes, if the fight was not worth it."

"And that fight was not worth it to you?"

"Of course not. It was just the company of our men for one afternoon. Surely, we have no right to be possessive."

I pondered her words as Victor accompanied us back to Blenheim.

"Lovely house is it not?" he said, "though now that I have considered choice after choice being made here, I daresay that I very much now prefer my seat at Errodin Abbey. Indeed, there is no place like home."

❧ 23 ❧

WHAT IS PAINFUL TO HEAR

Victor Whitfield was not impressed by the actions of the ladies in question, it was clear. But with the Shelby sisters, he could pardon, for the men were a novelty to them.

However, with Caroline Bingley, he could not be so kind, if he could be kind at all—which he could not be in her case. Her blatant disregard for all who were in her company by dismissing them so was repulsive in his eyes—and too cold.

Thus, when the next day came, they had returned to Matlock. Victor was happy to see Caroline Bingley thwarted by Henry Fitzwilliam's blatant intent of remaining by Isabella Gardiner's side, which he did whenever both the men and women were in each other's company.

A couple of times, Caroline did attempt to speak with Henry. Yet he kept his replies polite, simple and short, then he would part from her and single our Isabella and Mrs. Gardiner. The message could not have been clearer, and Victor observed Caroline sit down, doing her best to hide her dejection.

She then looked toward Acton, and while Victor could have felt sorry for poor Acton, he did not need to. Acton seemed to favor the

Bennet girls so much that he always was speaking with them. Clearly, he tore down that generalization that all men must enjoy the society of lovely ladies for the intent of stroking their vanity or flirtation. Acton just simply enjoyed being a part of their circle, for their simple and artless manners were infinitely to be preferred by any man of taste than the unpardonable Caroline Bingley.

However, passivity on a subject that he had best leave alone was never Victor's way. He did not, nor never had, the constitution of a man who thought it right to let fate teach everyone their due lesson. For he had often noticed that fate and justice were not always among the ton of England at that time of year.

Thus, when the opportunity came upon him one day at Matlock, he found himself unable to resist speaking his mind.

Three days after their visit to Blenheim, Victor was sitting in the library, reading, when he was come upon by an intruder. He looked up at the footfalls and saw that it was none other than Caroline Bingley.

"Oh, I am sorry," she said coldly. "I shall leave you in peace."

"That is not what you were planning to do to the man who you sought initially," Victor said, spitefully.

"What are you talking about now, Mr. Whitfield?"

"I mean that Acton was just in here not more than ten minutes ago, and you clearly heard of it, and so you came here looking for him."

"I needed him for something."

"Of course you did. For now, that the oldest brother has clearly set his sights elsewhere, you have done the same, exchanging your attention from his brother to him. How strategic and cold."

"Mr. Whitfield, do not speak nonsense."

"But it is not nonsense," he said, closing his book and standing up. "It is absolute truth. It is in your heart, and you are simply afraid to hear it out loud. Were you angry that Henry Fitzwilliam has set his sights on Isabella Gardiner?"

"Why should his actions affect me?"

"Because you were trying to draw him in."

"How dare you?"

"I dare, Miss Bingley. I dare anything."

"Really, Mr. Whitfield, you are so comical that you ought to perform as a court jester."

"Jesters deal in jokes; I deal in truth."

"Jokes can be the glimmer of truth with a smiling face."

"How witty, but it will not distract me from my purpose."

"What I do is not your business, Mr. Whitfield."

"You are right, it is not, but I do not care that it is not."

"This conversation is quite finished," Caroline said, turning her heels and beginning to leave.

"Leave now, Miss Bingley, and I shall pursue you."

Caroline stopped and turned to him.

"I beg your pardon?"

"I would like you to sit with me, and we should talk about you. If not, I will follow you, and then we shall cause a scene to which you shall not enjoy. For after all, your whole objective is to have no unpleasantness."

"Are you blackmailing me?"

"I am simply doing whatever it takes to do you a kindness."

"Kindness?"

"Yes, and in your case, the kindness would be to offer you the truth. So," he said, sitting down and gesturing to the seat next to him, "do we have a deal?"

Caroline looked at Victor, this man who was rash, presumptuous, and everything that was quite awful, and realized that she had no way out but to remain with him. Walking slowly, she sat down on the seat next to him, folding her hands on her lap.

"Well," she said, "what do you have to say that is so pressing, sir?"

"It is simple. I am going to save you."

Startled, she asked, "What?"

"Yes, I am going to save you."

"How so?"

"By telling you that you are the most unlikable woman ever."

"What!" Caroline was outraged.

"Well, not the most unlikable woman ever, but still, you are malicious sometimes."

"How can you say so? And how dare you?"

"How dare I? How dare you? I have learned much about you over these last few days, and I must say, Caroline, you are a piece of work. You are ambitious—too ambitious in the workings of matters of the heart. You also will cut and slight people, calling it proper. You will hurt another woman in the aims of gaining something from it, and do you not see how cold and cruel that is? Don't you care about their feelings?"

Caroline flinched at the mention of this.

"Well, I... I have gotten much better."

"From what I had seen a couple of days ago, you will hurt any woman who gets in your way, even if she does nothing to intentionally wound you—or even know she is wounding you at all. Don't you see that is malignant? You treat Isabella Gardiner with rudeness and contempt. All because a man that you have set your sights on, as flimsy as your feelings for him might be, fancies her. You cannot do such a thing, to punish a woman because a man chose her over you. And by so doing, you show him even more so that he was right to choose her over you."

Heat spread through her entire body. "You are horrid, Mr. Whitfield."

"I would rather be horrid now, and save you from your nature, than to be a gentleman and let you continue on to be so unladylike and vile. Do you not see that you hurt other women all for gain? How would you feel if a woman did that to you?"

"Women always do that to me!"

"What?"

"It is nothing."

"No, it is something, tell me what?"

"Other women always win!" Caroline said, unable to hold in her feelings any longer. "Because they not only triumph, but they triumph over me. How can I not take their victory as personal, as if they have come in and wounded me especially, for they always snatch away my happy endings? Is that not inspiration for my incivility if I am uncivil?"

"It is not a reason. For these women do not do this to wound you. And how can you expect to win, when you look at love in the wrong manner?"

"What manner do I see it as?"

"You see it as a conquest, a victory. Love is meant to be experienced and gained, not strategically acquired. It is meant to grow into, not to be forced upon. You push yourself upon the men who you tell yourself you fancy, but not because you actually care for them. Oh no, for if you had cared about them, then you would not so easily transition from brother to brother, or cousin to cousin. Your affections can be bought and sold, which makes them of no value to the man who is looking to have a love that is not mercenary."

"Unbelievable," she exclaimed, standing up and pacing, "This is the true double standards invented by the world, meant to make us women in a constant state of error because there is no right for us, because all is wrong. If we fixate on love for love itself, we are called foolish and willful. Yet if we set our sights on men of wealth and good breeding, then we are cold, malicious and mercenary."

She stopped and turned to him. "If we speak up and flatter the man we set our sights on, doing our best to show our respect for him, we are denounced as being false, too forward, and we frighten men away. Why do you all fear us women so much?"

"We do not fear you."

"Yes, you do," she argued. "If we flatter you or show any signs of life, you look at us as if we are breaking a rule. If we do anything with forwardness or integrity, you might as well fall on the ground and die of fright. But if we are demure and do nothing, apparently that is what you desire."

"For some men, that may be so, but clearly, being amongst our company, you have seen that many men prefer the opposite. And I am not afraid of you, Miss Bingley."

"But many are, apparently. For you all run from me, as you say, I am not likable, am I?!"

"You are not likable because you fear the world too much, Caroline. You have no definition to your character other than what the world presents as the standard. You are a chameleon, and you change yourself to adapt to anything, which gives you no chance at finding morality. I do not come here to hurt you for the sake of doing so. I come here for the sake of helping you."

"Helping me?"

"Yes. You may not listen, but for the love of yourself, you ought to. The right sort of men, not all of us, but the right sort, falls in love with truth. Kind Truth, but still truth. And if you alter yourself so much to please some, or maliciously slander or insult a woman just because another man chose her over you, then you have no truth to your character. You are shapeless and empty. No real man can fall in love with that."

Caroline Bingley was not made of ice, naturally, and therefore was steadily affected by his words, and was holding back her tears. To avoid looking at her, Victor walked to the other side of the room and looked out of the window. After his eyes left her, Caroline began to weep silently.

"I do not say these things because I wish to hurt you, but because

I must," he said gently. "Miss Bingley, whatever beauty you possess, every day you destroy with being intent on hurting others. Every good quality you have becomes invisible in the wake of all knowing that you are the sort of woman who has no sense of humility. And above all, understand that you can be wrong, like the rest of us. Until that time, you shall be as I so sadly had to tell you: unlikable."

"I cannot...you do not know what it is like to never win...you do not know."

"I am a single man in his forties, Miss Bingley. You think I never made any of your mistakes?"

Victor looked on her narrowly and then his eyes were filled with compassion.

"On the contrary, Miss Bingley, I was very similar to you once. Oh yes, I was very much like you. Why do you think it is so easy for me to read you so perfectly? I have the gift of age to add to my experience, and you do not. Therefore, I am telling you now, as someone who is a future version of yourself, let go of your jealousies, your hate, and your selfish disdain for the feelings of others. Find that source of truth within you, then find the goodness that comes along with it, and then let that define you."

Caroline wiped the tears with her handkerchief, and thus feeling too exposed, ran from the room.

However, Victor remained where he was, feeling the burden of being the one who told what is painful to hear, but it was a role he sadly had taken often in his life.

❧ 24 ❧

WHEN THE PAST AWAKENS

The evening for the ball at Matlock had arrived and many families from the entire county had come in their finest. Because we were guests of the household and not the hosts, we did not have to wait in line and receive all the guests as they entered. Therefore, in the many sitting rooms and ballroom of Matlock, we stood and waited as the guests continued to pour in, which they did in nothing short of hordes. There were so many guests that we did not get the chance to meet them all, honesty!

We also met Sir and Lady Hughes of Chatsworth, which was a great house that we had not visited of yet, but were planning to still do so, and among that company were the Shelbys of Blenheim.

"My goodness, we are all a merry party!" Fanny had exclaimed.

"Yes," I said, "I confess to not knowing that Earl and Lady Fitzwilliam would have so many to invite in their circles."

"It is a combination of many things," Mrs. Shelby had said to us, "for balls are so rarely ever given in this county that when it does occur, it is all the talk of the families."

"Truly?" Louisa asked. "I am amazed that it would be so rare."

"Oh, we are mostly a quiet sort of folk. All content to remain at home so often that we forget to ever do more than invite each other over for dinner and that is all."

"And you can imagine how little that pleases some of us younger folk," Maria said, "for every now and again, one gets restless. And feels like dancing."

"Well," Acton said, "you shall have your share of doing it this evening. And if I may be so bold, I would like to request the hand of every lady in this company while you are all still not engaged by a worthier man than me."

The Shelby women were the first to give their affirmation, them so did Sir and Lady Hughes' daughters, which meant that Acton was claimed by all women before those of us in his actual company could claim him. He looked at us, a little embarrassed, for he had not the slightest idea that so many would have taken him up on his offer.

"I must confess to not knowing that I would be claimed so easily," he whispered to me, sheepish.

"You really do not know that you are enjoyable to be around, do you?" I asked lightly.

"What?"

"Acton, your confidence in yourself may be lacking, but you actually are a most wonderful person to have in one's company. So do not worry, enjoy your time with the women and relish in being the object of so much attention."

He blushed. "Really? It actually makes me quite nervous."

"That is very well as well, just remember to keep talking to them, and you shall get over your nerves quite wonderfully."

Acton smiled at me and then he left my side to speak with Maria. He was to dance the first set with her, and then the next with Julia, then the third with Fanny, and the rest with the Hughes sisters.

When the first dance was prepared, Colonel Fitzwilliam approached me, for we were to dance the first set.

"I never understood the concept that one should not always start out dancing with one's own wife," he said, taking my hand, "for I am sure that Darcy wants to dance with you now."

"As you want to dance with our dear Kitty." I smiled as we went onto the dance floor and lined up with the couples.

"Is it so strange? I always want to dance with her."

"As you should. Oh Richard, I am so happy for you and her. You shall be a brilliant father."

"Thank you, Elizabeth."

The music struck up and we began our set while a little way down from us Jane was dancing with Darcy, Kitty was dancing with Lord Fitzwilliam, Henry Fitzwilliam was dancing with Isabella, I saw Caroline Bingley standing next to her sister and Mr. Hurst. For the last couple of days, she had seemed demure and a little subdued —almost despondent. I had often wondered what was ailing her, but I never felt our bond close enough to ever be intimate with her on that score. In fact, we were not intimate at all.

Also, her changed state had left little else to be desired, for her attitude ceased her often prudish and rude manner. Yet as my eyes looked further away from her, I beheld Victor Whitfield, looking at her most acutely, but not with an expression of curiosity, but gravity and silent despondence; it was then clear that something had happened between them, and it left its mark upon both.

THE DANCE BEGAN and Colonel Fitzwilliam and I began our set.

"Kitty and I have decided that immediately after we return to Pemberley, we shall soon travel into Hampshire. I have already written to your father, and he welcomes our coming."

"He shall already teach you about the estate?"

"Yes, and they welcome us living there with them. In truth, I believe that your mother is suffering from being a woman with an empty house when she has been used to having so many under her."

"I would not be surprised. Be brave and have a strong constitution, Richard, for she will dote on you."

"I expect it," he said. "And I do not fear anything at Longbourn. For she is very active, and your father is very sedate and witty. Now having someone to legally inherit his estate and maintain all when he passes on, hopefully he shall not look on my coming as an intrusion."

"As long as you do not invade his library, he shall be fine with you."

"I mean to run the grounds all day, oversee everything, or ride horses with Kitty. Oh, Elizabeth, it is so nice, that after looking death in the eye often enough, I can finally find some sense of peace and retire to quiet society."

"Does the past sometimes haunt you?"

"Yes, but I see that this discussion is not suitable for ballroom talk."

"Richard we are family now, and I am quite curious, if you are willing to talk about your experiences."

He released a sigh. "Very well, the truth is, after you fight in war, your spirit breaks. To take a life, and then to also have your life almost taken as well, one is never really whole again. And we past-soldiers walk around with a part of ourselves gone. I suppose that is why I cling to Kitty so desperately."

"She makes you feel whole?"

"She also reminds me of the man I was before I saw the worst of war. For some reason, when I am with her, I become the man that I was before I had led my armies. She keeps that section of me alive."

"In truth, when I had first met you, I always found it so ironic that you and she never got the chance to meet sooner. For I felt that your tempers were so much alike. Indeed, when her personality and manners overcame the most trying age and she bloomed into the woman that she now is, I knew that she could not be so good-natured for nothing."

"Yes, she was made for me—if it is not too egotistical to say so."

"No, it is not so, and those who believe so do not know the true possessive feeling that *true* love brings in its wake."

"Yes, true love...it is not something that all comprehend."

We both parted, for the dance movements required. We turned to our new partners, and I could not believe my eyes. Could it be that I was seeing hallucinations because there was no way that he could be here. But he was, looking at me with the same amount of alarm that I looked upon him.

"Mr. Brocklehurst!"

"Miss Elizabeth!"

I was staring into the face of Mr. Samuel Brocklehurst, the man who had proposed to my sister, Jane, even when he already had another wife elsewhere.

It felt like it had been a lifetime since we had seen each other last, for I was a different woman back then.

Once we had adjusted to the sight of each other, he took my hand, and we began to dance.

"It is pleasing to see you," he muttered, very much affected by my appearance.

"And it is a wonder to see you again," I replied, not wishing to call it a pleasure, for it was not so.

"How is your family at Longbourn?"

"They are all in excellent health, thank you for your kind inquiry. Yet they are no longer at Longbourn."

"Oh," he said, his cheeks reddening. "Where are...*all* of them, pray tell, Miss Bennet?"

"I no longer bear the name of Miss Elizabeth Bennet, but now I am Mrs. Darcy."

"Oh! I did not know when they said Mrs. Elizabeth Darcy that you would be her."

"Yes, I am she. My youngest sister Lydia lives in America with her husband, Mr. Henry Darcy, who is my husband's cousin. Kitty is here at the ball with her husband, Colonel Fitzwilliam."

"Who is Mr. Darcy's other cousin and is the younger son of the Earl of Matlock?"

"Yes."

"Then...your family has made splendid conquests, and that is very well. But what of your other sisters?"

"Mary is the companion of Lady Catherine De Bourgh's daughter, Miss Anne, and is at Rosings Park. And Jane is..."

"You need not soften it," he said suddenly and with harsh desperation, "I know what to expect, for if your fate is so large, then hers must be magnanimous. Has she wed an Earl herself?"

"No, she has not wed at all, and she lives with us at Pemberley, educating the children of Kent."

"She is unmarried? She? And she is at Pemberley now?"

"No, she is here, at the ball."

"But I had not—where is she?"

I could not help but look down the line of dancers and Mr. Brocklehurst instinctively followed my gaze, his eyes falling on her and they grew wide as a result.

"Mr. Brocklehurst..."

"No, do not speak to me now. I am sorry, but just do not..."

We were soon separated, and I went back to Colonel Fitzwilliam as my partner.

The dance soon ended and when Colonel Fitzwilliam led me off the dance floor, I immediately went to Jane and my husband. To have a private word with her, I asked Darcy to get me some punch while I spoke to her. He did so and then I took her hand and pulled her to the corner of the ballroom.

"Lizzy, what is it?"

"Jane, the most alarming thing has happened. Please do your best to keep your composure."

"I always do my best to do so," Jane said. "Lizzy you are frightening me. Whatever is the matter?"

"Mr. Brocklehurst is here!"

Jane's face went from curious to blanch as she stared at me in disbelief.

"Lizzy, is this some cruel joke? For it is not funny."

"When would I joke of something like this? Mr. Brocklehurst is here, Jane."

"But I did not see him enter."

"This ballroom is so full, that we did not see everyone as they arrived, and some did arrive late. He must have been in one of those parties."

"Dear lord, Lizzy."

"Can you withstand yourself now?"

"I... I know that it has been a long time since seeing him, but I fear that I am not up to the task of being near him once more. And I do not wish to do anything that would expose me to any improper remarks! Would it be amiss if I told Earl and Lady Fitzwilliam that I did not feel well, and that I wished to quietly remove myself from the company?"

"I think it wise to do so."

"Good, therefore I—"

"Miss Bennet?"

Jane and I both became still as statues, for the voice was all too familiar.

We both turned and Mr. Brocklehurst was before us.

"Mr. Brocklehurst," Jane stuttered, out of breath from the equal amazement and horror of seeing him before her waking eyes. Then remembering herself, she curtsied to him, and he bowed in response.

"Miss Bennet," he said, his eyes filled with astonishment, "You look remarkably well this evening, though it should surprise none, for you were always uncommonly pretty."

"Thank you, sir, and you are looking well also."

"I was hoping that I might have your hand for this next set."

"Well sir, I had not, I have not been feeling—"

"Please, you must allow me this privilege."

"No, she does not," I said for her.

"Mrs. Darcy, you must consider that if she refuses me, then she shall have to refuse any other gentleman who asks for her hand to dance."

"You are pressuring her?" I said, incredulous, and my temper was quickly rising.

"I do not wish to or mean to," he replied quickly. "It is just..." then he turned to Jane, imploring her, "Forgive me, Miss Bennet, yet I just wish to speak with you while I can, and I promise, I shall not trouble you for the rest of the ball. And Mrs. Darcy, we are in a public area where I can cause no harm. I know you must not trust me, but please pity me."

What a clever devil he was. He was playing up to Jane's compassionate nature and knowing that she could never cause any sort of pain to someone she once cared deeply for. He must have known that his words would have the desired effect—and they did.

"Lizzy," Jane said, "it is fine. I shall be well."

"But," I began to interrupt, however Jane acquiesced to Mr. Brocklehurst's request, he took her hand and led her to the dance floor.

As the dance began, Mr. Darcy came to my side with the cup of punch that he had for me.

"Who was that man who is dancing with Jane," he said, "for I saw him accost you both, and I could have sworn that you did not look happy."

"Fitzwilliam," I said with stern finality. "I need you to intimidate him."

"What? Why?"

I unfolded all of Jane's past with Mr. Brocklehurst, and when Darcy heard all, from Brocklehurst's willingness to remain married to Jane while he had a family elsewhere, Darcy was irate. But he hid it under his legendary scowl.

"The foul libertine!" he hissed so that only I could hear. "That is monstrous."

"Yes, it is," I said. "And I do not want him to pressure her into a second chance. Jane still has a part of herself that will always be partial to him, and he can easily bend that to his advantage."

"Aye, I know what to do."

Mr. Darcy walked to the edge of the dance couples, and he fixed his stern gaze upon Mr. Brocklehurst. Mr. Brocklehurst was originally speaking quietly to Jane as they danced, but then he caught my husband's eye, and they locked gazes.

Mr. Darcy and his look of wrath was a frightening thing to behold, thus as Mr. Brocklehurst danced with Jane, with my husband prowling around the group of dancers, never taking his eyes off him, was enough to unnerve him in every possible way.

The dance ended and while Mr. Brocklehurst led Jane off the dance floor, Fitzwilliam cut in and with a grave and demanding tone, he told Mr. Brocklehurst that he was sent to return the lovely Jane to her family. Jane looked at Mr. Brocklehurst with one fleeting glance, said her goodbye, then she took Darcy's arm and walked off the dance floor with him. She whispered something to my husband, and he nodded, then he took her to our company, leaving her there as he went toward Lady Fitzwilliam.

I took that time to casually make my way to Jane, and passing among the couples, I nodded to Isabella, who was dancing another set with Henry Fitzwilliam. I approached Jane.

"Jane..."

"At my plea, Mr. Darcy has gone to tell Earl and Lady Fitzwilliam that I am not well, and that I wish to retire for the evening."

"Did Mr. Brocklehurst say anything untoward to you, or base?"

"No, he was polite. He just wished to speak to me again, for he said that he thought of me often."

"As often as a pawnbroker laments his lost booty, no doubt," I muttered.

"Lizzy, do not say such things about him."

"Wait then... are you about to defend him?"

"I... oh dear, I was about to do so, wasn't I?" she whispered, astonished.

"Yes, you were."

"Dear lord! I thought I had grown stronger since seeing him. But now that I have, my weaknesses for him are still there. I do not know why, but I still feel sympathy for him, and I am easily swayed by his supplications—when they could always be false, or that of a man who only laments what he has lost. Yes, I must leave, for I am not up to the task of being around him for the whole evening—not when I know the truth now."

"And what truth is that?"

"That, if he asks anything of me with enough spirit, he can convince me to do anything."

"You must have loved him very much."

"Not just loved, Lizzy. But love... I still love him, I suppose."

❈

WHEN LADY FITZWILLIAM WAS INFORMED, Jane retired for the evening, and I escorted her up the stairs to her room. I knew that I had to return no later than a quarter of an hour's time, so I helped Jane out of her gown so that we did not have to call for a maid.

She got on a simple dress and requested that she sit in the nursery with Caiden and William, for they would bring her some peace.

I went with her there, and both of my sons were asleep, as Jane and I sat there for a couple more minutes before I had no choice but to return.

"A painful thing," Jane began, "when you wake up and realize that you are no stronger today than years ago."

"It is not so easy to overcome the powers of love," I said. "You have no reason to look down upon yourself."

"Oh, but there is. There was once a fleeting moment in the past, where I had preferred ignorance over truth. A part of me had wished that I had never found out about his double life, and that we had wed. For what I did not know would not hurt me. Eventually I overcame that foolish intention, but I fear it rising again."

"I understand," I said, not surprised at her having that wish for one moment in time, for love did have a blinding effect on us all at some point.

"And so, I did not trust myself, and that was why I had to leave the ball. In truth, I feared that base impulse rising in me again. When the past awakens, sometimes so can our worthless desires."

"Jane..."

"You must return to the ball, and do not worry, we can speak of this later, but right now, all I need is solitude, Lizzy. And to look on my nephews now would be enough peace for me."

I looked her over and understood her need for quiet contemplation, for her inner turmoil must have been great indeed.

"Stay until you get tired, Jane, and I hope you feel better."

"Thank you, Lizzy."

I stood up, left her and went back to the ball.

25

DANCING PARTNER

By the fourth dance of the evening, it became clear to Aunt Gardiner that Henry Fitzwilliam favored her daughter with much indiscretion. It made her heart soar. Harriet was in the midst of securing her future, but with Isabella, who was secretly her favorite, but objectively would be less likely to get a husband, this was a most welcome surprise.

Left in pleasant astonishment, she hoped that an offer would be made to her dear Issy, but also feared that Henry Fitzwilliam, like other wealthy men before him, would change his mind quickly in realizing that Isabella came from a background of trade. Thus, within her was a conflicting mindset, one who hoped and one that prepared for disappointment. And the side of her that was ready for no offer to be made hoped that her dear Issy would not be left too much in heartbreak.

Yet while Aunt Gardiner was sitting in careful contemplation, further down the row of seats sat Caroline, much occupied in her thoughts, but thinking on a different subject. She had danced a couple of times, but her spirits were so uninviting that she received very little notice from others around her. She smiled and said pleasant things when spoken to, but she never furthered conversation by behaving enticing in any way. Thus, she sat alone, losing all the desire to appear brighter than she felt.

This was all too difficult and distressing. For, despite all her hubris, her self-confidence, it now made the revelation that much more painful to endure. Was she really wrong about the way she went about things? And were all the enemies that she made her own fault?

So much was she occupied and self-possessed that she did not take heed to Victor Whitfield when he sat down beside her.

"Well," Victor said, lightly, "sitting out this dance, I see?"

"I was not given an offer," Caroline replied, "which is why I remain here."

"I am surprised at that. With your pleasing features, I was sure that you would never want for partners."

"You do not need to flatter me, Mr. Whitfield," she whispered, "for I see what your design is."

"You do?"

"Yes, you were hoping that the grace of a compliment would ease the sting of your critique of my character from before. Well, you need not trouble yourself."

"Very well, if you wish to be frank then so shall I. I have noticed how you are remote and low in spirits tonight. And yes, I knew that it was because of all that we have said to each other."

She answered, "I was foolish to think I should come to the ball tonight. I told myself that I would be able to set aside my wounded pride, but I cannot just now."

"One thing can always do so, for it is the way of lifting one's spirits always. Or at least, it is called so."

"And what is that?"

"Dancing, and I daresay that it can move any woman to greater vitality, energy and bring a spring to her step."

"You only say so because you have heard me give speeches on

the subject of how a ball is most invigorating," she challenged. "And when you did overhear, did you not think, Mr. Whitfield, that I expressed myself uncommonly well just then, when I teased Mr. Shelby to give us all another ball at Blenheim?"

"With great energy—but it is a subject which always makes a lady energetic."

"You are severe on us."

"It will be your turn to be teased if you still do not wish to stand up with me."

"Then...you really are asking me to dance?" she asked, surprised. "I only thought you were speaking in jest."

"I have only recently argued and lectured you, Miss Bingley. I therefore know it is too soon to pull such a joke on you."

"Well then, if you should like to, I am not engaged, but I do not know if I wish to dance with you."

"You had better say yes."

"What?" she scoffed, amazed that he was giving her an order. "How dare you—"

"How dare I help you? Miss Bingley, I can see that our past verbal altercation has hurt you. If we stand up together, we can speak much on the matter while also helping you find your feet again. After all, I am the one who knocked you off balance before, and now I ought to set you back to rights. For it is only fitting, don't you think?"

Caroline was torn, for she was still angry with him. But she was curious to speak with him for whatever reason her mind could concoct. She was left much in doubt and uncertainty, therefore perhaps conversation could stabilize her. And thus, despite her reservations on accepting his hand, she did so. They both stood up at the beginning of the next set and joined the other couples as the dance began.

"Tell me something," Victor began, "What did you feel after our conversation in the library?"

"Mr. Whitfield, I do not think this is the best time to speak of such things, for I do not wish to leave the ballroom weeping and making a spectacle of myself—scenes might arise that are unpleasant to more than just myself."

"I admire your forbearance, truly, but Miss Bingley, understand that I do not wish to make you cry."

"You already have."

"I said what needed to be said, for I wish someone had said that all to me once upon a time."

"Did you?"

"Yes. So, tell me, how did you feel after I had reprimanded you so boldly?"

"First it was anger, and then I was greatly disturbed, unable to make light or reason of anything. Indeed, I could not. I was uncomfortable enough. I was very uncomfortable, I may say unhappy. And with no one to speak to, of what I felt, for even Louisa could not comfort me and say that I had not been so weak and vain and nonsensical as I knew I had! Oh! How I wanted a release from my revelations!"

"So, you found yourself to be weak, vain and nonsensical?"

"I do not wish to confess that to myself, but I suppose—and yet I meant to be uncommonly clever in taking so decided a dislike of everyone in my way, without any reason. It is such a spur to one's genius, such an opening for wit to have a dislike of that kind. One may be continually abusive without saying anything just; but one cannot be always laughing at a man or woman without now and then stumbling on something witty."

"You toy with yourself now."

"No, I merely make fun of myself so to decrease the feeling of the sting of self-doubt. But you must tell me something."

"Yes?" he asked.

"You have called yourself a villain in the past and said that you wish someone had told you what you told me? What did you mean by that?"

"I meant what I meant."

"And what I meant was what did you mean behind that confession?"

"It is simple. Caroline Bingley, I know your kind most intimately, because I was once you."

"How were you once me?" Caroline persisted. "Was your character similar to my own?"

"Yes, I was the oldest, the inheritor to Errodin Abbey, and while I was taught good principles, I was left to forget them because I dwelled often in self-conceit and idleness. I gave into the ways and workings of society so easily and never had the courage of my convictions, unless it was convenient to have them. Like you, I did not care who I cut with my intentions. If I wanted something, I would seek it, not caring who posed as an obstacle to me. My ambition made me emotionally cruel and thoughtless to the feelings of others. And you were similar, were you not?"

"I... I wish to say that I was not."

"But were you?"

"Yes, I was."

"Precisely. Therefore, I do know you intimately, don't I?"

"Well, if you were the way that I am now, for you to lecture me feels like hypocrisy."

"You are only saying that to wound me for me wounding you."

"Is that all?"

"Yes, you are replying in self-defense."

She gave him a sidelong glance. "You did offend me."

"Because, as I said before, it is to save you from forever never improving yourself. But at the remains of the day, that shall not be my choice to make. It has to be yours."

"I suppose."

"Besides, if there is one sort of person who has the right to tell you how to improve, it always ought to be those of us who were like you. We do not speak from hypocrisy as often as you would think. We just know the outcome of your story, and we serve as a warning for what you should not continue to do."

"Then...one day you woke up and improved?"

"Yes, I did. Well, it was more like it took me weeks to realize that a change should take place within myself."

"And...what inspired it?"

"It is a strange thing."

"What is?"

"I cannot really remember the day that it began. It is all so amusing and astonishing, because in the world of fiction and history, there is always the concept that it takes a great action or sight to awaken the better halves of ourselves. As if, for us to change, something had to have occurred within us to bring about that change. And yes, that is true, for often a drastic measure that was taken can often lead to someone realizing the deficiency in their character. Yet that was not what I found. Sometimes a person could wake up one day and feel different. Sometimes it is only the work of a moment that makes us want to be better people."

"That was the way with you?"

"Yes, I was a bit of a rake who thought he was a saint, a bit of a bigot, though I thought myself an unprejudiced man, and a bit of an idiot, though I believed myself to be a man of the world. And then one day, while running Errodin, I found myself to be deficient in all the things that I believed myself to be proficient in. I was quite a foolish man, who made nothing useful of his education—and was missing much. I suppose that was when I began to become funny."

"How so?"

"Self-realization always leads to all sorts of joking remarks. For you see, with our lives, we understand that one thing everyone hates: regret."

"You have many regrets?"

"Too many to count."

They were separated in their dance, and then came back together.

"Mr. Whitfield?" Caroline asked.

"Yes?"

"How did you overcome this feeling of self-disgust?"

"You can't, for it is something that needs to be felt."

"Then tell me, does it get any easier of a memory to bear?"

He smiled down at her. "Now *that* I can say yes to. And see, do you not feel better now that we have spoken?"

"Much still feels unresolved," Caroline said. "But I cannot say it is anyone's fault. Yes, you were right. I did feel better after all."

And thus, the set ended and Caroline, who walked onto the dance floor feeling herself the most unfortunate woman in the world, now walked off the dance floor feeling lightness to her spirit. For her dance partner proved to be worthy of her, in the sense that they both once weren't worthy of much.

26

WHEN FATE DEALS YOU
ITS HAND

T he ball had come to an end late in the evening, or very early in the morning, we occupants of Matlock were sluggish all the rest of the next day. We were allowed to sleep in late, or for the entire afternoon.

Many of us who were married took advantage of the lax schedule and had our meals served to us in our private rooms. I spent my day in between lounging with Darcy or sitting with Caiden and William. Jane joined us. I let Lucy take the day to herself, and she ran skipping down the halls while Jane and I remained with my boys.

"Do you feel better now, Jane?" I began.

"Yes and no," she replied. "But I suppose it is as it would be. I feel better in that he is not here anymore, but I feel equally bad for a part of me wishes to see him again. It is altogether a bad business."

"Yes, I can imagine it being so."

She turned to me. "But I will say this. It is nice that it occurred in that it now has given me something to talk about, for that is always the one good thing about an unfortunate circumstance or trying time; it gives a person something to talk about instead of repeating the same things always."

"Yes, that is a good way of looking at unfortunate incidents. They occupy our conversations and save us, albeit temporarily, from being redundant."

"Well then...a bright side to problems. They decrease boredom."

"Oh, Jane...only you could find a way to absolve and defend the concept of 'crisis' by giving it a purpose."

"I can and I do. But all I can say of this is that I shall now free Mr. Brocklehurst from my mind. There, I am done! And I shall be myself again. I shall be perfectly content."

"Are you sure?"

"Yes, very much so."

"Good, for Darcy was worried over you as well."

"He has a good heart, your husband does, under that rocky exterior."

"Are you calling my husband a rock?"

"Yes, for he cannot be moved or broken easily, can he?"

"No, and I daresay only time shall be the only thing to dissemble him, but nothing else."

"Tell him I thank him for coming to my aid."

"Do not worry, Jane. He already knows. He always did."

◈◈◈

THE NEXT DAY, we were off to Chatsworth, which was the seat of Sir and Lady Hughes, whom we had already met. They had a lovely park around their estate, and that park would prove to be the trial that put a growing affection to the test.

We rode on some phaetons that the Hughes had, through the grounds of Chatsworth, with the Hughes giving us the tour of their lovely park.

However, when we descended from the phaetons, one of the

wheels on one of them broke as it was rolling away, and it began to land upon Henry Fitzwilliam. Isabella, who always possessed quick reflexes and much nerve, rushed to him and pulled him out of the way just before the phaeton came crashing down on him. Though her actions were quite impulsive and instinctive, it was still a very heroic thing! Henry Fitzwilliam could have been injured, as well as her in helping him, but she had not cared.

Aunt Gardiner rushed forward as well as Lady Fitzwilliam, as they both wanted to attend to their children.

"Oh, my lord!" Lady Hughes cried. "I am quite mortified, and I am sorry for it, Mr. Fitzwilliam and Miss Isabella and I—"

Yet all of us halted; Lady Fitzwilliam and Aunt Gardiner froze, and Mrs. Hughes gasped as Henry Fitzwilliam suddenly grabbed Isabella, pulled her toward him and kissed her savagely.

Isabella, one possessed with great compassion and gusto, did not shy away or act mortified. She was surprised clearly but she only allowed him to continue his kiss and then rested her hands on his forearms.

One of us should have attempted to separate them, but no one was up to the task. For how could we be? Whether Henry's rash action was of a man who was so glad that she had come to keep him from being crushed that it threw reason to the winds, or of a man who was already in love with Isabella and now had another reason to love her, or of a man who wanted her so terribly that his impulses told him that if he kissed her, his parents would have no choice but to allow him wedding her, despite her low connections.

For yes, Isabella was regarded as being below the Fitzwilliams, but she had a sufficient enough dowry for our uncle was successful at his trade. To add to her charms now, she had saved Henry's life. His parents could never deny her now.

At last, Henry released Issy and looked red in the face as he had done so.

"Forgive me," he whispered hoarsely. "I was not thinking of you."

"It is well." She sighed, out of breath. "I have never been kissed before, I know not how to..." she began to collapse into his arms, half-fainting, and he caught her. But then she awoke as soon as she had passed out. "Sorry," she said, "I was merely overcome for a moment. Henry, I..."

"You saved me from injury," he said.

"Of course I did, I..." she said, looking deeply into his eyes. "Yes I... I have not the words for what I am feeling right now."

Out of another burst of emotion, Henry pulled her to him and embraced her, to which Issy responded in kind by wrapping her arms around his waist.

Again, we knew not what to say. For such a strong display of emotion that resulted from a strong deed that was done could not help but be so beautiful that we could not reprimand them or tell them to cease.

There, in each other's arms, they remained for a whole minute, seeming desirous of melting into each other as his tall form over-looked her shorter one. The beauty of Chatsworth was miniscule to their moments of affections that were not sprung from forced emotion or propriety obeyed. It simply sprang from mutual affection that had been rising organically for some time and therefore had the most fruitful of results.

Henry Fitzwilliam, who had been heartbroken in the past, had only endured so much so that he could walk toward his happiness in another quarter. Yes, Henry Fitzwilliam had found his joy, and there before us, he was clinging to it as if it would escape him if he let it go.

Still with his arms wrapped around Isabella, he looked over her hair and at his parents.

"I will not hear otherwise," he said. "I shall marry her! She is my match!"

"Yes, of course," Lady Fitzwilliam said, feeling in Isabella's debt.

"Well," Lord Fitzwilliam said, "since marrying such women has proven to be the lot of the young men in this family of this generation, Henry... I suppose maybe, I shall be happy that it is your turn."

Henry Fitzwilliam smiled, but Isabella looked up at him with spice in her eyes.

"Oh, really!" she scoffed. "And when did you ask me for my hand in marriage?"

"Oh dear, I realize I quite forgot that."

"Yes, you did, and that was most high-handed! Now, I believe you should ask me with sincere affection. I shall allow you to begin now."

"Very well," he laughed, still holding her. "Isabella Gardiner, also known as Issy, you must allow me to tell you how much I adore and love you. Please, marry me, my lovely savior, and be the woman who helps me stay strong. For you are stronger."

"That was..." she sighed, "that was precisely as I would have wished it to be spoken."

"Was it?"

"Yes. And now it is my turn."

"What?"

"You have asked for my hand, and how could I not desire to tell you how I feel? Henry Fitzwilliam, I will be your wife, I will very much...if you will have me, for I promise that I... I love you as well."

"You do? Truly?"

"I do not know how long it has been coming on, but it has. So, will you have me?"

"Of course."

"Then, there is one more thing left to do." Isabella turned to her mother and smiled gently.

"Mother, I know that I have quite erred against decorum again, but I cannot care for it now—not when it has gotten me such beauty."

"She called me a beauty," Henry Fitzwilliam whispered, more to himself than us.

"So please, write to Father, and tell him that whether by his will or not, I now obey Henry Fitzwilliam, and I will marry him."

"Of course, my dear!" Aunt Gardiner cried. "And I am so glad, that I... I..."

And it would be Aunt Gardiner who had fainted in the end.

However, Lord Fitzwilliam had caught her before she fell to the ground.

⊗⚘⊗

THE JOY that this news brought all around was one of unparalleled exclamations of well-wishes.

Lord and Lady Hughes, who would have once found the phaeton fall as an embarrassment to their party, now could regard it as a blessing in disguise and proclaim it as the means through which Henry Fitzwilliam and Isabella had become united. Their mutual affection had already been growing steadily and was only marred by their social differences. So their relationship just needed an extra push and it had received it on Chatsworth. Lord and Lady Hughes expressed that it would be a story that they would tell for years to come, and their daughters seconded this half-heartedly, for I could tell that they secretly were upset that such a romantic circumstance had not happened to them.

Returning to Matlock, Isabella and Henry remained close to each other, and Georgiana was seen whispering something to Jason, who nodded his head, and then stood up.

"Mr. Fitzwilliam and Miss Isabella," he said, "forgive us if this is not your pleasure, but we figured that we would ask in case you wished. Our wedding is to occur soon, and since you both are clearly very much devoted to each other already, we were wondering if you would fancy a double wedding?"

"Truly?" Isabella said. "You would be content with us sharing your happy day?"

"We could not be more delighted," Georgiana said. "For the Fitzwilliam cousins have always been like siblings to Fitzwilliam and me, therefore, if you like, we shall look forward to the day when we all can have our happiness fulfilled, united."

This scheme was easily accepted, and now, the joyous event that would secure the domestic tranquility of so many would occur and enter us into a new path that more of us would walk down.

"And," Henry Fitzwilliam said, raising up his glass, "I shall propose a toast, for not only to my beautiful fiancée, to my brilliant cousin and her soon to be husband for letting us share this event, but now that I think on it, when fate deals you its hand, it all is meant for a reason."

He looked at Kitty. "Kitty, you were meant for my brother, it was fate, and fate was right. Just as it was right to bring Darcy and Elizabeth together, Georgiana and Jason, and to have Miss Bennet among us, always saving children from the harsh reality that not all can be educated, to the Hursts, Mr. Whitfield, and Miss Bingley being here to support this dynamic family.

"We are such a collection of odd parts, but we fit together. We create one large masterpiece. One time, I did my best to take matters into my own hands and deny the destiny that each of us had. It led to catastrophic events, when it turned out that providence was correct. Now I am no philosopher, and I cannot tell you where is that line that determines when one should give way to fortune, or to decide one's own future. But in matters of love, yes, providence has its own plan, and it will find you. It found me. Therefore, let us raise our glasses, in honor of all of us here, for all the parts that make this family whole."

We all raised our glasses and drank.

27

PROVIDENCE HAS A PLAN

The second to last day of our stay at Matlock, I was sitting in the nursery room, rocking Caiden in his crib with my foot and holding William in my arms. The men had gone out for shooting, the rest of the women remained in the parlor room, and I sent Lucy away, giving her another day off to enjoy the holiday in Matlock. In truth, I knew very well that she would spend her day being flirted with by Jefferson and he might have been able to persuade her to kiss him, but that was all out of my hands.

As I sat there, enjoying the peace of seeing my boys older now and healthy, there was a knock on the door.

"Come in," I said, expecting it to be Jane or Kitty. Thus, when the door opened, I was surprised to see that it was Caroline Bingley.

"Miss Bingley," I said, immediately put on my guard. "Hello, does someone need me?"

"No," she whispered, "I just wished to speak with you."

"Miss Bingley—Caroline—if you wish to speak with me on matters that would cause discord between us, I shall tell you now that I will rise to the challenge. I do not want strife at the moment, only peace."

"Do not worry," she said, "I did not come for discord to continue, but rather to end it."

"Did you?"

"Yes."

"Do sit down."

Caroline smiled gently, sat down, and looking at her lap, she immediately began to speak.

"When you first confronted me at Canterbury, I should have taken more heed to your words, and...no, I must go further back. Mrs. Darcy, Elizabeth, since the first day I met you, I despised you."

I leaned back, not fazed by what I already knew.

"And why, might I ask?"

"Because you had the one thing that I always wanted."

"Mr. Darcy?"

"Love."

I flinched, surprised with that confession.

"Oh."

"And I'm not excusing myself," she continued. "I am just explaining. When my brother met you, he found you intriguing and lovely. Mr. Darcy fell in love with you immediately and all else around you seemed ready to enjoy you, and you never even had to try. You have no idea how hard it is on us women who have to try often when we see those find love when they do not try at all."

"Love is an organic thing, Miss Bingley, whether it is through effort or none, it flows its own way."

"Yes, I should have known that, but all that I knew then was my own jealousy. And I reaped the rewards of a vanity working on a weak mind and how it creates all sorts of mischief. I let my envy turn me into a monster, it seems, and it should not have been born."

She stared at the child in my arms. "After the first circumstance, it should have ended, and I should have learned my lesson. Yet we humans, sadly, oftentimes need many lessons before we actually learn it well enough to see the reality that is right in front of us. I continued to cling to irrational sentiments, and it all led to me being jealous of anyone connected with me who took the fate that I thought I deserved. I offended you terribly, wronged you often, as well as I was unjust to your sister, Lydia.

"I offer no excuse for my actions, but only explanations. The only thing that I can say to ease your sense of feeling wronged, is that my actions were never out of any wrong that you committed, but out of pure venom on my own mind, born from jealousy because I could not be of the same heights as you Bennets."

"Oh Caroline...this is so much to hear."

"I know," she sighed, "and I ask for your forgiveness, even though I do not deserve it. For you were quite blameless, and I was full of flaws that I took too long to see."

"How does it feel now? To see them?"

"I," she chuckled, startled by my question, "it feels very crippling, but refreshing all the while."

I offered a smile. "Well, that is marvelous to hear, for revelations can feel quite life changing, as they ought to. And Caroline, if you mean all that you say—"

"I can assure you that I do."

"Then I shall believe that you are sorry. And you shall be allowed to start anew in my eyes."

"Thank you. Mrs. Darcy, you are too good. I admit that I do not deserve it."

"Yes, you do. We all do in turn."

"Then may I be worthy of it," she said, standing up. "And I shall not overstay my welcome, so thank you again, Elizabeth." Before she left, I looked on her retreating form and acted upon an impulse.

"Miss Bingley?"

"Yes?"

"Why do you apologize now? What has changed that made you feel apt to do this so suddenly? What inspired you to seek penance for your actions?"

"I cannot say for sure, but all I can say is 'providence has its own plan'. And I should cease to get in the way of it."

She nodded to me and left. While I remained alone, I felt a rush of many emotions, but most of all, I felt shaken. It is a great deal easier to go on with an enemy at bay, but when that enemy yields and you must reconcile, it can be quite disarming. It can make you confused and unnerved when seeing them again. As it also can be for the one who apologized. Either way, Caroline Bingley had sought reform, and bless be the ties that bound her to it. For may they always bind her.

❧ 28 ❧

CAROLINE'S CONFESSION

Different paths can often lead to different courses that are taken, or the same course taken by different routes. For Victor Whitfield, he simply awoke one day and began a transformation of his vice-driven self, but for Caroline, there had to be a life-changing event, something to show her the ultimate victory for changing her character.

Thus, when Isabella risked her life for Henry Fitzwilliam, only then did Caroline see the benefits of having a pure heart and mindset. She had despised Isabella, and like many others before her, she despised her for the simple fact that Isabella was the woman that she, Caroline Bingley, thought herself to be and ought to be, but was not.

Thus, seeing a selfless act done in the name of love, she was overpowered by the sight of what true heroism was. Caroline knew very well she could not aspire to such greatness, but she would begin where she may. Thus, when she heard that Victor Whitfield was in the billiards room by himself, she took that opportunity to find him and begin as she thought it best: with an apology that was long overdue.

When she entered the billiards room, Victor looked up from the table and stood up, then bowed.

"Miss Bingley."

"Hello Mr. Whitfield."

"Does Jason need me?"

"No, he does not. I came in search of you."

"Did you?"

"Yes. I just wished to thank you."

"For what?"

"For not giving up on me. You may not have known that was what you were doing, but you were. You chose to fight me, for the sake of *me*. You dared me to learn from my flaws and see myself for who I truly was. No one else has ever succeeded at that."

"I see that they have not," he chuckled, getting closer to her. "But, if it makes you feel the compliment, you were worth the fight. Improved now, I see?"

"Yes. And while stubbornness is often called a vice, in you, it is quite the virtue. I...um, I wish to tell you something else."

"What more good news do you bring in your wake?" he said gently, his gaze warm.

"I did apologize. When you fell from off your horse, and you were riding off, I called out to you. But you were too far away. I called out, apologizing, for I had realized that I ought to have. It took me too long, but I finally understood how to get past my own selfishness and think on you. Now I shall have to learn how to find my compassion swifter. But I just needed you to know, even though my telling you is shamefully overdue, that I did feel sorry. I did feel something."

"And I felt much remorse in almost hitting you and being insulting. Yet ironically, it appears that providence was there with us. For apparently, we needed to crash into each other, or you never would have stood up as you are now, do you agree?"

"Yes," Caroline chuckled. Victor walked up to her, took her hand in his and kissed it.

"Caroline," he said, "now you are capable of great kindness. Chase it."

"Victor—you—you are a great man. Aren't you?"

"I don't know. Am I?"

"Yes, and I think I owe you much. Thank you! I know that I have said it before but thank you."

"And as I said, your soul was worth the fight."

Caroline's confession was enough to make her feel light as a feather as she curtsied to Victor and left him, skipping lightly down the hall.

THE SUCCESSION OF INCIDENTS

O ur return to Pemberley and Kent was not a retirement to quiet, for we brought a whirlwind of action with us. Henry Fitzwilliam joined us as the Hursts and Miss Bingley went to Allenwell. Victor joined us as well, but wished to stay at the Inn in Kent, for as he put it 'he could always dash away one day, or the next, or the next, and it was all down to how he felt when he woke up'.

Very soon upon our return, Miriam went into labor, and we had all arrived as she was giving birth. We all sat downstairs, with Mr. Bingley sitting there, pale in the face as he heard his wife's screams from above. Then, after what had felt like an eternity, the midwife came downstairs and told Mr. Bingley that he was now a father, Mrs. Bingley was out of danger, and she now held in her arms their beautiful baby girl.

Overjoyed, Mr. Bingley rushed up the steps to be with Miriam. We all waited for longer to give them their moments as parents alone as well as a chance for Miriam to be cleaned up.

When we entered the bedroom, Mr. Bingley sat on the bed,

holding his daughter while Miriam lay down, her head resting against Mr. Bingley's shoulder.

"Charles," Mr. Darcy said, "I believe that this might be the best Bingley yet, and what will her name be?"

"Well," Charles said, "What say you to Elizabeth?"

"What? Me?" I gasped.

"Yes," Miriam said, "for if you and Mr. Darcy had not fallen in love and come to America, then I never would have met Charles, and I never would be as happy as I am now. Therefore, our little girl here owes a lot to the path you both chose to walk down. So, would you give her name your blessing?"

"Of course," I said, on the brink of tears, "that is all so wonderful!"

And thus was Elizabeth Bingley brought into the world.

❦

THE NEXT LARGE event was the double wedding of Georgiana, Jason, Henry and Isabella. The days leading to the wedding rolled onward with alacrity and, in the style of Kitty's wedding to the Colonel, their wedding would be out of doors. But this time, in a light set of woods on the grounds, where the low hanging branches were decorated with lovely decorations.

Many families in Kent came, as did our families of Matlock, Gracechurch Street, Errodin Abbey, Lucas Lodge, and Longbourn. Families from Chatsworth and Blenheim came as well, including Lady Catherine, Anne De Bourgh and Mary. Naturally Lady Catherine objected to it being outdoors, but her arrival was too late to allow anything to be influenced by her. So the plans remained as they were.

It proved to be a wonderful picture, with Henry and Jason standing at the altar while Lord Fitzwilliam and my Uncle Gardiner walked their daughter and niece down the aisle. Both women looked beautiful in two different ways, as their men eyed them both with warm affection and adoration.

With Jason, there was the conquest of marrying a woman who stirred him from the day they met in the most intriguing of circumstances. With Henry Fitzwilliam, he was a man who took his past heartbreak with Kitty to heart so much, that I doubted he thought destiny would offer him a second chance in gaining the perfect woman for him—and it had, and he was happy to see that he was not forsaken in matters of the heart and mind.

After the ceremony, we had the wedding feast in the ballroom of Pemberley where all was set up for a party of sixty people—there ended up being eighty people, yet all were still able to eat.

After the wedding, both couples remained at Pemberley for a couple of days before Georgiana and Jason travelled to Spain for their honeymoon and Henry and Isabella went to Italy. They were the first couples in our family to have a normal honeymoon where they did not take family along. Oh, how boring they might turn out to be... that was merely a gentle joke.

After the newlyweds had left Kent, all the families naturally returned to their homes, but we lost another two in number ourselves. Kitty and Richard joined our parents in going back to Longbourn, where our father would teach Richard how to run the estate. While a part of me was content with this, for it proved to be that Longbourn would always be in our family, I was sad for now we were losing many of our household. When Georgiana would return to England in a month's time, Jason and she would live in London, Kitty would remain at Longbourn, and luckily Jane was the constant. It was made very clear that she would remain with us at Pemberley.

However, the surprises had not left us in our past, but there were still some that awaited us. The first would come when we had travelled to Allenwell to have a dinner with the Bingleys. When we arrived, we were surprised to see that Victor Whitfield was there.

"Mr. Whitfield," Jane said, "I am astonished, for we thought you would have returned to Errodin Abbey."

"Oh, I can see your reasoning, for I have been wicked and have not paid my respects recently to Pemberley," he said. "But I have been most preoccupied here."

"Oh, Allenwell suits your taste?" Mr. Darcy said.

"Yes, it has very much, but it is not the grounds that hold me but matters of the heart."

"We have a most wonderful announcement," Mr. Bingley said as Miriam stood beside him, holding little Elizabeth in her arms. "Not more than a week ago, Mr. Victor Whitfield visited Allenwell, with the express desire to tell me that he had requested a courtship with my sister, Caroline, and she had accepted."

"Indeed?" Jane exclaimed. We all turned to Victor and Caroline, who stood next to each other and blushed a bit.

"Yes," Caroline said, "Mr. Whitfield and I are courting."

❦

THE SURPRISE WAS AMAZING. Though I now saw that it should not have been unexpected, for Victor and her clearly had hidden words between them, Caroline's personality suddenly improving would have sprung from somewhere, and Victor was the sort to bring it about.

We all offered our congratulations, and I did the same, but it took a while to become comfortable with this courtship. It was so alarming because I was foolish enough to not see it when there were perhaps many signs that could have been explored.

Yet as the night went on, Caroline enjoyed Victor's company most pleasantly and she never really took her eyes off of him. When finding a moment to be alone with her as we waited for our carriage to be drawn, I whispered to her.

"I confess myself surprised as to how all this has come about," I began.

"As you should be," Caroline Bingley chuckled quietly. "As I was. I know it seems shocking and sudden, but in truth, he was the one who helped me to improve my own nature. But I had no idea that while he did so, it would grow to become more in his and my eyes."

"How did it happen?"

"He visited Allenwell a couple of times. While normally a male guest would command the time on my brother, Victor proved to be most welcome because he always told Charles to not worry on him, for I was sufficient company. We therefore had many chances to have easy conversations, and he always came to see that I would continue to improve myself. I know now that I could not have succeeded in my alteration if it had not been for him. Then one day, he came and as we walked along the grounds, he told me that he had grown to develop a strong attachment to me, and that it could not be denied any longer. I cannot believe how foolish I was, for I had never noticed his growing sentiments, and I had only seen a man who just wanted company and who I enjoyed being around. He and I are so honest with each other, that it is comfortable and simple."

"It is perhaps best that you did not see it at first. For this way, he could see the part of you that was true as opposed to you always attempting to make a good impression."

"Yes, and now I have learned what it means to try too hard as opposed to letting things take their course. Now that we are romantically attached, I can be partial to him all that I desire. But it is natural, unlike forced, which is what I did too often before. Yet when I heard him speak his adoration of me, I was amazed to find that I never had heard happier news. Is it so idiotic of me to not have realized that I had been falling in love with him the whole time?"

"No, it does not," I answered warmly.

"Thank you, for I know it seems as if I have been coming upon these feelings so suddenly, but they had been growing, deeply as if they were like roots within me. Now I cannot understand how I did not like him sooner."

"Well then, Miss Bingley, I am happy for you. Victor is an honorable man, and his sharp tongue will always keep you on your toes, which I believe you will like."

We moved away from each other, and I began to go to Darcy for him to help me into our carriage. Yet before I did so, I brushed past Victor and gave him a fleeting message.

"I should have known, Mr. Whitfield, that when you had come, something about you would change things."

He gave me a wicked smile. "Yes, that often is my way."

I smiled at him, and our company was off to Pemberley, with us all speaking of this new turn of events.

News of their courtship spread throughout our families, and as it grew to become clear that Caroline and Victor were on their way to forming a more permanent attachment, we sent letters to Matlock, London, and Hampshire. All expressed their surprise at the news, but the reply from Matlock and London was the most amusing. Between the marriage of Captain Wentworth to Charlotte, then Georgiana to Jason, Issy to Henry Fitzwilliam, and now Caroline Bingley to Victor, it had been a year of many marriages, and all to the satisfaction of everyone around them to witness these bonds being forged.

However, at London, where Jason and Georgiana had now returned to, when they received the letter, Georgiana laughed, because for too long she feared that she would result in being Caroline's sister-in-law if she married her brother. But being married to Victor changed it all. Georgiana now no longer feared Caroline Bingley, for even she sensed that Victor had a nature that would complete Caroline's.

And while her reaction was one that chuckled at the irony of all things, from Matlock, we received a letter from Lady Fitzwilliam.

Her letter told us that she enjoyed the news and would send an invitation for us and those from Allenwell to come back to Matlock so she could host another party. Below her letter, the handwriting changed, and Acton had written a few words:

This news of even the happiness of Miss Bingley and Mr. Whitfield stirs me and makes me feel as if I am quite the unfortunate singularity, for everyone is now becoming more than one in number, and here I remain as I ever was, only Acton. Yet perhaps it is my fortune to be the single one, or perhaps it is not. Either way, I still smile.

When Darcy showed me the letter, I sighed.
Poor Acton!
Why did it always seem as if it was the fate of those who most deserved to find love were sometimes the last ones to receive it? Even when it was their due.

❧

ONE SUNDAY, after church, I was sitting with Jane in the sitting room, and she was sewing while I was reading a letter from Rosings Park.

"Mary is ill at Rosings," I said to Jane, as I finished reading it.

"Is she?" Jane said, looking up from her needlework, "Dear lord, it is not serious, is it?"

"I cannot make out if so or not," I said, a little unnerved. "Mary writes that she is not so ill, but she had been bedridden for four days now. When Anne and she had visited the tenants on Rosings, all of the family's children were very ill, and when Mary tended to them, she caught what they had."

"Oh dear, what are we to do?"

"She is not alone, however. She has also written that Kitty and

Richard have visited Rosings, and when seeing that Mary was ill, Kitty asked if they could remain at Rosings for which Lady Catherine and Anne immediately said yes. Anne is worried as well, but Mary continues to assure her that she will recover."

"Do you think..." Jane began, a little apprehensive. "No, I'm sure she shall recover, for she has Anne and Kitty to remain there. Their company shall raise her spirits and raised spirits can do much for sickness."

"You are recalling when I walked to Aginfield for you, aren't you?"

"Yes, and you being there was a vast improvement to me being alone. Kitty's company will work wonders."

"Yes, Mary has been ill before, but surely, she has grown stronger. Yes," I said, more encouraging myself than certain, "yes, I am sure that she is going to be well."

"Yes," Jane said, flexing her hand nervously. "Yes, but if we were to receive another of these letters, I think it best that we ask Mr. Darcy if we may travel to—"

We were interrupted by our steward, who entered and bowed to us.

"Mrs. Darcy and Miss Bennet, we have a visitor who claims an acquaintance with you both. He wishes to have you humbly receive him now."

"Oh," I stuttered, "I was not expecting to receive anyone. What is his name?"

"He has just driven up the lane in his chaise and four, and his name is Mr. Samuel Brocklehurst."

Jane and I looked at each other in alarm.

"Shall I show him in?" the steward asked.

"You should inform him that Mr. Darcy is not in at the moment," I said.

"Yes, but he called to expressly speak with Miss Bennet."

I turned and looked at Jane, and she nodded to me gently.

"Very well. Show him in."

The butler bowed and left.

"Jane," I warned, "are you certain that I should allow him entry? Is this wise for you?"

"Perhaps not," she replied, "but sometimes what is necessary is not wise. I... I need to see him again."

Filled with worry, I stood up and waited for Mr. Brocklehurst to enter, which he did with confidence mingled with trepidation—if both could be held within a countenance at one time. Jane stood up as we both prepared to receive him.

"Mrs. Darcy," he said gently, "And Miss Bennet." He bowed to us, and we curtsied. "You both look as lovely as ever."

"Thank you for the compliment, Mr. Brocklehurst," I said, "and I trust that you are well."

"Yes. Or at least as well as can be expected."

"Do you come into Kent for business or for amusement, sir?"

"Both, if that can be called for penance," he replied. "I... forgive me, I do not know where to begin. But you must forgive my frankness, for I cannot help but see the absence of Mr. Darcy as providence."

"Do you offend my husband sir?" I stated firmly. "For that I shall never allow."

"No, never would I insult him, for he is clearly a stronger man than myself. I simply acknowledge that if he were here, I would never get the chance to say all that I need to say. Please, Mrs. Darcy, you were always a woman who never feared the truth being spoken, but also too generous to shun someone when they seek reform. I humbly ask that I be given a moment to speak with Jane."

"No," I said boldly.

"Lizzy," Jane said, raising her hand, "I know that it's wrong for me to care, but please..."

I looked at her expression of supplication, his look of shame, and

I could not help but soften my resolve—though I refused to fully forget it.

"Very well," I relented. "However, I shall sit here and write a letter, never looking at you or interrupting, but I will not leave you alone. That is as far as I shall bend, is that clear to you both?"

"Thank you, Lizzy," Jane sighed.

"Yes, thank you so much," Mr. Brocklehurst echoed. I nodded to them both and then sat down at the writing desk, pulled out some paper and pen, then began to compose a letter to Kitty and Mary.

While one could do one's best to ignore a conversation, it is impossible to do so when it is so engaging and within hearing. Therefore when Mr. Brocklehurst began his pleas, this is how I remembered it.

"Miss Bennet... Jane..."

"Mr. Brocklehurst," Jane replied evenly.

"Would there be a chance that you would call me Samuel once more? Or Edmund?"

"Is it important that I do so?"

"It was what you used to do."

"Yes, it was." She sighed, emotional. "However, that was when I was allowed to do so. When I was allowed to admire you."

"But please, for the sake of us being friends once, call me so again."

"Samuel," she said, and I could tell that her voice was shaky—she was holding back tears.

"Please do not cry, Jane, for I am not worth it."

Very much so, I thought, he was not worth it.

"Jane," he continued, "I know that this must look as if I am simply returning to see you only because we danced together at Matlock. But it is not a sudden fancy of mine just to satisfy my curiosity. I have thought of you often since that day that I showed myself to be the worst of libertines. And I want you to know now that I never meant to hurt you. And it was not right for me to have gained your love and then abused it in such a way."

"No, it was not. And while there is much within me that will always wish to never cause you grief, I shall speak now as I wish. For not doing so has left too much inside of me that I wish to unleash."

Jane took a deep breath. "Samuel, while I wish that I could see all the goodness that has come into my life because of your actions, I wish that I could only see how now I teach children, how I mean something to so many, how now I shall always be the best of aunts to my nieces and nephews, how I shall always be allowed to be here at Pemberley, where I can make a difference always. I still cannot look on them without wondering what happiness I could have found if you had proven to be the man I had fallen in love with."

Jane stood up and she paced back and forth.

"What do you want from me now?" she cried quietly. "What do you expect out of all this, Samuel?"

"I expect to let you know me," he said desperately. "I desire that you know me."

"What more is there to know?"

"That I loved you as well, Jane. That I loved you terribly."

"How can you say that?" Jane said. "When you have another woman and children elsewhere?"

"I will never say that I am good, or singular in my passions, but only that they were real. This is a frightening thing to confess, but some of us in this world, we can love one, as well as love another."

"That is disloyalty."

"I know, but it is true."

"If it is, sir, I am sorry to say it, but I am glad that I am not of your heart or mind. I am glad that I find devotion to one to be the highest form of honor and goodness."

"I will never ask you to excuse my behavior."

"Then what are you asking?"

"I am simply asking that you believe that I did love you terribly. And that you deserved to have been loved!"

I closed my eyes as I heard Jane cry. I wished to go to her, but I had promised them faithfully that I would remain as if I were not there. And to that I had to hold fast onto.

"You were loved, Jane Bennet," he continued. "By me. And if I had been a better man than the one I was once, I would have been worthy of you, and you would have been all that was best in me."

"I loved you terribly, Samuel," she said through her tears.

"I know, and I with you. I just wished for you to know that there was some goodness in me, and it was you—and her. Her devotion to me is something I have, but am not worthy of, as it was with your devotion. Hate me, be disgusted with me, but never feel that I did not adore you terribly."

"I cannot hate you now," she said, "and that is what makes this all the harder. She and I deserve better, that much is certain, but I cannot ever forget how I felt with you."

"Then that is all I ask."

Out of the corner of my eye, I saw Samuel walk up to Jane and kiss her on the cheek.

"My dearest Jane, my almost wife, and one of my great loves."

I stood up and turned to him before he could fully kiss her.

"Fine, now that is enough."

"Yes," Mr. Brocklehurst said, "yes it now is."

He moved from Jane and put his hat back on.

"Mrs. Darcy, I know what you must think of me."

"Yes, I do," I replied, for his heartfelt manner was engaging enough to have affected Jane terribly. When someone has such powers of address that they can make someone pity their crimes, they can be dangerous, even if they meant what they had said, "But my feelings mean nothing now. Only Jane's."

"Yes." Then he turned to her once more and nodded.

"I will never forget you."

"Nor I with you. Goodbye Samuel."

"Goodbye, Jane."

With one last nod to me, Mr. Brocklehurst quitted Pemberley. When we were finally alone, I rushed to Jane and caught her just before she collapsed. There, on the carpet I held her as she wept uncontrollably.

"He did love me!" she cried.

"Yes, perhaps he did."

"Should I feel better, Lizzy, or should I feel worse?"

"I cannot tell you, Jane. Yet I believe that it is natural to feel both those things at once."

We continued in that position, with Jane speaking of her feelings and lamenting her fortune while also praising it. For if she had married Mr. Brocklehurst, she would not have become the woman she became, and the woman she became was important to us all.

Yet, when Mr. Darcy was returning to Pemberley from the farms, she wiped her tears and appeared as her pleasant and lighthearted self, concealing every disturbed emotion. For while she loved my husband truly, there were some things that she wanted to keep within herself, locked away from prying eyes. And her undying love for Mr. Brocklehurst was one of them.

"Elizabeth!"

The next day I was sitting in William and Caiden's room. Lucy and I were lifting them into the air, letting them bounce on the bed, when I heard Jane's voice call for me. From what I had heard, her voice seemed desperate even before she rushed into the room, with her face matching the tone of her voice.

"Jane," I said, "what is it?"

"I have just received another letter from Kitty. Mary is very ill, and we need to go to Rosings."

"What!" I gasped in disbelief. Since the last letter sent from Rosings, I had convinced myself that Mary's ailment was a passing one and that any worry on the matter would be me overreacting to a small crisis that would easily be overcome. Had I been lying to myself?

"Yes," Jane said, handing me the letter. "Read it, and please convince Mr. Darcy that we must go."

I took the letter hastily, opened it and began to read.

> Dear Jane,
>
> I hope I find you in good health, but that will be more than I can tell you now. Please, after reading this, take this letter to Elizabeth and Darcy and have them learn of its contents.
>
> As you know, when I came to Rosings with the Colonel, Mary had fallen ill, and I decided to stay and tend to her. I am sorry to say that she is not improving. In truth, she is getting worse, and every day, the doctors tell me that I need to prepare myself for the worst. Mary fights, but—Mary is losing.
>
> Please, if the worst does come to pass, I wish for Mary to have us all here to see her one last time. I have written to our parents, and I know they come in haste, but please, Mary needs to see you, Elizabeth and Mr. Darcy. If she does not recover, please let her have that.
>
> Do not take the time to reply, but only come, for I know with your silence that you will.
>
> Your loving sister,
>
> Kitty

I closed the letter and stood up immediately.

"Where is Mr. Darcy?" Jane asked.

"In his study," I said, rushing past her. "Jane, pack quickly, for we are going to Rosings!"

WHEN I HAD TOLD Mr. Darcy of the news, he moved with all speed, arranging our transport in no more than an hour's time. We had to leave Caiden and William at Pemberley, for it would slow our progress. Lucy promised she would look after them well, and we had Jefferson stay behind, for we knew that no harm would befall them while he oversaw all of Pemberley.

Thus, we were on the road that exact day, each believing that when we arrived at Rosings, Mary would be well. And with the succession of the incidents that had fallen into place one after the other, all had always ended well in the past. We hoped it would so this one last time. May Mary live, I prayed, may she live.

✣ 30 ✣

THE LAST MOMENT

At Rosings, Kitty was just beginning to wake up. Over the last couple of days, she had stayed with Mary in her guest room often and sometimes fell asleep in the chair that was next to her sister's bed. When waking up, she realized that she had done so again, for it was Mary's coughing that awoke her.

Kitty immediately walked over to the nightstand, poured some water from the pitcher and offered the glass to her. Mary took it and drank it swiftly.

"Do you want me to get you some tea?" Kitty asked.

"No," Mary sighed, handing her the glass. "Water is enough, and..."

"How are you feeling?" Kitty asked, feeling the foolishness of her question. Mary was pale white, her skin sweaty and her eyes were glazed over, as if she were barely even there. "Miss De Bourgh was here earlier, but she was called away by her mother."

"I am stronger now," Mary said. "I am... I am who I am."

"Yes, you are," Kitty replied, agreeing with anything Mary said, no matter how nonsensical it was. The day before, Mary had been speaking gibberish all day, her mind plagued with hallucinations from the days before. With her body being so seized, her mind filled with false images, and her health constantly under attack, Kitty had feared leaving her for fear of Mary getting up and ever doing harm to herself.

"I was just dreaming," Mary began, her eyes almost vacant, for she was stricken with fever and pneumonia. "And if you might remember—we were children. A swing was set from our tree along the bushes of Longbourn. Do you remember, Kitty?"

"Yes," Kitty whispered, "I remember it."

"Well, you might not remember...but I was the one who taught you how to swing on it."

"Yes, I remember that too."

Mary's voice then grew husky and heavy as Kitty rubbed her face. "And I never told you something."

"What was it?" Kitty continued, eager to keep Mary talking, for she was worried that if she ever were to stop doing so, she would fall asleep...and never awake again.

"I told myself, that I would be the best older sister ever to you."

"What?"

"Yes, I did."

"Why did you never tell me this?"

"Because I was angry."

"I... I don't understand."

"When I was born, I was the third daughter. What was special about me? Nothing. And Jane and Elizabeth had each other, and they were nice to me, but they were so... so, so devoted to each other always, and then you were born. I remember thinking that now was my chance, now I could be the older sister. And now, I would have someone look up to me. And you did, Kitty, you did."

"I... I was too young. I can remember none of this."

"I know, but I do. And then it happened."

"What?"

"Lydia was born. And it was time for you to be the older sister, and I was angry, for Lydia clung to you, and I felt that there ended my chance."

"But..." Kitty began, desperately hoping that Mary was saying all this out of being delirious and that none of it was real. "Naturally I did my best to be so to her, to the point where I lost my way a bit, but I did not forget you."

"You might not have, but I thought you did. I felt that you would now care nothing for me as a sister, and so I turned away, and that was when it began."

"When what began?"

"When I turned to my studies, to books, learning, and—and—and music. Books became my great companion. Intelligence became my sister."

Kitty rubbed her eyes, not knowing how to take in what Mary was confessing.

"Mary...please do not speak anymore of this. Please—"

Mary suddenly seized Kitty's hand and held it tightly.

"No," she cried, "it is better that you should know me. You must know me! For I feel... I know that I am..."

"No, Mary! You will be well, I promise that."

Mary looked up at her, her face relaxed and her eyes losing life by the moment.

"Kitty, you must know me."

Holding back her tears, Kitty pulled up her chair and sat down close to the bed.

"Very well, Mary, I am listening."

Mary's eyes closed temporarily, she smiled but it was hard to tell if she did so because of intent or vacancy of feeling.

"Well," she began, "all day I played on the pianoforte, gathered extracts, and prided myself—yes, yes, yes, prided myself on my superiority of mind. And in this frightening time, in this painful place, I see that all of it leaves me. All that I learned, and only emotion remains. It took me so long to awaken to the fact that I did not see things clearly. And that I did not ever allow myself to be filled with life and take joy in what I had when I had it. But now, I have come ever closer to understanding how I ought to have been. I have just begun to discover how to care for people, to forgive—to laugh. I had even thought of falling in love, so why now? Why have I just learned all of this right at the moment when all is leaving me? What cruel joke is this?" Mary whispered, tears coursing down her cheeks. Kitty leaned forward and cradled Mary's face.

"Is it pointless...the word 'regret'?" Mary said. "Am I horrible Kitty, for looking back on my life and seeing all the paths I could have partaken, now that it's too late for me to walk along them? My life was without action, direction...passion. I lived from passivity to passivity, thinking myself intelligent. Yet now I see that it was mere vanity. There is nothing smart about not living. And I did not live, Kitty, I did not live! I breathed, I moved, but I was a corpse who simply had the gift of air and movement. Humanity was my business! The common man and woman were my neighbors! My ilk, my kin, and I chose to take their existence for naught but non-importance. I lived so selfishly, Kitty! So empty. If I could go back in time, if I could breathe life in myself once again, I would be brought anew. I would not turn away from my fellow man because they can hurt me. I would never lose faith, hope, and the instinct to love. Humanity would be my business, Kitty! It would be my life!"

"I did care for you, Mary," Kitty said, "I did."

Mary gave a ragged sigh. "I know now that you did. All of you did. I just waited too long to see it."

"No," Kitty declared, "you will not die. You will live, you shall grow to be as old as us. I shall see you become the aunt of my child. I shall see your hair gray, your skin wrinkle, and I shall see you fall in love, believe me, and then fall out of it." Mary laughed, though it was hard for her to do so. "I shall see you make mistakes, then feel remorse for it, and then evolve, as we all shall. I might even see you have children and cry out about your pains. But I shall see you live, Mary. I shall—"

Kitty's attention was taken by a carriage rolling down the lane. Recognizing the coach to belong to Mr. Darcy, Kitty stood up and felt her heart soar.

"Mary! Stay awake, our sisters are come!"

❧

KITTY RUSHED DOWN the steps of Rosings, threw the doors open and hurried down to the carriage as it came to a halt. When Mr. Darcy stepped down, followed by her sisters Jane and Elizabeth, Kitty did not hide her alarm.

"You must all come quickly, before it is too late!"

They tried to question her, but Kitty was insistent, and therefore they all followed her up the steps quickly. Lady Catherine appeared on the landing with Colonel Fitzwilliam.

"Nephew, you are arrived!" she announced.

"Yes!" Mr. Darcy exclaimed, annoyed at her casual manner in the wake of a sick woman living in her home. Thus, Kitty, Elizabeth, Jane and he rushed down the hall.

"Is she worse?" Colonel Fitzwilliam asked, striding after them.

"Do not run!" Lady Catherine cried." It is unseemly!"

"Shut up, Aunt!" Darcy declared.

Upon hearing the reprimand, Lady Catherine felt as if she had been stricken across the face.

"Fitzwilliam," she said, pursuing them down the hall. "How dare you?"

Not paying her any heed, they all burst into Mary's room and cast their eyes upon her still form.

Elizabeth moved past them the swiftest, knelt down and took Mary's face in her hands.

250

"Mary?" Elizabeth cried. Mary's eyes opened slightly and, upon seeing Elizabeth, Jane, followed by Kitty, she smiled weakly.

"You came for me," she whispered.

"Of course we did," Jane cried. "You're our sister."

"Yes," she sighed. "I am... and you came for me! You came to—"

Mary's eyes drained of life, her breathing shortened and then ended altogether.

Thus, with her three sisters weeping over her, Mr. Darcy, Colonel Fitzwilliam and Lady Catherine entering soon after, the last moment of Mary Bennet was witnessed, for she had gone to sleep...to never awaken.

OUR LAST GOODBYE

C an you define loss?

Whatever poem or book that does its best to describe it to you can never portray it properly, for it is beyond definition.

When Mary breathed her last, I wanted to deny that it was real, for her to only be offering a joke, and that any moment she would awaken and we would see her again, **alive** and well. But Mary was never one to joke. Therefore, I could deny it no longer. As her eyes finally closed, I wept uncontrollably, with Kitty and Jane doing so as well. Behind us, Mr. Darcy and Richard stood there, stoic, not understanding how to ease our grief...and Lady Catherine. She was as still as a statue. For a time, I had quite forgotten her existence, not even remembering her until Kitty stood up suddenly and glared at her.

"This is all your fault!"

"What?" Lady Catherine whispered hoarsely.

"Do you have no sense of responsibility that it has not crossed your mind, Lady Catherine?" Kitty hissed. "Are you that devoid of proper feeling? This never would have happened if you had taken heed of Mary's health! Or if you had taken it more seriously earlier! Our sister is dead, because of you!"

"Kitty, you will stop this instant!" Lady Catherine declared.

"No, I will not! How much of life is marred or is destroyed by Lady Catherine always thinking herself to be right? How many wrong moves will be made on the chessboard that is this world, and how many of them were by your doing!"

Kitty rushed to Lady Catherine and grabbed her hands, equally demanding and in supplication.

"Why can you never see how wrong you always are? No, you will know yourself now. Look upon my sister's form! Look upon her, and see a young woman dead because you did not care for her welfare, because you did not notice that you were unwise? You sent her to sick houses over and over and did not see how it was affecting her. And I tell you now, Lady Catherine, no more! You will see yourself for what you are. You do not see how your selfish disdain for the feelings of others and only to rule them but not listen to them has brought you here. You killed my sister as much as any disease did!"

While Lady Catherine was in Kitty's clutches, the rest of us stood transfixed, motionless but taking no step to pull Kitty off of her. Whether it was due to our shock, or because we wished for Lady Catherine to hear all that she had said, we did nothing but watched and listened.

And witnessed!

Lady Catherine began to weep and shake uncontrollably.

"I didn't mean to be wrong," she whispered.

"But you were," Kitty cried. "Look upon my sister. You were wrong."

"I..." Lady Catherine looked at Mary, then at the rest of us as we looked on her with grief. The most astonishing thing began to occur.

Lady Catherine's body went limp, losing all strength and energy, and she sunk into the closest chair as her shoulders shook. Beginning to weep, she looked at all of us. "I did not know that I could be wrong. I could be—I can be wrong. I..."

Lady Catherine's words trailed off, she looked lost in shock, and it was the result of a woman who had spent her whole life filled with mean understanding, to which it all now untwined, and she was finally forced to see herself for what she always had been. It was a painful revelation for her, but it was one that needed to be experienced, even if it was experienced too late.

Even though the tears flowed down my eyes and blurred my vision, my judgment of her state was clear; Lady Catherine had finally been humbled—here at the end of all things.

The next day our parents arrived and when they heard the news, it was a painful message to give them. At first, they met the news with utter disbelief, but then after the truth of the matter became evident, our mother wept continuously, and in utter despair.

Anne De Bourgh sat there, watching us, and was so filled with guilt and sadness that she continuously kept apologizing for not standing up for Mary and demanding that she no longer visited the sick when she was becoming ill.

Lady Catherine was in bed, afraid to see my parents. She told us to inform them that she would pay for the funeral service and arrange everything out of debt. Naturally this was not enough a penance for our parents, who despised to hear the very mention of Lady Catherine for a while. But they accepted her offer as recompense.

And my father, he was silent for so long that it frightened us. A man who spent so much of his life in indifference or amusement, now was forced to feel the emotions that he never thought he would have to experience. No parent should have to bury their child. But they would do so, and it would take a long time for anyone to recover. With my father, I was not sure how long it would be for him, but I knew that it would leave a mark on his soul terribly.

Lady Catherine used her influence to make certain many came to Mary's funeral, and from Hampshire, the Lucases came, including Samuel, Charlotte and Captain Wentworth, along with our Aunt and Uncle Philips. From London came the Gardiners with Georgiana and Jason, and from Kent came the Bingleys, added to the people who lived on and around Rosings.

The service was beautiful, yes, but I cared for none of it, nor took heed to it. For Mary's absence could not be substituted by grandeur so easily.

Transport was offered immediately after her funeral and we all traveled to Hampshire, with her coffin. When we arrived, we arranged for her to be buried in the main cemetery of Steventon. News spread quickly that we had brought her home and people from all over the town had come to see her as she was lowered into the earth. Among those people were the Longs, the Crofts, and the Austens.

While the rest of us stood over the grave, Jane and Cassandra stood beside me, each holding one of my hands.

"Mary," I said, "despite her flaws, had a good heart. And was a great woman, without a doubt."

"We none of us is perfect," Cassandra said. "All we can hope to be is our best. After seeing Mary grow, I can say that she found her best."

"Yes," Jane Austen said, and then she walked behind me and hugged my shoulders while I collapsed in her embrace.

"She will always be remembered, Lizzy," Jane Austen said. "Both the virtuous and the amusing in her will live. And though nothing can bring her back, I can only promise you this. I have my pin and my paper. Though she will sadly suffer the same fate of all my characters and be a subject for fun." Jane laughed, and added,

"And some might not recognize her funnier moments and see how she learned over time, I shall put much love into her, and she will be remembered. Believe me, Mary Bennet shall live forever."

The next day, I had felt restless and wished to visit Mary's grave alone, so I woke up early, left Darcy a note and then walked to the cemetery. I was surprised, though I should not have been, when I found my father standing in the midst of it and looking down on his middle daughter's grave.

At first, I hesitated when I saw him, then I walked forward.

"Father."

He turned to me and I saw the sorrow in his eyes.

"Oh, yes well...hello."

I stood beside him, and we looked at the headstone in silence. Words seemed to fail us briefly, and after a few minutes, he chuckled.

"I was just thinking of something."

"What?"

He began. "With each child a father has, there is always one memory of them that sticks out the most. With Mary, it is not her playing always on the pianoforte or her moral speeches—oh no. It is much more precious. It was of when she was a child, and I was walking with her somewhere. She looked up in the sky and she saw a bird fly overheard, and she declared to me that one day, she would fly herself. I told her that it was not possible, but she said she would. And I still denied it to be so until she looked downhearted, accepting that I was right."

He shook his head. "I limited her. And now, I am heartily ashamed of myself. I told her that she could not fly, but that was not what should have been said. I should have told her that she could fly, in her mind, and in there, all was possible. And her dreams ought to be without limitation. I know it is too late, but if she can hear me, then Mary, you always could fly, you could have gone everywhere that you had wanted. And I am sorry for having said otherwise."

"Do not worry, Father, for she hears you."

And I hope you did, Mary. Wherever you were, you could have done anything. And now you can do everything. For now, you are free.

May you hear us, Mary, for this is our last goodbye.

❦ 32 ❦

FAREWELL

In time, our company parted. Kitty, Richard, and our parents remained at Longbourn while Jane, Darcy and I made our way back to Pemberley.

Along the way, we all sought solace in our own individual ways. Jane was quiet, Darcy was attentive to me, and I decided to begin writing a journal, in hopes that words would help me recover.

I knew that I would overcome the sadness eventually, but I wanted my sister's memory to still be keenly felt within me, for one should not forget some things so swiftly.

❦

IT IS A STRANGE BUSINESS: grief and acceptance. One is hard enough to endure, but when one does overcome it, was it in proper time?

I knew our mother would lament over it for months, and our father, for once, could not find any fault with her nerves. She would cling to Kitty even more now and always wish to have at least one daughter with her till the end of her days.

For Lydia, we sent a letter to her, but it would be weeks before she would receive it and learn of her sister's demise—if she would even get it at all. War was agonizing in its natural course, but the rift it can cause is always hard. Would it be years gone by before Lydia would learn of Mary's end? I hoped it would not be so.

Yet as we rode on, I thought of how Mary had wanted to know my sons and believed herself on the road to being the aunt they deserved, and it would not be so.

But my sons!

As I would return to Pemberley, they would be there, as constant sources of joy, of life, and the continuation of our family. I would tell them about Mary, and they would at least know of her.

For at Pemberley, there is always constancy, memories, and family.

There we would be whole again.

Soon we arrived back into Kent, and when our carriage rolled before the steps of Pemberley, Mrs. Reynolds came down the steps, ready to receive us.

"My goodness," she cried. "I am so happy to see you all, but... I am so sorry for your loss."

We thanked her for her condolences and then Mr. Darcy offered me his hand. Looking down on it I had seen the promise of unity and affection. I took it in mine and Jane followed us into the house where we all felt the comfort of family.

There, at Pemberley, I had faith that family would always be strong with us.

I had faith that this loss would bind us even tighter.

I had faith that we would be happy.

"Well," Mr. Darcy said, "we are home."

I inhaled, smelling the air that was pungent with the fertile grounds of Pemberley. "Yes, my dear, we are home."

And as it turned out, faith was all that I needed.

EPILOGUE
MANY YEARS LATER

For one of the last times in his life, Mr. Darcy picked up his diary again, to write the last entry that he felt it necessary to make. He raised his pen and as he considered, he felt a change in the winds.

A difference of perspective.

A diary was something to reflect one's thoughts. But also, it was history—personal history that always makes a name, a character—into a three dimensional being.

If someone were to pick up his diaries, long after he was gone, they would wonder about the man he was. And the man he was not.

Stricken with a desire to be remembered, not as a name, but as a man, Mr. Darcy had an idea. For what makes a person feel true, was not an entry. It was a letter. A letter would do. And so he began to write…

> *Greetings,*
> *For whomsoever this letter that I now write, whether you are my grandson, or great-grandson or granddaughter, I write this missive in hopes that you know me. In hopes that you learn of*

*my existence long after I am gone. This letter shall remain
stored in our records, always secured with previous wills, and
testaments, prepared to be read and discovered again.*

*I am Fitzwilliam Darcy, who was the master of Pemberley in
the year 1810 and onward until the day that I pass. I was
married to a woman named Elizabeth Bennet, whose journal I
shall fight to always have preserved. If you come upon it, it is
yours to read, and here are some things that she never was able
to mention.*

*After the death of Mary, the family went through a long
reign of peace where happiness and luck did find us always. To
add to my two sons, we had three more children, and they were
all girls, as we had hoped. Helena, Josephine, called Jo, and
Hero.*

*Eventually Anne De Bourgh did marry and become mistress
to Rosings Park. She showed her stronger will in being set to
wed Nicholas Heywood, a man who was a farmer. Aunt
Catherine de Bourgh was against this match initially, yet with
her will dissolving gradually, mingled with the encouragement
of the rest of the family in support of Nicholas's suit, Nicholas
and Anne de Bourgh did wed. Lady Catherine, discovering that
we did not despise her for the loss of Mary any longer, was
reconciled to us. And she learned that she would never lose us
as family again.*

*As for Acton Fitzwilliam, oh dear Acton! To his surprise, he
finally made the acquaintance of Maria Lucas. Who would have
thought that Charlotte Lucas's little sister had been the perfect
match for him? Well, except for my Lizzy, who had thought it a
happy concept from the second they met. Their tempers and
personalities were in fact so much alike, that no more than a few
months after they met, they were in love enough to wed. My
cousin Acton got his romantic ending after all.*

Colonel Fitzwilliam and Kitty remained at Longbourn after

the death of both Mr. and Mrs. Bennet, who lived their lives complete, and to no one's surprise, with much affection to the very end. In her late eighties, Mrs. Bennet finally passed, and her husband, who spent much of his life in between indifference for his wife and affection, lost spirit at her passing, and not four days after she died, he did as well, from grief of missing her. Richard and Kitty would end in having six children.

Mr. Bingley and Miriam had a family as well, and they remained our constant and loving neighbors. I have outlived Mr. Bingley, as I have outlived my wife. Yet Jane Bennet still lives, and she and I sit in our old age, looking on my children as they begin families of their own. Elizabeth asked her older sister to look after me when she was gone. Jane, who loved my Lizzy as much as myself, agreed. Even in death, my wife still chose to look after me.

Captain Wentworth did survive serving in the War of 1812, and he returned to Charlotte Lucas whole and happy. In America, Lydia did eventually learn of Mary's passing, and she returned to England after the war to visit her sister's grave, along with Henry Darcy.

The reason I write this all, is to show you that nothing ever fully ends, does it? Even I do not, for I live through you.

Yet to the purpose of why I am writing you, my descendant, is not only because I want you to know me, but I also want you to know the grandmother, or great-grandmother that you belong to. My late wife, Elizabeth Bennet, Mrs. Darcy. Even when we were parted, I thought of her every day, I remember every look, every smile she gave me, and it warms me to this very moment. Some will remember me, Mr. Fitzwilliam Darcy of Pemberley, but now you must remember the woman who made that man, who kept me from the darker parts of myself, who fought for myself and changed me. I was not the man I was because of self-discipline, oh no. Rather I was the man I was because she loved me. Every amount of goodness that was in my soul, the love that I learned to give, the hope I found in life, was because she decided that I was worthy of her. She was Elizabeth Bennet, and she was a heroine of mine.

So please if you read this letter, and you know who I am, remember her. Remember Elizabeth Bennet. I have faith that you will.

Mr. Fitzwilliam Darcy
Of Pemberley
July 8th, 1873

THANK YOU FOR READING

Did you enjoy this book?

We invite you to leave a review at your favorite book site, such as Goodreads, Amazon, Barnes & Noble, etc.

DID YOU KNOW THAT LEAVING A REVIEW...

- Helps other readers find books they may enjoy.
- Gives you a chance to let your voice be heard.
- Gives authors recognition for their hard work.
- Doesn't have to be long. A sentence or two about why you liked the book will do.

ABOUT THE AUTHOR

Ney Mitch has been a long-standing Jane Austen enthusiast, having written forty novels that were inspired by her various works. Since stumbling on Miss Austen's books after graduating from college, she has always dabbled in Austen inspired literature, ranging from writing works for teens to adults. Originally, her desire was to adapt Jane Austen's writing in a way to help young adults connect with her, however over time, she has spread her aims to other genres and styles. Having received her BA Degree at Desales University, she is a writer, both literary and dramatic, as well as being a Historic Reenactor.

 facebook.com/courtney.mitchell.589

x.com/CMMitchelPsyche

 pinterest.com/shebaanna

❧❦❧

The Memory Series

Moments of Moments Past

Moments of Moments Present

Moments of Moments Future

Moments of Moments Infinite

❧❦❧

Romance & Revolution Saga

The First Impression

❧❦❧

Chances Series

Chances Are

Chances Come

Chances Fade

Chances End

❧❦❧

Considerations Near Christmastime

Curiosities at Christmastime

❧❦❧

Novels

The Tale of Mr. & Mrs. Bennet: A Pride & Prejudice Christmas Tale